Brand Warriors

CORPORATE LEADERS SHARE THEIR
WINNING STRATEGIES

Edited by Fiona Gilmore

HarperCollinsBusiness

HarperCollins*Publishers*
77–85 Fulham Palace Road,
Hammersmith, London w6 8jb

This paperback edition 1999

9 8 7 6 5 4 3 2 1

First published in Great Britain by
HarperCollins*Publishers* 1997

Copyright © Springpoint 1997, 1999

The Authors assert the moral right to
be identified as the authors of this work

isbn 0 638892 2

Set in Janson and Ellington

Printed and bound in Great Britain by
Caledonian International Book Manufacturing Ltd, Glasgow

Fiona Gilmore is a founding partner of Springpoint Ltd, one of the leading brand positioning and corporate identity consultancies in Europe. Over the last fifteen years she has contributed to the development of corporate branding architecture and positioning programmes for some of the leading global organizations. A regular speaker on the role of visual identity in business, Fiona Gilmore also writes articles on corporate branding, and has appeared on 'The Money Programme' and 'Question Time'. She is married with three children.

Contents

Acknowledgements

Putting this book together has been quite an adventure. Every step of the journey has been very demanding and yet immensely rewarding; a book of this nature is demanding in its structural ambitions and logistical complexity. What has been most rewarding for me is the team interaction and enthusiasm.

My colleague Katrina Symons deserves special mention. She joined the project at an early stage, bringing the team together, unwavering in her support and tenacity.

I would like to give special thanks to Sarah Butterworth, my assistant, who has demonstrated remarkable gifts of diplomacy and patience, and to other colleagues from Springpoint, in particular Gary Broadbent, Patricia Perchal and my business partner, Mark Pearce.

My deep thanks also to Lucinda McNeile of HarperCollins, who has provided excellent editorial guidance, and to Bob Garratt, who has added insight and new ideas, right up to the last moment.

I gratefully acknowledge my debt to the contributors: Bob Ayling, Richard Branson, Jos Brenkel, Alain Evrard, Chris Gent, John Hawkes, David Heslop, Shigeharu Hiraiwa, Nick Hodges, Robert Holloway, Tim Kelly, Archie Norman, Alan Palmer, Robert E. Riley, Fred Smith, Sir Clive Thompson, C. C. Tung and Allan Wong.

My grateful thanks go to Meg Carter, Laura Mazur and Alan Mitchell, for their assistance over many months.

I would also like to thank the following: Kim Balling, Valérie Banino, Pat Barry, Terry Barwick, Rick Bendall, Eddie Bensilum, Jim Carroll, Simon Chalkley, Eric Delamare, Lynn Downey, Kate Ecker, Anne Forrest, Sylvie Gagnot, Cindy Gallop, Martin George, Clarence Grebey, Charles Grimaldi, Michael Harvey, Michèle Heyworth, Jackie Holmes, Richard Hytner, Prue Jeffreys, Joyce Jui, David Kisilevski, Jill Kluge, Annie C. H. Loi, Gordon McCallum, Greg Rossiter, Justine Samuel, Gregory Sendi, Stanley C. Shen, Geoff and Rachel Skingsley, Emma Smith, Robert Triefus, Charles Tugendhat, Stephen Webb, Will Whitehorn, Dominic Whittles, Elin Wong and Jim Wood-Smith.

Lastly, I would like to thank my husband, Richard, for taking over some family responsibilities during the eighteen months I was working on this book, and for his support.

Fiona Gilmore

Contributors' Biographies

Robert Ayling

Bob Ayling was appointed chief executive of British Airways in January 1996. He joined the airline in 1985 from the Department of Trade, and headed the legal side of the British Airways privatization in 1987 and its acquisition of British Caledonian in 1988. He has also held the positions of group managing director, director of marketing & operations, director of human resources and company secretary.

Bob originally qualified as a solicitor and has been involved in air transport and international commerce throughout his career.

Richard Branson

Richard Branson founded Virgin as a mail-order record retailer in 1970, and shortly thereafter opened a record shop in Oxford Street, London.

He has since expanded the interests of Virgin Group through over 100 companies in twenty-three countries, encompassing international music retailing, financial services, the Internet, book and software publishing, film and video editing facilities, clubs, travel, hotels and cinemas. In 1984 he formed Virgin Atlantic Airways.

Richard has been involved in a number of world record breaking attempts. In 1986, his boat *Virgin Atlantic Challenger II* crossed the Atlantic Ocean in the fastest-ever recorded time. This was followed a year later by the first hot air balloon crossing of the Atlantic Ocean in *Virgin Atlantic Flyer*. In 1991 he crossed the Pacific Ocean from Japan to Arctic Canada by balloon, breaking all existing records. In July 1995 he announced his intention to undertake the non-stop circumnavigation of the world by balloon.

Richard is a trustee of several charities, including the Healthcare Foundation. He was born in 1950 and educated at Stowe School.

Jos Brenkel

Jos Brenkel is director of the Personal Systems Group at Hewlett-Packard's European Marketing Centre and is responsible for ensuring the company's success in the European market for personal information products, such as portable notebook computers and PC products. He joined Hewlett-Packard in South Africa in 1986, moving to Grenoble the following year where he held various management positions within the marketing centre.

Alain Evrard

Alain Evrard has been L'Oréal's zone director Africa, Asia Pacific since 1990, and his work covers Africa, the Middle East, East and South-East Asia, the Pacific and French foreign territories. He joined L'Oréal in 1981 from Solvay & Cie of Belgium, where he held management positions in Austria and Italy.

Alain graduated in Economics and Finance from the University of Brussels. He has been Conseiller du Commerce Extérieur de la France since 1988.

Chris Gent

Chris Gent is chief executive of Vodafone Group Plc, and chairman of Vodafone Australia, Panafon (Greece) and other Vodafone Group UK companies. He was managing director of Vodafone Ltd from 1985 to 1996.

He began his career at NatWest Bank (1967–71), before joining Schroder Computer Services (1971–79). In 1979 Chris joined Baric Computing Services, where he was managing director from 1983 to 1984.

Chris served as personal political assistant to the Home Secretary in 1974 and National Young Conservative chairman from 1977 to 1979.

He is currently a member of Goodwood, the Lords' Taverners and Hampshire Cricket Club.

John Hawkes

John Hawkes is senior vice president of McDonald's UK. He joined the company in 1982 as marketing executive, was promoted to marketing manager and from there moved to McDonald's Development Company as marketing director, with responsibility for Scandinavia and other Western European countries. He was appointed to his current position in April 1994.

David Heslop

David Heslop is chairman and managing director of Mazda Cars (UK) Ltd. He joined Mazda in 1984, and worked his way through sales and dealer operations before being appointed managing director in 1991. He began his career as personal assistant to the chairman of Trebor.

David is a graduate of the London Business School, and is a member of the Institute of Directors.

Shigeharu Hiraiwa

Shigeharu Hiraiwa is director and president of Mazda Motor (Europe). After graduating in Industrial Engineering from the Tokyo Institute of Technology, he joined Mazda Motor Corporation (then Toyo Kogyo) in 1965. Since then he has worked in a variety of roles and is now responsible for overseas marketing and sales and European R&D.

Nick Hodges

Nick Hodges was appointed group chief executive of London International Group plc in 1993. He joined LIG in 1982 as sales director of the UK operation, LRC Products, rapidly moving through the ranks to managing director of LRC Products and Regent Hospital Products with worldwide responsibilities. In 1991 he became divisional managing director, Europe/Middle East/Africa, joining the main board in 1992.

Nick previously worked for Kimberley-Clark, Golden Wonder and Johnson & Johnson. He is a graduate of London University.

Robert Holloway

Robert Holloway joined Levi Strauss & Co. in 1982 and has held a wide range of marketing and merchandising positions in Europe. He was a key member of the team behind the Levi's® brand's European marketing successes over recent years. In January 1996, he relocated to the company's San Francisco global headquarters to become vice president of the new Global Marketing team.

Tim Kelly

Tim Kelly joined Guinness plc in 1995, and is based in Dublin as marketing director for the Guinness Ireland Group. He is responsible for marketing the Guinness brand, and franchise brands such as Budweiser and Carlsberg.

Tim began his career at Unilever in 1982 and worked for Van den Berghs for four years on a variety of brands. He left in 1986 to join Coca-Cola & Schweppes Beverages as brand manager on Coca-Cola, and later held the position of marketing director from 1994.

Tim is on the Board of Cantrell and Cochrane (a joint venture between Allied Domecq and Guinness) and is on the editorial board of the *Journal of Brand Management*. He was educated at the Oratory School and Warwick University.

Archie Norman

Archie Norman joined Asda in 1991 as group chief executive, from Kingfisher plc. He became chairman of Asda in 1997. He was educated at Cambridge University and Harvard Business School, and his early career took him to Citibank and McKinsey and Co. where he was a principal.

Archie is a non-executive director of Railtrack plc, a Fellow of the Marketing Society and Member of the Council of the Industrial Society. He was voted Yorkshire Businessman of the Year in 1995 and UK Retailer of the Year in 1996. Archie is vice chairman of the Conservative Party and Member of Parliament for Tunbridge Wells.

Alan Palmer

Alan Palmer was appointed marketing director of Cadbury in 1993, and has been involved in drawing up a programme to focus investment and development behind the Cadbury brand.

Alan began his career as a graduate trainee with Cadbury Schweppes in 1974, from where he broadened his experience at Cadbury Typhoo, before beginning a six-year period at Cadbury Ltd. He later moved to Schweppes as marketing director, and has also been marketing director of Trebor Bassett.

Robert E. Riley

Robert E. Riley is managing director of Mandarin Oriental Hotel Group. He holds a Bachelor's degree from Randolph-Macon College, a law degree from University of Virginia and has extensive experience in the real estate and hotel businesses.

Robert E. Riley began his career in 1974 as an attorney practising corporate and tax law in New York. He first became involved in the hotel business when he worked for the Ford Foundation which supported various urban redevelopment projects in the USA. In 1979, he changed his career and joined a Texas-based commercial real estate and hotel developer. He continued to work in the fields of real estate and hotel investment, development and management and joined Mandarin Oriental Hotel Group in 1988.

In 1994, Robert E. Riley became chairman of the Asia Pacific Hotels Environment Initiative in liaison with the Prince of Wales Business Leaders Forum.

Frederick W. Smith

Fred Smith is chairman, president and CEO of Federal Express Corporation, the world's largest express transportation company.

Fred graduated from Yale in 1966 and served as an officer in the US Marine Corps until 1970. He founded Federal Express in 1971.

Fred serves as director on the boards of various transport, industry and civic organizations.

Sir Clive Thompson

Sir Clive Thompson is chief executive of Rentokil Initial plc which he has led for the past fifteen years, transforming it into an international service group operating in every country of Western Europe, North America and Asia Pacific.

Sir Clive graduated in Chemistry from Birmingham University and began his career in marketing with Shell. He subsequently moved to Boots, becoming the company's general manager in East Africa before returning to the UK in 1971 to join the Jeyes Group.

He is a vice president and a Fellow of the Chartered Institute of Marketing, a Fellow of the Institute of Directors, and a Companion of the British Institute of Management. He is deputy president of the CBI and will become president in July 1998. He is a member of the CBI President's Committee, the CBI Finance and General Purposes Committee and of the CBI National Council.

Sir Clive is currently a non-executive director of BAT Industries plc, Sainsbury plc, and vice chairman of Farepak plc. He is also a member of the British Overseas Trade Board.

He was knighted in the 1996 Queen's Birthday Honours.

C. C. Tung

C. C. Tung is chairman, president and CEO of Orient Overseas (International) Limited (OOIL), a position he has held since October 1996. His involvement in the company spans twenty-five years and from 1986 to 1996 he was vice president.

He studied at the University of Liverpool, where he received his

Bachelor of Science degree, and later acquired a Master's degree in Mechanical Engineering at the Massachusetts Institute of Technology.

C. C. Tung currently holds the following positions: 2nd vice chairman of the Hong Kong General Chamber of Commerce; chairman of the Merchant Navy Training Board of the Vocational Training Council; chairman of the Port Welfare Committee of Hong Kong; a member of the Port Development Board, a member of the Hong Kong/Japan Business Co-operation Committee and a member of the Hong Kong/United States Economic Co-operation Committee.

Mr Tung is also a non-executive director of Sing Tao Holdings Limited; chairman of the Hong Kong-America Center; a member of the Council of the Hong Kong Polytechnic University; a member of the School of Foreign Service, Georgetown University's Board of Visitors and a member of the University of Pittsburgh's Board of Trustees.

Allan Wong

Allan Wong is chairman of VTech Holdings Ltd. Educated at the University of Hong Kong and in the United States at the University of Wisconsin, he obtained degrees in electrical and computer engineering before joining NCR Manufacturing as a design engineer in 1974.

In 1976 he founded VTech to pursue the design and manufacture of microprocessor-based products. VTech has since grown to become the largest and most successful electronics company in Hong Kong and China, with worldwide sales exceeding $700 million, with 18,000 employees in thirteen countries.

In 1991 Allan was awarded Industrialist of the Year by the Federation of Hong Kong Industries. He serves on various business and technology committees and is also a director of the Bank of East Asia.

Introduction: Brand Championship

FIONA GILMORE

Business is war; the objective is competitor destruction through superior industrial economics. *Brand* warfare is different: the brand warrior identifies the key conquest as the customer, not the rival. Beating the rival follows inexorably from winning over the customer's heart and mind, so the process of nurturing a brand is a crucial aspect of the warrior's attack.

Branding is ultimately about securing the future of a company, its products and services, by building loyalties using emotional as well as rational values. Such values matter because they are exchanged for cash in the marketplace and affect the perception of a company's products and services as well as its ability and its freedom to manage its future.

The companies which are rated by marketeers as the rising stars for the future are those with very clearly positioned, confident corporate brands. These companies deliver through their core competencies and, more importantly, have a coherent core value and emotional brand proposition for the consumer.

A brand is inclusive. It is the tangible and intangible benefits provided by a product or service: the entire customer experience. It includes all the assets critical to delivering and communicating that experience: the name, the design, the advertising, product or service, the distribution channel, the reputation.

Brands need to be cared for in much the same way as parents care about their children: brand custodians need to know and understand the quirks, the specialness and the faults of their brands.

Increasingly, however, business leaders do not have the same parental relationship with the brands in their care. For reasons which are understandable, the typical brand owner cannot give the required time to managing brand equities as he or she used to. So, just when consumers are more open than ever before to buying into well constructed, motivating brand positionings, many brand owners have reduced the amount of time they spend thinking about their brands.

The economic case for branding

Sometimes the marketing hype overshadows the economic advantages of branding, but, as *Brand Warriors* shows, branding survives because it enhances the present value of future cashflows. This simple economic value comes from both the price premium justified by effective branding, maintaining and growing markets, and from building brand loyalty, to deter new entrants and substitutes, thereby making future earnings more secure.

In purely financial terms, the importance of brands is clearly shown by the price that companies have been prepared to pay for them. Nestlé, for example, paid £2.5 billion (more than five times the book value) to win control of the Rowntree group in 1988. Similar acquisitions can be seen in Figure 1. Virgin only came to realize the value of their brand over the last few years – when they wanted to break into financial services a new partner was willing

Figure 1: Examples of goodwill payments

Acquirer	*Target*	*Goodwill (% of price paid)*
Nestlé	Rowntree	83
GrandMet	Pillsbury	88
Cadbury Schweppes	Dr Pepper	67
United Biscuits	Verkade	66

Source: Greig Middleton & Co. Ltd

to put up half a billion pounds to Virgin's half million, for only 50 per cent of the company.

Branding is *the* differentiation strategy. The cost of differentiation must naturally be less than the perceived value, but companies must be alert to the temptation to erode differentiation by cost cutting, or other short-term tactics.

Good business leaders set about the nurturing and caring inherent in good brand management because they know it pays off. Investment bankers and other financial professionals become uneasy because even though the cost of differentiation can be quantified, its benefits cannot: shutting an inefficient factory is easier to justify than building cost into a product or a significant investment in marketing.

The economic arguments concerning brands might be characterized as the 'cost fixation' versus the 'art' schools of management: to the cost fixated, branding adds cost of uncertain value, so it is driven out and joins the other downsizing initiatives. This to me is the classic short-term view. Renting a brand share encourages brand promiscuity, where a customer shows little loyalty.

Most, if not all, consumers like choice. Observers of the British supermarkets' struggle for share attribute part of Tesco's dramatic overturn of Sainsbury's historical leadership to Tesco's commitment to brand choice. In many other product categories, consumers like the intrinsic or extrinsic reward of branding. Who buys training shoes without explicit branding? The secret, surely, of good marketing is understanding customers' underlying motivations, the deep psychological needs and moods. For this reason, it is dangerous to assume that 'mystique' per se is still credible or relevant. Even today, there are brand custodians who, when asked to sum up their brand's positioning, confide knowingly, 'Well, it's mystique, isn't it'. Today's customer cannot be bought so easily. *Brand Warriors* shows that mystique has to be replaced by a true psychological contract between customer and company.

Charismatic branding must go hand-in-hand with delivery of the functional product values. The equation is not based on an addition but on multiplication:

Brand values × product delivery = customer satisfaction.

If either brand values or product delivery equals zero, you will not deliver customer satisfaction.

The two schools of management ('cost fixation' and 'art') illustrate the perennial dilemma of the director's task. The multiplier effect can give significant leverage. How do you strike an appropriate balance between the two sides? Careful benchmarking of where your brand *really* is, rather than where you have convinced yourself it should be, is central to this process. Successful brands operating in aggressively competitive markets have acquired these disciplines out of necessity. Brands which have flourished in monopolistic environments have greater difficulty in coming to terms with self-criticism. While companies will never achieve perfection in both product delivery and soft values, *Brand Warriors* confronts this dilemma.

The economic arguments are more difficult for the 'cost-fixated' manager. Branding needs the sustenance of investment, but everyone knows that at least half of it is wasted. It is easy to see that successful brands command a price premium and that their branding creates a volume demand, which can provide scale economies in procurement, manufacturing, distribution, R&D and even marketing. Plus, critically, once these are achieved, they are *real* barriers to entry.

Cost-fixated managers, even if they are not comfortable with the art of branding, ought at least to know about the risks of high sunk costs in market entry caused by better-scaled branded competitors. The final nail in the coffin of the cost-fixated view is the inexorable temptation to reduce price. The quickest way of eroding profits is by reducing prices; and it is very hard to raise them again. Low cost and differentiation are not alternative strategies. Most of the greatest branded businesses have always pursued both with vigour; exploiting all possible economies of scale to deliver lowest cost and differentiating via product, service and branding. This combination is the key to superior returns, higher profit margins and less likelihood of disruption by new entrants.

Short-term pressures on performance have destroyed the Procter & Gamble paradigm of 'brand manager as managing director of the brand'. Today's brand manager is often the custodian of tactics to maximize short-term profitability, not the custodian of brand positioning and brand values. In these circumstances, the custodian of brand positioning and brand values clearly needs to be the CEO with the support of the team. Only he or she can balance the short-term/long-term trade-off. *Brand Warriors* illustrates the importance of not being distracted from managing the brand.

The custodian's role should not be underestimated. Brands need a lot of love. Fred Smith, founder and chairman of FedEx, has a clear view about his role: 'maintaining [the FedEx] reputation and its brand image is a top priority for me, since it is one of the most valuable things the company has.'

Allan Wong, chairman of VTech, has admitted that many companies in the Far East are only now starting to appreciate the importance of developing a brand: 'being too focused on cost and not nurturing and investing in the brand has been typical of many companies in this region. Perhaps people here are very good merchants but are not necessarily also good at building brands.'

Brand warriors need courage to take difficult decisions. In 1997, British Airways chose to cut costs, rationalizing its workforce, and also decided to build on traditional values and invest new values in its brand through a costly redesign programme.

For maximum effectiveness, everyone must work together towards the same goals and with a realistic degree of harmony. The old adage of partners sharing the same bed and dreaming different dreams is an issue for every business. As Archie Norman of Asda once put it: 'a company like this tends to be like a large orchestra: it's no good having the lead violins ahead of the rest.'

Realizing the dream: local or international

The senior management team may not always agree about their international aspirations and strategy. Nick Hodges, responsible for the Durex brand, refers to the pitfalls of local baron warfare. Clarity of vision and acceptance of that vision are crucial.

Otherwise, life becomes ambiguous and tiresome for everyone involved, resulting in a weakening of brand positioning and management drive. When British Airways decided to become a global brand, a massive change in structure, attitude, behaviour and communication was required. As *Brand Warriors* shows, a lot of energy and management time must go into similar exercises.

The single-minded, global strategy has been embraced by American brands such as Levi's and Coca-Cola, and Japanese brands such as Sony and Canon. Few other Asian home-grown brands have become universal household names, but this is all changing, as the Asian entrepreneurs realize the benefits of developing the brand.

In Europe, there is a growing number of companies recognizing the value of an international vision. Two of the biggest fast moving consumer goods (FMCG) companies, Unilever and L'Oréal, have been moving towards greater focus on core competencies and commitment to global branding. There are certain attractions to developing brands in new regions: remarkable market growth and significant consumer respect for international as opposed to indigenous brands. Achieving economies of scale through harmonization, such as product format, advertising and design, can obviously bring huge rewards. These emerging regions, however, bring new challenges and some of these are described in the chapters about L'Oréal and McDonald's.

Brand Warriors illustrates dilemmas and challenges both local and international. For example, Durex (LIG) is looking to adopt one brand-name worldwide and Guinness is capitalizing on the universal appeal of the 'Irish soul'. The imperialistic approach is rejected in favour of a listening attitude. Nick Hodges of LIG suggests: 'You always see the corny expression, "think globally, act locally", well, even big brands must take local action . . . We can't decide to roll out a brand globally and just do it. Local attitudes, approaches and sensitivities must all be taken into account.'

McDonald's makes certain that its menus reflect the cultural framework; so the Maharaja Mac™ is the Indian version of the Big Mac™. The brand's emotional values remain unchanged, but the 'rest is about tailoring it for local markets'. As Robert Holloway of

Levi Strauss suggests: 'The emotional chords any global brand needs to strike will have many similarities worldwide. It is how you hit them successfully in executional terms that ensures the brand's continuing success.'

Effective implementation and relevance can only be achieved using strong local teams which understand the particular cultural, historical and economic nuances that are likely to influence brand appeal. The conversation should never be one-way. L'Oréal's management team is open to ideas and insights from anyone, anywhere: 'We soon realized it would be very difficult to develop an effective long-term strategy ... without our own organization, our own "family" to give us feedback from the ground.'

Sensitivity manifests itself in executional terms. The Mandarin Oriental Hotel Group's fan symbolizing the Eastern quality standards of personal service is central to its service proposition, but given increased relevance as well as charm by being interpreted differently for each market. As Robert Riley says: 'This kind of originality gives life to our identity – it's not a rigid, static thing.'

Deeply committed to being a global brand, British Airways symbolizes its intention through its new visual identity introduced in June 1997. British Airways has chosen to dispense with the Union Jack motif and heraldic crest, replacing them with a logo, suggesting wings and speed, but curved to create a warmer feel, adorning the tailfins with ethnic and abstract works of art. The British Airways plane feels less like a flying bus and more like a feathery friend, showing off its bright plumage.

This is a fascinating change as it represents a swing in mood within society as a whole. The 1997 identity suggests a more open, less arrogant and jingoistic spirit for the brand. Those who choose the British Airways badge, in the future, will by association be showing an interest in a multi-cultural world and a curiosity to discover diverse, creative forces. The pre-1997 identity now looks not only dated but is a perfect historic icon of the mood of the 1980s, where a more didactic corporate tone of voice was admired. The new identity has lost any possible imperialistic overtones and suggests 'we come in peace'.

British Airways is, at the very least, demonstrating both orthodoxy and unorthodoxy (the paradox of Britishness) in its new identity; namely, respect for relevant heritage and equity combined with courage and vision to break new ground. An identity can be both fixed and flexible. It is fixed in the sense that there are familiar icons suggesting the inherent consistency in the brand and its offer. It is flexible in the way it has been dramatized through the variations of art form, reflecting the creative characteristics of the brand. In this way, it has life and spirit; it is a true living brand.

Many see there are strengths in combining globalization and localization. Jos Brenkel of Hewlett-Packard states: 'Centralization means cost saving. Localization means being closer to your customer.'

Figure 2: Brand architecture options

Monolithic (single dominant corporate brand)	Fixed Endorsed (strong, strait-jacket endorsement)	Flexible Endorsed (flexible in terms of high level, low level variations, depending on relationship to heartland)	Discreet (corporate brand is not used overtly with consumers)
Levi's			
Canon	Kellogg's	Cadbury's	
Sony		L'Oréal	Procter & Gamble
FedEx		Guinness	(e.g. Ariel,
OOCL		Mazda	Pantene, Pampers)
Rentokil Initial			
Mandarin Oriental	Durex		
British Airways			
VTech			
McDonald's			
Hewlett-Packard	There are many endorsed strategy options ranging from high		
Asda	level to low level, strait-jacket through to flexible		

Developing the brand architecture

I use the term 'brand architecture' to define the strategic relationship between corporate brands and product brands and I have identified four types of brand architecture. (1) The 'monolithic' approach, with a single dominant corporate brand, such as Levi's, is highly focused and cost effective. (2) The 'fixed endorsed' approach, with a strong strait-jacket endorsement, such as Kellogg's, allows clear product line differentiation but ensures the 'master brand' remains all-powerful. (3) The 'flexible endorsed' approach, such as Cadbury's, allows sub-brands to become heroes, with the Cadbury's signature acting as endorsement. (4) The 'discreet' approach, deployed by Procter & Gamble with brands such as Ariel, Pantene and Pampers, ensures that the corporate brand is not used overtly with consumers (see Figure 2).

Clearly there are pros and cons to each approach. The 'discreet' approach is costly – each brand needs clear differentiation and support – but the 'monolithic' approach can be limiting. Then again, 'monolithic' and 'fixed endorsed' approaches are the most economic methods of support, as it is difficult to afford a range of product brands without a corporate umbrella endorsement.

In 1989 I ran a worldwide assessment of corporate architectures and predicted that more and more companies would focus on their corporate brands, as competition and economic pressures increased. *Brand Warriors* illustrates how this refocusing is taking place. Vodafone's Chris Gent had no doubt about the benefits of reducing their twelve brands down to just the single Vodafone brand. He wanted to give transparency to the customer, and maximize their marketing effort.

British Airways has recognized the primary role of the corporate brand, and is now reasserting its commitment to the brand's status, appeal and reputation. It has rejected its 1980 'pillar branding' strategy which, although it was created to *support* the corporate brand, ultimately placed too much emphasis on product brands and thereby diluted the core brand.

When Nestlé took over Rowntree, it wasted no time in introducing a corporate brand endorsement to all the original Rowntree product brands, which had historically been most coy about their corporate brand. Owing to the range of products in Nestlé's portfolio, it is unlikely to choose an even stronger corporate branding approach which could become too rigid and too limiting. A range of endorsement strategies is available and has to be tailored according to the proximity between the core brand values and products.

Successful brand champions assess the complex value matrices of each individual brand, and endeavour to communicate the varying offers without alienating particular customer groups. There will be those who buy BA First for business travel, but BA World Traveller, or another brand, for holidays. Other consumers will buy Marks & Spencer's underwear but insist on Jaeger or Armani for business clothes. This is a more complex jungle than the choice between Nescafé and own-brand coffee. A great challenge for more dominant corporate branding is to manage these apparent value gaps successfully without eroding one side or deterring the other.

Brand dilution has often been the result of greedy expansion, diversification and meaningless extensions. Today, there is greater awareness of the benefits of concentration. As Alan Palmer of Cadbury reflects: 'it is probably no accident that those branded entities that have survived and prospered under a single company's ownership owe their success to deep-rooted management competencies and considered investment over time in the core values of their products.'

The other dimension is the discipline of concentration on core competencies. Rentokil Initial's growth was based on this belief: 'over time, we have carefully developed and extended the brand according to our core competence', the core competence in this case being a range of service activities.

Levi's has survived the pitfalls. According to Robert Holloway: 'Perhaps the most common mistake when you become successful is to try to stamp your brand on everything ... It often takes a calamity to focus a company's collective mind. When you're doing very well the temptation is to keep adding bits here and there. Ultimately you risk losing your core consumer.'

And as Nick Hodges of Durex says: 'Diversification had led to management losing sight of the core business – the Durex brand and Biogel surgical gloves – and the heritage of the company.'

One of the benefits of the monolithic approach is, as Sir Clive Thompson of Rentokil Initial says: the 'leverage from one activity to another. The down-side is potential dilution of the impact of the brand, because it acts as an umbrella rather than being sharp and focused on the single activity.'

Another confident, highly respected corporate brand is Virgin, an exception to this principle of core competency focus. This is a brand based on a highly seductive proposition, 'I'm one of you', that is, not one of them, one of those corporates. A 'people's champion' brand is very pertinent to the mood of the late 1990s, and building a brand on a psychological plane, rather than on functional product offer, allows for much more elasticity. Virgin can credibly cruise from music to airline, from vodka to financial services. Richard Branson has an appetite for this kind of challenge: 'Ultimately, Virgin will go where we can have fun and where there's an angle.'

So many companies are excited by what Virgin has achieved that they too will be developing their corporate brand architecture in a similar vein. This more fluid, organic development of a corporate brand is certainly inspirational, particularly for young marketeers. Virgin's protagonist, Richard Branson, is a folk hero in parts of the world and in this respect a traditional corporate monolith cannot so easily engage young wannabes. This winning strategy still requires guaranteed product delivery and value justification. Consumers loyal to Virgin forgive certain disappointing experiences on their trains because they like the attitude of the brand, but ultimately there are limitations to how far loyalty can be stretched. Retailers who own conventional distribution channels have also demonstrated brand elasticity; major multiples, such as Asda, can offer a wide range of products and services and are beginning to challenge the conventional high-street banks.

The world is big enough to accommodate contrasting types of corporate brand and endless brand elasticity is not necessarily appropriate. Perhaps, more importantly, it is a question of deciding what you want to be, and doing it in full knowledge of the implications. L'Oréal builds its own brand on emotional, aspirational values as well as product superiority, and, like Cadbury, has a powerful signature.

Some products have the same values and emotional offer as their parent brand, but they carry additional and specific benefits for smaller, niche audiences. These offspring are sometimes called sub-brands. They should be clearly positioned (as, for example, Durex Fetherlite) and their differentiation should be consonant with the corporate brand values. Mutual reinforcement, the multiplier effect, can be a central benefit in a brand architecture strategy. A symbiotic relationship can often be particularly beneficial to the parent corporate brand, as in the case of Mazda MX5.

Sometimes, the sub-brand begins to contradict rather than reinforce the parent's core values, resulting in loss of brand coherence. In certain markets, such as toiletries, product brands have proliferated to the extent that the consumer is more likely to be bewildered than bewitched. *Brand Warriors* shows that the ultimate decision-makers have to determine how those relationships should be developed, but they need to do so in collaboration with the ultimate brand champion: the consumer.

The benefits of mutual reinforcement, such as credibility, impact, cost efficiencies and product brand freedoms (frameworks within which to operate), have been central to the debate for many of the brands discussed in this book. Building business alone is not enough. 'The moment you produce something that disturbs ... the soul of the brand – you're in trouble,' says Robert Holloway of Levi Strauss & Co.

Cadbury too has achieved a sophisticated and successful model where the positioning of a new product is considered carefully in relation to the core values, and all aspects of communication, including visual identity, reflect that relationship faithfully. The coherent and yet inherently flexible Cadbury architecture provides an increasingly attractive strategy for FMCG brands, which need the strength of a single brand proposition and product offers individually designed with precision. European FMCG brand companies such as Unilever and L'Oréal have been particularly inventive in this respect in recent years.

Keeping the brand relevant

It takes skill to understand the needs and moods of your customers, to connect them with the brand proposition and then to *deliver* it. First Direct is a perfect example of making the right connection with users who were frustrated with the traditional methods of banks and were open to new distribution channels.

Many admit to past failures because they did not understand customer needs and moods. For example, Mazda admits: 'For too long we have been product- rather than market- and marketing-led.' The mature brands have often learned this lesson the hard way: the challenge for Levi's 'is to remain relevant to a target audience that regenerates itself every four or five years; and . . . to avoid the distractions of success . . . History is one element of the brand-building equation. The other part is adapting our history to a lifestyle that is relevant and interesting to today's consumers. A classic mistake brand managers make is to become too obsessed with their own culture, talking to consumers in ways that are too remote from actual experience – preaching history.'

Guinness is another mature but outward-looking brand whose management is directly and constantly involved in consumer research. Stimulated by creative methods of research and serious benchmarking, the Guinness managers teach their people to listen hard.

Not so long ago, a worldwide brand leader still claimed 'the *mysterious* beauty fluids help'. Consumers in both developing and advanced economies will no longer be patronized. Today, customers seek greater knowledge about products and services. The 'smart home' (real or virtual) gives more power to the consumer, so the product or service performance benefits are more crucial than ever. Activism on the part of the tourist, the patient, the mobile phone user, the utilities' user and the investor is increasingly evident. In this environment, the people own the brand.

While trying to maintain relevance to the consumer, the company must also tread with care. The opening of McDonald's in Russia is a case in point: 'We keep reminding ourselves of what makes us successful. We cannot just rush into new countries if it means we cannot achieve the level of quality and consistency our customers expect. It is much better to do the right thing and guarantee quality than to go for speed. And it works: the Moscow McDonald's is now the busiest in the world.' In Levi's case, in Europe, 'by hitting the right note, sales for the Levi's brand went up 800 per cent'.

With any brand, the offer has to be coherent in every aspect for a brand's appeal can be fragile. A few years ago Asda lost its appeal, and since then the company has worked hard to regain it. A feeling of Asdaness or Guinnessness can be engendered through delicately balanced messages, themes and variations.

The level of sophistication employed to ensure brand relevance varies among the companies featured here. At Levi's, for example, a European research pilot covered 500 of the core youth target group in each of seven key territories. It has now been rolled out as 'a measure of total brand image strength, breadth, depth and salience across Europe'.

Anticipating future needs is both a skill and an art. Insights from research, combined with imaginative leaps can create exciting opportunities. Fundamental needs never change, but the way in which these needs can be reinterpreted and given new meaning is one of the most rewarding activities of a brand engineer.

Creativity and its value

Imaginative leaps are not the preserve of consultants bearing the title 'creative'. Everyone involved in the development of a brand should be encouraged to make leaps in thinking. Ultimately, a brand dies if it is allowed to stand still, and therefore the culture of an organization has to be dynamic in order for it to progress. Shigeharu Hiraiwa of Mazda believes in continuous progress: 'brands are not static things, they have to evolve.'

The brand custodian must never neglect his or her duty to encourage the team. An organic, creative process begins with the tone of the leadership. Brand warriors encourage their colleagues to think freely. Lateral thinking is a rare gift and should be valued much more than it is.

Technology industries welcome change: it is in their bloodstream. Hewlett-Packard's Jos Brenkel comments: 'We have to hire people who like change, but who understand that change must never affect product quality, or compromise our core values.'

Anticipating needs has been of prime concern to Fred Smith of FedEx: 'for a growing number of major corporations, our air fleet has become their 500-miles-an-hour warehouse: we take over their entire logistics functions ... And now, FedEx is ready to provide the distribution infrastructure the Internet commerce needs. What the clipper ship and railroads did for nineteenth- and twentieth-century trade, we are ready to do for the twenty-first century ... That skill – the ability to meet the needs customers don't know they have – is what continues to drive our business forward.'

Brand supremacy cannot be assumed. Competition is a positive trigger. Bob Ayling has no doubt that British Airways has to give customer service new meaning: 'the quality of customer service we give and the reputation we have for customer service must get better and better. What some people might think are dangers to our business could be stimulants to its growth.'

An unconventional corporate identity can attract new prospects who may have hitherto rejected a brand for being too staid. That's fine, as long as the core loyalists are not alienated. A niche sponsorship programme aimed at opinion-formers can appear indulgent, but may in fact be part of a focused, long-term campaign.

Take Mazda's approach to sponsorship. The idea of sponsoring is an old one, but the idea of reflecting the spirit of your brand in a new concerto commissioned by your company is exciting. The striving for harmony is fundamental to Mazda and therefore to this new Michael Nyman concerto. Thematically linked communications, where the core values of the brand are echoed consistently, require imagination. Otherwise, the result can be ponderous and dull.

More and more companies are exploring scenarios for the future, matching advances in technology and design trends with projected needs. The 'leapfrogging' approach is particularly favoured in the Asian region, where companies learn from others' mistakes, thereby avoiding pitfalls. VTech recognized that its competitors suffered from the absence of an in-house technology capability. VTech has the know-how to produce a constant flow of unique offers.

Making proper time to *think* is tough in a world obsessed with instant results. Brand champions make the time. They also know there will be disappointment as well as success. Guinness' Tim Kelly accepts: 'you won't succeed unless you make an effort, and in making an effort, sometimes you will fail.' Fred Smith, with over twenty-five years' experience, professes: 'our goal is perfection, but we live in an imperfect world.'

Mobilizing creativity through fluid structures

The value of the people who can make creative leaps is increasingly recognized. Seeing things differently will be a greater valued skill, particularly in markets where standard performance differentials are eroded.

The most effective brand developers are structured to allow these creative leaps to see the light of day with, for example, global marketing teams who stand distinct from the day-to-day local or regional management, as in the case of Unilever and Levi's.

Levi's Global Marketing group was created in 1996 to 'act as visionaries, outside national and regional constraints and to build and manage global developments such as the Internet, media, sponsorship, Original Levi's Stores and brand equity management tools.' It allows Levi's to 'transfer best practices from local markets to global markets, bringing a new perspective to the individual and local businesses that previously didn't exist.'

Hewlett-Packard's 'entrepreneurial flexibility is fostered by decentralized business units which have a fair degree of autonomy'; its consistency, in terms of consumer perceptions across a wide range of products, 'has arisen from both culture and behaviour'. As Jos Brenkel states: 'We have had over fifty years to build up values based on our people, customer support and service, the products, innovation and active citizenship.' He admits, though, that 'trying to cement together this very diverse company with its 112,000 employees can still be a challenge.' For the global brands such as Hewlett-Packard, the intranet has transformed work processes and enabled a faster, more comprehensive exchange of ideas.

McDonald's franchised structure allows it to work 'based on long-term commitment' so it has built an infrastructure to facilitate that. As John Hawkes says: 'In order to achieve consistency, we need partners who can not only understand us, but also live by our standards.' McDonald's identify its franchising system as one of the organization's greatest strengths: 'franchisees ... bring a wealth of individual flair into the business ... and the franchisees have typically signed up for twenty years and because it is their livelihood, they bring a great deal of dedication and energy to a restaurant's development.'

For many featured in *Brand Warriors*, the direction, tone and style with which things are done are established at the top. That means that not just the intellectual tone – the strategy framework – but the way that people work, and what they do, can now be assessed by the use of competencies.

L'Oréal's structure, with its segmented approach to brands, as well as giving it a prominent position in the three main channels, allows each signature to function as its own business. It fosters the notion of internal competition which, the company believes, is vital to keep it fit.

Many companies are adopting a more mobile, less hierarchical shape. Flat structures have replaced pyramidal structures and the benefits derived from this include more accountability, greater speed and efficiency and, crucially, real focus. Holistic strategy with local implementation is the most attractive approach. A recurring theme from each contributor is the importance of this creativity. It's apparent in the way each tells his story. The L'Oréalian idea of 'poet and peasant' is the very heartbeat of the company's culture. Imaginative people who are both ambitious and generous are selected early on and then they are valued, respected and motivated to stay.

Respecting your roots

Giving a brand some meaning, something engaging and appealing to consumers is crucially important. Keep things simple, but not simplistic, otherwise you patronize your audience.

Perhaps the most important question for the contributors to address is, 'What meaning do you attribute to your brand?'

We often gain insights into the culture of a country by exploring the essence of a brand. We can sometimes understand a brand better by knowing the culture of the country of the brand's origin.

McDonald's and Levi's are symbols of the casual, unpretentious American lifestyle. L'Oréal's personality exudes French charm, flair and finesse. British Airways reflects some of the British virtues of stability, subtlety and yet unorthodoxy. OOCL mirrors typical Hong Kong characteristics: boldness, pride, free spirit. Guinness reflects much of the attraction of Irish soul; in fact, Guinness seems to be doing a grand job for the Irish tourist industry. The Mazda philosophy is a product reflecting Japan: renowned for its high quality, high standards and modern technology.

In other instances, the roots of a brand have less to do with the culture of one specific country and are more concerned with the founder's moral and philosophical motivations. This is true in the case of Cadbury and FedEx.

When Archie Norman proclaims 'to thine ownself be true', as Asda returns to its Yorkshire roots for inspiration, perhaps there is a message here for all brands. Take care not to throw away your cultural roots, jettisoning your equities. A business, in its bid to act globally, can become enfeebled by its acceptance of lowest common denominator values. While certain aspects of a traditional culture convey parochialism, these characteristics may be some of the brand's most distinguishing and motivating assets. A defensive move towards putative commonality can herald the beginning of decline.

Living the brand

OOCL and VTech are corporate brands that have recognized the importance of sharing the brand vision. Chinese companies have historically been typified by the brilliance of their merchants. Now, they are building expertise in long-term branding and this will encourage people to articulate their brand values in a more deliberate way.

Perceptions of the ideal corporate brand vary widely from country to country but, in many countries, social status brands still hold sway. Recent research conducted by Springpoint shows that, in advanced economies, the ideal corporate brand is friendly, enjoys life and has imagination. It is interested in profit, but considerate to staff and suppliers. It is not dogmatic and hears others' opinions. Many Europeans say, 'they promised us the caring 90s, it's turned into the scaring 90s'. That is why brands which mouth platitudes such as 'We are a caring, trustworthy brand' may no longer be credible. The didactic, authoritarian approach to building trust values can alienate people.

Security is a deeper, warmer, more human notion. A 'caring brand' can gain meaning through its ability to understand the psyche of its customers. The British Airways Business 'larder' for the middle-of-the-night snack is a good example. Levi's 'Personal Pair' jeans, tailor-made to your size, is another.

Getting it wrong *within* a company can also alienate people. Motherhood and apple pie propositions which are not followed through are a waste of space or, at best, a sop to a divisive board. Levi's teach people to 'walk the talk'. Hewlett-Packard believes: ' "Just be." In other words, don't advertise your values, just live them.'

A mismatch between the external and internal protection of a 'caring' brand is upsetting to employees and suppliers. When you get it right from within, as is now the case with Asda, your brand attains a deeper resonance. 'Getting it right from within' is echoed by every service champion. For example, OOCL, Mandarin Oriental, FedEx and McDonald's recognize that *the brand is delivered by the people*. This message is not only pertinent to service brands, but is more relevant than ever today for FMCG brand champions than it was when times were easier.

Branding in the future

Some argue that brands will wither away, particularly in the supermarket arena. Certainly, the trends in economies such as Western Europe suggest that more discerning consumers, prompted by increasing fragmentation of distribution channels, greater knowledge and, in some respects, greater insecurity, show increasing willingness to buy own label. Retail Own Brand can, of course, be a brand. The retailer is a trusted supplier and the major multiple retailer can offer any product or service relevant to his customer, where he has an edge. Fuel, OTC products, insurance and financial services – there appear to be no restrictions.

Retail Own Brand has eroded traditional brands' shares across many parts of Europe. Carrefour, the French chain of supermarkets, has been selling own label computers since 1995. Décathlon, the French sports goods retailer, sells own label sports goods across France and Spain. Its own range includes sports shoes, clothing, bikes and trekking kit. In 1997 this retailer had become the sixth biggest sports manufacturer in Europe, and the second in France. Corte Ingles is one of the main distributors for credit cards in Spain. Sectors which historically were exclusively branded are now open to this retail competition (see Figure 3).

The reality is that own label has lost any social stigma it once had (see Figure 4). Interest and experience can provide people with the confidence to buy own label and avoid well-known brands.

Once upon a time, there was a simple world where a stable line

Figure 3: Acceptance of own label brands – not just FMCG products. Those who could imagine buying the following own label products when offered for sale by their local supermarket

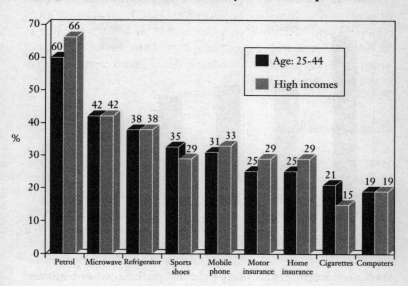

Source: The Henley Centre, *Frontiers: Planning for Consumer Change in Europe 1996/7*

of manufacturing brands dominated a market. Retail Own Brand has now gone so far that the old order of Brands and Commodities has disappeared for ever in certain parts of the world. The conventional model has gone and, as in chaos theory,* a bifurcation has occurred: there are now FMCG brands and retail brands. Within this turbulent environment, there appear to be new 'spikes' of order, breaking into four, then eight lines, as distribution channels fragment. For example, Eismann provides home delivery of frozen foods and First Direct promotes telephone banking.

Within this apparent chaos, however, a new regularity will emerge. In the future, with the convenience of shopping on the

* *Chaos* by James Gleick (London: Heinemann, 1988; Minerva, 1996).

Figure 4: Percentage of high earners who agree, 'I would be prepared to pay more for a supermarket "own label" champagne if I thought it was better.'

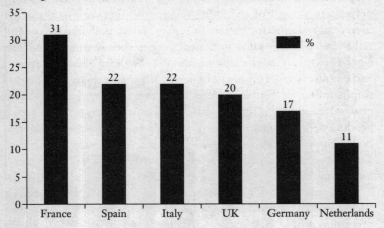

Source: The Henley Centre, *Frontiers: Planning for Consumer Change in Europe* 1996/97

Web, product choices are likely to be more concerned with quality/value trade-off. Interactive media can be regarded as both a threat and an opportunity for companies. Technology is a key driver, changing the way markets are and will work. Ultimately FedEx, UPS and DHL may become the channel; and the mechanics will be the Web, mail, phone. There are risks to conducting transactions simply on the Web, however. If you reduce all your exposure to a consumer down to a transactional, rational level, do you undermine your own ability to create the myth which is the heartbeat of a brand?

Levi's raises this question and many companies today are grappling with this issue. However hard we try to be rational about product choice, we are not purely logical in our responses. As we have discussed earlier, brand appeal and reputation are created not only through the product experience but as a result of both controlled and uncontrolled communication (such as the hostile publicity that Unilever's Persil Power received in the mid-1990s in the UK).

Intangible values may evoke a range of emotional benefits, ranging from self-enhancement, romance, fun, through to deeper, spiritual yearnings. Even City analysts are liable to form opinions about corporate brands in this way. For many years the City has tried to perpetuate a myth of a rational relationship between institutional investment and performance. In reality, many individuals buy and sell shares with the same fickleness as they choose which premium lager to drink. The challenge is therefore to own *both* the rational and emotional high ground and, in this way, own the total relationship. Product performance superiority continues to be a desirable goal, whether this is judged in terms of customer service or actual product delivery. The emotional high ground will always influence brand choice, but in new ways. For example, the ethical stance of a company, projected through its corporate brand, will engender a moral contract.

Perception will always be crucial. As Robert Holloway says: 'What makes Levi's different, and allows them to be priced at a premium, is how they are branded and *perceived*. As a result, Levi's earn Levi Strauss & Co. twice the profit that other manufacturers' jeans earn them.'

To cope with the diverse challenges of fragmented distribution and more sophisticated competition, the warrior must demonstrate his ability to resist the temptation to compromise on the big ideas. He or she will need to reduce layers of bureaucracy even further and empower innovation or breakthrough groups to create the revolution in corporate brand positioning, architecture, concept, creation and product development. These groups will be so structured, as to be able to form and re-form according to the nature of the project. A headache to manage well, such teams are immensely effective.

Recruitment and management development policies will adapt as corporations build new kinds of teams, where creative talent is allowed to shine through and make an impact.

Brand positionings will be more distinctive and more engaging. Trademarks will be respected as only part of a brand identity and a brand identity will be seen as an important part, but only one part, of a brand experience.

Brands are about people and ideas. *Brand Warriors* explores the ways in which people and ideas come together to make a profit. United in a common mission, the brand is fuelled by an inner fire. The warmth and glow of this fire radiates and creates the *charismatic* brand. The brand warrior can light and tend the fire, controlling its flames. Unmotivated people let the fire rage out of control or allow it to die. Motivated people deliver a fire that glows and radiates warmth. In *Brand Warriors*, all the brands selected have in common an inner fire.

Marketing in the third millennium will be tougher than ever before. Brand warriors, as individuals, will be thinking in unconventional ways about new kinds of distribution channels, media strategies, distinctive brand positionings, architectures, moral dilemmas, quality of life aspirations and a new vocabulary for brand development. The challenge for every business leader, outside commodity sectors, will be his or her ability, every day, to be a true brand warrior.

1 | Asda: The Accelerated Repositioning of a Brand

ARCHIE NORMAN, *chairman*

To thine own self be true

If there is one lesson to be drawn from the Asda experience it's this: the secret of successful branding is 'to thine own self be true'. In retailing especially, your shoppers define your brand, and knowing what your brand stands for and how it appeals to its core customers is key. The successful revival of the Asda brand was the result of a determined return to powerful core brand values that had once made it popular, but had been lost, forgotten or deliberately rejected.

From its origins in the 1970s, Asda was a pioneer. It had a unique positioning as the place you could go to get everything you needed at the lowest prices. It was the UK's first superstore, selling a wide range of groceries and non-food items such as clothing, washing machines and toys. It pioneered the idea of permanent low pricing before it became a fashionable concept. And, long before others began to see the vital importance of the shopping experience, it consciously tried to craft a better way to shop – one that would appeal to the whole family.

By the late 1980s, the business had comprehensively lost its way. Its roots had been abandoned in an attempt to copy the strategies of rivals J. Sainsbury and Tesco which were more upmarket and up-margin. At the same time, the group had invested heavily by diversifying into other businesses such as furniture and carpets.

Asda had started chasing after the customers it thought it would like to have and, in its search for higher margins and a more upmarket customer base, it had begun to suppress the very brand identity that had made it so popular. In doing so, Asda became caught up in a vicious circle, losing customers, pushing up margins to compensate for that loss, thereby accelerating the customer exodus, responding by pushing up prices even further, and so on.

By the time a new management team took over in 1991, sales per square foot were two-thirds that of the market leader, a £1 billion debt mountain was piling up and the group's share price had entered a tail-spin. The organization was in the grip of a triple crisis: a crisis of confidence, an identity crisis and a financial crisis. If it was to survive, all three had to be tackled. Fast.

By 1996, Asda's debt mountain had been eliminated, the company's profitability was restored and rising and, in fierce competitive conditions, its sales growth was outstripping its rivals. The brand had staged a dramatic and comprehensive recovery.

Move fast and focus on your strengths

To turn Asda around, everyone had to understand that things had to change if the organization was both to survive and to thrive, and that the change would be major, radical and painful.

Clear overall directions were set out – directions which came from the roots of the business. Asda's stores are in areas of Britain with lower-than-average demographics and tend to be older and larger than those of the competition. So it was clear that Asda had to trade in a way that exploited its floor space while tapping into the powerful brand heritage.

To create scope for the radical change needed, two new projects were set up within the first hour I was in the business. One was called Renewal; its task was to create an idea of what the Asda store should look like in the mid-1990s, what it was aspiring to achieve. The other project subsequently became known as Dales; it was all about creating Britain's best wide-range discount formula.

This overall direction was quickly confirmed by research, which showed Asda's customers still remembered the old things about it: an honest, no-nonsense 'Yorkshire' brand synonymous with value. Everything subsequently centred on reinterpreting those brand values for the 1990s, and focused on four key elements:

- Asda is a family shop. A greater percentage of people who shop at Asda have children and shop with children. They also stay in the store for longer. So Asda must stock a range wide enough to satisfy customers' basic needs; it must be a place where they can solve problems such as what to give the kids for tea on Friday night; and it should have a cafeteria so that customers can sit down and relax for a moment too. As such, the Asda store should be closer to the community than its rivals.

- Asda has 'Yorkshire heritage'. That means it is honest in what it does. It is authentic. It has integrity. It is ordinary and every day, without pretensions.

- Asda is committed to value. Instead of adopting yo-yo pricing policies and promotional gimmicks so that customers are never sure how much things will really cost, it opts for steady, permanently low prices. This delivers recognizable value to the customers, and it reduces the manipulation, thereby positioning the brand as the housewife's champion. Any promotions must be authentic. In other words, if Asda buys for less, the customer buys for less. If it gets a good deal on pineapples, or finds a way of engineering better value into the system, it is passed on to the customer.

- It must be an enjoyable shopping experience. Partly, this is connected with Asda's family focus, but it is also about the experience in store: Asda is a place people enjoy going to because it contains a lot of interesting things, things customers didn't expect to find, things which solve problems they have been worrying about. It's all about creating a sense that this store is for its customers and that staff are there to serve. And that means integrating service throughout Asda stores, actively helping and stimulating the shopper.

Live the legend

Once these brand values had been clarified, Asda set about living the legend. First and foremost that meant cutting costs. If Asda were to offer value for money, which means lower prices on goods overall than its major competitors, then there would have to be lower costs. That meant starting from the centre. For the first year, there was a complete wage and salary freeze. Overheads were quickly reduced by a third, by trawling through each department and store to find ways to cut costs.

At the same time, Asda had to find ways to express all the core brand values, using a process called 'sauna-ing'. It involved an intense review of every aspect of the business and the store: from cost structure to store layout, design and format, and the way customers were served. For example, before the new team began, the first thing a customer encountered on entering a store was clothing. But food values are fundamentally important to Asda, and so food is now right up front. And, to communicate a no-nonsense, market trader feel, it is now displayed differently. Whereas in some rival stores everything is arranged so perfectly that the shopper feels afraid to pick up a piece of fruit, Asda piles it up, giving the impression of relative abundance; the place looks lived in.

At every twist and turn, Asda looked for ways to express its brand values. One way which emphasized the value-for-money proposition was to put prices on blackboards as though the local produce man had chalked up the price of tomatoes that morning. Wider aisles were installed for easy traffic flow for the whole family. Samplings and tastings were introduced to involve and entice customers and to create a sense of personality, warmth and theatre. And the store layout was planned as though it were a good book. As they come out of the store, people should be able to tell you what the highlights were, what the chapter headings were, and why it had an exciting ending. What you don't have is a really exciting first chapter, a boring bit in the middle and a punch-line at the end. It has to be paced – at the end of each aisle there must be something exciting.

Only after the sauna-ing process was well under way and Asda was truly delivering what mattered, was mass media advertising appropriate. The whole idea of 'Asda price' (which had been abandoned) was revived, re-creating Asda's once famous tap on the pocket, 'pocket the difference' imagery.

The challenge in retailing is that your customers experience your product directly. They actually walk through the store for an hour every week. That has much more impact than any amount of media coverage or advertising. They see everything, buy everything, and talk about it. What they experience in the store is the brand. So stores have to be both internally and externally coherent. The way the brand is projected and advertised externally reflects the way it lives and works internally.

The new advertising campaign fulfilled three key objectives. First, it announced to the world that 'We're back', that Asda had returned to its roots and its heritage. Second, it was a clear statement of intent. Some change, some improvement, was already visible. Asda was effectively promising that there would be lots more to come. And third, we were signalling all this to our own staff.

From the beginning Asda had worked on the assumption that whatever it said externally would be said internally too, and this was an extension of the theme. It was not always easy to unite a workforce consisting of tens of thousands of staff, many of them part-time. But as soon as they saw the TV commercial, colleagues understood the mission statement. They knew what they had to do, and for many it was back to the Asda they grew up with.

Finally, it was consistent *brand* advertising. Unlike a lot of retail advertising, which is about this 'summer saver' or that 'half-price meat offer', in every commercial we focused on our commitment to value for money.

Align the culture and the brand

To create, live and communicate an Asda culture, it was crucial to change the way people operated and felt about things.

One of the most important initiatives was the teams set up to look at the future of Asda stores. They were 'risk-free zones', working outside the main body of the organization, resourced with some of the best people, regardless of cost. This was important in two ways.

First, people in a crisis-ridden company lose their ability to help themselves. That's because innovation generates a high proportion of failure to success, but if you are in a position where you don't dare fail, then you don't dare take risks. For this reason, the project teams were specifically briefed to collect all the ideas that people had, to push the boat out, to create a sense that everybody was wanted and had a chance to play a part. This was critical to mobilize staff for the long haul back to viability.

Second, people from outside were hired to help with the creative process and search for good ideas. Being able to do this without feeling defensive is a good test of a company's culture. Many people become tremendously defensive at the notion that an outsider can think of anything they have not thought of. So the successful repositioning of Asda results partially from its ability to gather and apply ideas from organizations like Wal-Mart in America, or from people like Julian Richer, who concentrates on customer service and staff motivation. The key, however, lies in knowing how to translate these ideas and turn them to advantage in an Asda sort of way; retailing especially is a very cultural, people-based business and just because an idea is good, it doesn't mean it's right for Asda.

Another crucial step was the formation of a close leadership team to see through the programme and to live the vision. The leadership tone was essential to what had to be achieved. The direction, tone and style with which things are done are established from the top. That means not just the intellectual tone – the strategy framework – but the way management works and what it does.

If you set the right leadership tone, the right direction and the right mini-examples – ones that deliver solutions with a high degree of understanding, detail and quality (so that you can focus on the issues that are central to what you are trying to achieve) – then the organization starts to take care of itself.

One such mini-example was the way the stores were visited. Thus, instead of the chief executive arriving in an imperial caval-cade, informal wandering around taking notes became, and has remained, the norm. Initially, store managers were amazed that the chief executive was writing down what they said. It gave them a tremendous sense of importance. It positioned the chief executive as being there to listen, and it positioned the manager as someone who had something to say for the company.

Another effective cultural change was to give store managers their head, focusing them on sales rather than costs. That is what Asda is about: driving sales. If you drive the sales, customer service naturally follows. And selling is something everyone should be involved in – a universal responsibility.

As a result, store managers became confident that they were central to the success of the company. They then started doing things locally that they wouldn't have done otherwise, the vast majority of which were highly productive for the company.

Also central to the Asda proposition is straight talking. It would have been a mistake with a company like Asda, which had been drifting downwards for so long, to try and pretend that things were better than they were. Trying to motivate and lead employees using the feel-good factor in such a situation would not have been cred-ible: they knew too well what things were really like. What was needed was a sense of grip. So, right from the start, everyone was told it was going to be tough and we might not make it. With the management at last openly facing up to reality, the main reaction was one of relief.

Likewise, from day one, the strategy was explained to share-holders. They were told it would take three years before Asda would have a sustainable basis for profit growth and that the new team was not focused on short-term growth. Indeed, if reducing the next year's profit happened to be the right thing to do, that's what would be done.

Continue the revolution

Once the main direction has been established and results have started coming through, in retailing especially it's essential to maintain momentum. You have to move on, avoid complacency, be relentless. And, to move with pace in a high employment business – Asda employs 75,000 people – you have to have a strong culture. It's this that helps you manage behaviour. It creates a way of doing things, a set of principles that people recognize and work with.

We have deliberately tried to create an Asda culture, encompassing three words: Selling, Personality and Involvement. Our attitude to service, for example, starts from a different base from our competitors. We believe in service with personality. Good service comes from the heart. It has to be experienced, not advertised. And it doesn't come from a training manual. It should not be necessary to say 'Make sure you have good eye contact and smile'. It's much better to recruit people who smile in the first place and to put them in a position where they feel they are respected and where they think this is a smiling sort of place, that this is a bit of fun.

The next task is to get them motivated about the business – to believe that the business is trying to do a good thing in the marketplace and trying to help its customers. Everybody can subscribe to that; it gives them an incentive to sell. Then you start to deliver service. It will happen in a way that combines selling and personality.

The same goes for involvement. We seek to involve customers in stores with tasting and samplings. And we seek to involve staff. We are an open sort of company. If you walk around our headquarters in Leeds you will find people who don't actually work for us foraging around, hopefully making a contribution. We feel at ease with that. We also have the biggest employee share-ownership plan in Britain. Since it was launched in July 1995, 36,000 colleagues have taken up share options.

And we have pulled down every partition wall in the building. There are no offices, no meeting rooms that don't have windows. Why? Because we try and operate a single status business in which people are not judged by the size of their office. We want open communication. It's lively, vocal, noisy and sometimes it seems a bit chaotic, but it's got personality.

We are also maintaining the momentum in communicating the Asda brand values. Having revived 'Asda price' and the famous 'pocket tap' in our advertising, we moved on to create a Yorkshire farmer to express some of the things which are central to the Asda proposition: calling a spade a spade; good honest value; a little bit of old-fashioned craft skills; bringing back to supermarkets some of the things that used to belong in the High Street, such as fresh food; plus a sense of trust and being on the customer's side.

This sense of 'being on your side' is very important – and it's another area where we have expanded the Asda brand. Being a champion of the consumer was always part of Asda's stance but we have deliberately added a crusading element, campaigning on issues such as perfume prices, the Net Book Agreement and retail price maintenance in medicines. To some extent, we enjoy being a northern, anti-establishment company. More importantly, by becoming 'Britain's value crusader' we are bringing our customers and colleagues together, allowing them to feel good about what they are doing.

Some people say that there is a PR, gimmicky element to our crusading. Certainly, there is a PR element to it. It does create enormous opportunities for expression in store. But then, all good marketing relies on strong communication. Asda is not the biggest and cannot afford the marketing budgets of some of its competitors, but we can find campaigns that matter. This is not a stunt. We do not enter these campaigns for cheap publicity. We do and will go to court to see things changed.

We have also changed our policy on own label. In the beginning we cut back on many own label lines. They were lower quality, me-toos and failed to offer genuine added value. Now we are developing a theme of 'only at Asda', starting with an excellent fresh food offer, with the George clothing brand, and with an improved own label offer. Own label is a crucial method of delivering customer value. If own label is as good as leading brands (as ours is now), and if we sell it at a discount of 10 to 15 per cent, the more the customers buy own label, the better value they get. Therefore, own label penetration is essential to delivering value in the basket overall. Also, we believe we are a food company first and foremost, and therefore developing a unique product is part of what we should do. Early on Asda had to catch up, but now we believe we can do some pioneering.

We are also exploiting assets like our larger stores to enhance that sense of personality. Take a little thing like doughnuts. After three hours, a doughnut loses its freshness. But with an operation where the doughnuts are fried in-store and sold within the first three hours, you will have a product that nobody can match. It may not be the cheapest way of producing a doughnut but it's not expensive either if you sell the volume. And, of course, the margins are tremendous.

Asda's competitors which have smaller outlets don't have the facilities to do this. Nor do the discounters. Asda, as a result, has more personality. Bakers baking the bread, people making up the salads, butchers cutting the meat – this is how you start creating a sense of humanity, personality, theatre and excitement. These are the things that shoppers hanker after.

Themes like these are coming together under our new strategy of Breakout. Breakout is about continuing the revolution, creating not just a good business, but something that is special and which is capable of sustaining profitability and growth even where the market is competitive and mature and even when we have to accept we will never be the biggest grocery multiple.

Being the biggest is not an option for Asda. Instead, we have prioritized something we do have control over. We want to be the biggest operator of large-scale, wide-range superstores at the best value. We want to have the best value, fresh-food operation in

Britain and to re-create the craft skills which can deliver, in-store, prepared and finished fresh foods that nobody else can match.

Accelerated repositioning is possible – but it still has to be real

Many people believe that Asda's performance has improved basically because of price. We have improved on price. We are better value for money. But our performance improvement stems from the whole renewal programme: refocusing the Asda brand. The small moves, central to repositioning and integrated right across the business – the display, merchandising, presentation, ranging – make things happen and make the difference, not a single idea.

You certainly can accelerate things. At Asda, there was no time for exhaustive strategy reviews. We simply had to create a tremendously accelerated run at change and get the organization moving very, very fast. Nevertheless, a company like this tends to be like a large orchestra: it's no good having the lead violins ahead of the rest. It just won't work. In the end, you cannot be a different type of store or retailer unless you have a different type of business behind it. In retailing, the store is the business. You can't reposition the brand without repositioning the business.

2 | British Airways: Brand Leadership Results from Being True to Our Long-term Vision

ROBERT AYLING, *chief executive*

When British Airways started using the slogan 'The World's Favourite Airline' in 1983, it was perceived to be extraordinarily arrogant and self-regarding. It was. That was the whole point. It was not something that British companies did. At the time it was probably quite unjustified in the sense that British Airways was by no means everyone's first choice. Today all that has changed. People no longer say that British Airways has no right to call itself the world's favourite airline, but how terrific it is to have a company that is one of the world leaders in its industry based in the UK.

One of the most critical elements in that success has been the concentration on our customers: you have to give customers not only what they expect but more than they expect. And that is a very difficult thing to achieve. Understanding what customers want better than the competition does has to be at the heart of everything we do.

The crucial role of branding

The balance between functional and emotional delivery has taken years to fine-tune, and branding plays a crucial role in this. We have created certain expectations of the British Airways brand: it stands for a professional Western style of service of the highest calibre where passengers are treated politely, professionally, in a friendly way and where they are cared for.

The British Airways brand experience is of course not just about the tangible aspects of the airline – seats or food, for example – although we are constantly improving what we offer. It is also about softer values – the emotional side of the brand. Creating and sustaining these softer values is critical in creating and sustaining the success of the company.

Good design and innovation are central to the brand proposition. For example, the new seats in First give a significant product advantage for British Airways, and have won numerous design awards. They also build the brand equity for a key customer group. Research among our most loyal passengers clearly indicated how we could reduce yet more of the stresses of travelling: they wanted privacy, space and flexibility, and we've been able to deliver in a way that's never been done before.

The need to relaunch

The first time we transformed ourselves, culminating in privatization in 1987, we changed the airline from being a company criticized for its bad service into one of the most profitably privatized companies and the world's leading international airline.

Since then we have enjoyed fourteen good years of profit to become the 'world's favourite' airline. It became clear, however, that more of the same just wasn't good enough. We had overhauled a good many parts of what we offer our customers, but the company itself clearly needed to be relaunched.

Our research confirmed that we needed to change again if we wanted to continue to be the industry leader into the twenty-first century. So, over two years, we planned a new corporate identity which would create a global personality for British Airways.

The new identity is a visual promise to our customers and staff of the many improvements that will come from the company's repositioning for its customers – 60 per cent of whom come from outside Britain. We are blending the best of traditional British values with the best of today's Britain – diverse, creative, friendly, youthful and cosmopolitan in outlook.

Our new identity represents an outward sign of significant change within the organization. It is part of a larger programme, launched in 1996, to prepare the airline for the next millennium.

It is linked to a £6 billion investment programme which covers new aircraft and new buildings. Hundreds of millions of pounds are being ploughed back into improved services and products for leisure and business travellers. A programme of new training initiatives will ensure even better customer service. As part of our programme for the new millennium, we are improving our efficiency by ensuring that all of our activities match external cost levels, and by working our assets harder.

The aim is to ensure it is fully equipped with the right people, with the right skills, in the right places to meet the challenges of the new millennium. Driving the overall programme is a new corporate mission – to be the undisputed leader in world travel. British Airways is aiming to set new industry standards in customer service and innovation, to deliver the best financial performance and to evolve from being an airline to a world travel business, with the flexibility to stretch the brand into new business areas.

The new livery, the efficiency programme and the change in staff skills are all designed to show employees and customers that the airline is changing, as we need to do. To become the world leader in world travel, we have to do again what we did in the last decade – put clear blue sky between us and our rivals. We have to reach out to people around the world and deliver a service that meets their needs. Our customers want to deal with people who speak their language, and eat food that suits their palate. In short, they want to feel as if they are travelling home from home.

British and global

The airline's British heritage is reflected in our corporate colours of red, white and blue, but the heart of the new identity is the creation of more than fifty 'world images' which will appear on the entire fleet. They will also be seen in the designs on ground vehicles, stationery, signage, timetables, baggage tags and ticket wallets – everything that bears the British Airways name.

Through these world images, British Airways is turning its fleet into a flying gallery – one of the world's largest art commissions. The new identity is aimed at presenting British Airways as an airline of the world, born and based in Britain with a community of people passionately committed to serving the communities of the world. To show this, what we have done is to find art that represents different communities, which we then take to other communities on our tailfins. We are sending an important message to our existing and new customers everywhere: British Airways wants to be your favourite airline and is responsive to your needs.

We are moving the brand's formal British style of the 1980s to a more international one. Instead of being perceived as 'professional but reserved', British Airways is becoming less formal and more flexible, catering more to our customers' individual needs.

Our change ensures we are now British *Airways* instead of *British* Airways. We are proud of the name of the company, and we never considered changing it. Keeping British in the name is a strength because, although the British are perceived in some countries as being a bit reserved, they are also seen as caring, ready to help and responsible. These are all very good characteristics to have if you are running a business in which people trust you with their lives, because uppermost in people's minds is their safety.

Customer needs in the new millennium

Global demographic trends were a factor in the change in brand focus. In addition, we are aiming to enhance our customers' experience by delivering an individualized service.

Ultimately, each of our customers expects to be treated as an individual. Each one has a different reason for travelling, a different reason for choosing British Airways, and different expectations of us.

Recently, in order to understand better the needs of our customers as individuals, we have been listening to them and exploring their social values. We have found that they are the kind of people who like to explore all new options. They take nothing for granted, and do not necessarily accept the status quo – so our challenge is heightened. In our favour is the fact that many of our passengers have 'heavily invested' in British Airways. They tell us that, as well as investing commercially (choosing to give us both time and money) they are committed to British Airways at an emotional level.

Breaking down the 'them and us' between British Airways and its customers is important. Many of our passengers are as involved with the company as are the staff themselves. They wish to be recognized for that and treated as 'insiders'. In fact, they tell us they want British Airways to succeed and feel let down when things do go wrong.

Not sub-brands but segmentation

The brand is British Airways. In the 1980s, it all became too complex – sub-brands with distinct personalities. What we learned was that our customers ultimately purchase British Airways.

The British Airways brand has been developed in close collaboration with our customers. The research findings conclusively showed that they wanted a global airline, by which they meant big, safe and reliable. However, they also wanted an airline that cared for each customer, addressing individual needs wherever they came from. In all our communications we therefore aim to combine scale with humanity, to appeal to the heart not just the head.

The aim became, and remains, to be the airline that customers choose first in all the markets we serve. Ultimately, all who travel with British Airways should feel so much at home with us that they choose us in preference to their national carrier.

We have to segment the market to some extent, however. That is why we offer a number of services like Club World, Club Europe, and World and Euro Traveller. But to call them sub-brands can be misleading. What we have is the one main brand, British Airways, which offers a number of different services. Travellers know what they will get depending on which service they have selected. For example, travellers in First and Club Class know they will get off first, their baggage will be in the hall first, and that they have the use of a lounge.

Concorde is a different case. While it is part of British Airways, it is seen as a brand in its own right. The British Airways name is on the outside of the aircraft, but otherwise all the branding inside the aircraft is Concorde. The Concorde brand stands above all for speed, for getting from London to New York in three hours, twenty minutes. It represents a very exclusive means of travel, and in some ways it is also an exclusive club.

It also stands for a particular form of engineering excellence. It might be twenty-five years old but it has never been bettered. It is still the most remarkable sight in the skies. When it flies over everyone looks up, and not just because of the noise. In fact, the British Airways and the Concorde brands are complementary. Concorde helps the British Airways brand by giving it cachet.

The implications for the brand of strategic alliances

Apart from the competitive issues, one of the most difficult branding issues British Airways is facing is what happens to the brand as strategic alliances are formed with other airlines. The laws in Europe forbidding foreign airlines from having a majority stake in domestic airlines have recently been liberalized. We took advantage of this by taking stakes first in TAT and then in Air Liberté in France and in Deutsche BA in Germany. In these we have control over their operations, but the way the global aviation market is moving means that we will have to form alliances with players as big as ourselves to stay alive.

When British Airways formed a relationship with Qantas in Australia, in which we have a 25 per cent stake, all sorts of possible corporate branding ideas were considered. It soon became obvious, however, that none of the ideas – such as, for instance, Global Airlines – would work. Both James Strong, chief executive of Qantas, and I were clearly of the view that his airline should remain Qantas and ours should stay British Airways.

Changing the name of an airline might be fraught with danger, but there are times when it can be done. When British Airways took over British Caledonian it was rebranded overnight. We were in one market and both operating out of the same airport, so it made sense. Changing 'British Caledonian' to 'British Airways' worked because we told the British Caledonian employees about our values as a company and helped to make them keen to project them. Many of the British Caledonian staff still work for us.

Qantas and British Airways are both resonant, motivating brands with loyal customers; they are discrete propositions which risked being diluted if combined. However, over time, there will be aspects of what we do with alliance partners – the seats on the aircraft, the style of our catering, the sort of cups and glassware we buy – where it would be crazy not to seek economies of scale. None of this will affect the brand in a significant way. If people believe that travelling on Club World on British Airways has similarities with Business Class on Qantas or other partners, that is fine. But the personalities will remain different. When we sell British Airways and Qantas services together, customers are offered the airline of their choice.

In terms of brand protection, the key issue on alliances is that there must be an alliance of equals when it comes to the quality of service. We have taken the view that passengers prefer one carrier or the other so market share might be lost if the two were merged. However, the service levels clearly need to be in line with customer expectations: if a customer is transferred to the partner airline, the comfort and quality of the alternative provider must be the same, throughout the journey.

Franchising has also proved an effective way of developing our business. Franchising at British Airways dates back to 1993 and is central to our growth strategy. We tend to franchise where we don't have the right size of aircraft, or expertise in a particular market, or legal rights to fly. For example, we cannot fly from

Johannesburg to Durban for these reasons, so Comair flies it as a franchise.

For many of the routes operated, the best way for British Airways to earn money on them is from the licence fees. For example, British Regional Airlines flies football fans from Shannon to Manchester under our name. Our franchising agreement allows other airlines to use British Airways' intellectual property – logo, style, trademark and service standards – provided they deliver product consistently to our specifications. As with Hertz, which has franchised 70 per cent of its operations, the customer would be hard pushed to tell the difference.

Staff levels have increased from 55,000 to 60,000 as the business has grown and, of these, 1,000 extra members of staff have been employed to service the franchisees. We already have ten franchised airlines carrying about 6 million passengers a year, and we have ambitious plans to continue to develop in this way.

The staff as embodiment of the brand

A vital part of the brand's personality is its closest interface with our customers: the staff. Good customer service is essential. It is central to our competitive edge as it increases our customer retention and our overall efficiency.

Our approach can work only if we have a clear vision, deliver the basics reliably and consistently, and employ staff who have a passion for delivering excellence in customer service. Their personality and attitude will project the image of the brand.

A culture has to be created which is strong enough to transmit the brand values without having to repeat them every day to every person. You have to persuade everyone who works for the company that customer satisfaction is the only criterion that matters.

Keeping a finger on the pulse of the brand

The chief executive has to act as the guardian of the brand. Keeping a finger on the pulse of the brand means that when I fly, which is at least once a week, the key thing is to look around. I notice the way our staff treat our passengers. We don't want people to be gushing but polite, friendly, helpful, always thinking of something they can do to make passengers' lives easier.

I notice things like the quality of announcements. If they are being made on a flight from Frankfurt, can the staff speak German or do they put on a tape? How do the captain and co-pilot cope with things like delays – are they informative without being overly informative? Do they keep the passengers in touch? I look at the quality of the service, not just the meal service. I look at the interior of the aircraft, whether there are any broken seats, whether the carpet is stained, and I do this almost without thinking about it because it is all part of the brand. If there are things that are not quite right, everyone needs to know. Feedback is a very powerful tool for upholding the brand values.

It is like visiting someone's house. When someone comes to your house you want a certain impression to be created. It would be different from the impression created by anyone else. Your house is organized and presented in a particular way, and it is the same with the aircraft.

My job is to be responsible above all for the reputation of the company. The day British Airways starts losing its reputation is the day it starts losing money. So, looking after the company's reputation is my job since the branding of the company and of our products and services is really about our commercial reputation. It has to be taken very seriously.

For example, in summer 1996 Egon Ronay said some really quite unflattering things about our shuttle breakfasts. There was a lot of press coverage at that time about the American Airline alliance and the share price, which was all very important, but the one thing that really caught my attention was this criticism about our breakfasts. That is what our customers are going to be interested in. If people really don't like the breakfast on the shuttle, then we have to find out about it. After all, it is the brand's reputation that is at stake.

Global consistency

It is also crucial to protect the brand by being consistent on a global scale. That means having strict controls over advertising, the use of the name, and representation of the company's products in the marketplace. There has to be a high level of discipline but the marketing managers in different countries must be able to say what they need for their particular markets.

We now translate the offer to meet local needs with appropriate food and local cabin crew. Regular tracking, worldwide, ensures we stay alert to our customers' evolving needs. Our research has stressed the need for multi-cultural and multi-functional teams. Although this approach involves more work and debate, it is important to involve people early and encourage their input.

With this in mind, we have developed our marketing team over the last six years to build our knowledge, understanding and sensitivity with regard to different markets.

We also needed to work more closely as a team with our creative partners. In the early 1990s we reviewed how we were communicating worldwide and were concerned at how patchy things were, particularly in view of the plethora of ways in which we have contact with our customers. Whether via computer screen, letter box, or sales shop, the brand needed to be managed consistently across these channels to ensure clarity for our customers.

One area that is harder to control is publicity. We think long and hard about the impact any form of publicity has on the company and the way we deal with it. We have to ensure that we communicate in a tone of voice that is consistent with our brand. British Airways will do so in one way, while another company would do it differently.

Growing the brand

British Airways is fortunate because we are in an industry which is growing. More people each year want to travel by air. Provided that we can maintain our share of the market, then we will continue to grow. Over the next few years the objective is to make British Airways more international, in the sense that people from other countries identify with the brand as much as people in the UK do. Beyond that, the quality of customer service that we give and the reputation we have for customer service must get better and better.

Our mission to be the undisputed leader in world travel means that we must move forward. We have been relaunching the various sub-brands every three or four years. In future we will have to do it more frequently, to match evolving consumer needs and to respond to aggressive activity by the competition, which is always trying to catch up.

In addition, there are many international marketing opportunities for the brand. 'Brand stretch' is a central theme of our mission to be the undisputed leader, and it comes from our desire to offer more to our customers. Extending our brand into other travel-related products fits our business well, and is of great interest to our customers.

There is a limit to how much we can stretch the brand, however. The brand is so closely associated with travel and air travel in particular that it would be impossible to market something like a British Airways motor car.

There are a number of things that could change the nature of the industry over time, such as electronic communication. On the whole, more communication leads to more travel, because as more people contact each other by non-physical means, they want more contact with each other by physical means. What some people might think are dangers to our business could be stimulants to its growth.

One of the big branding challenges British Airways has faced over the last few years is that as a 'mature' brand it has to keep the brand fresh in the face of 'new' brands. The many new entrants not only make us increasingly aware of the competitiveness of the marketplace, but also make the company think more about what it stands for. New entrants coming into markets which have been dominated by large, previously state-owned businesses, challenge the establishment and status quo, and we are forced to react.

It would be a mistake to compete on others' terms. We will never win with that. It can sometimes be rather frustrating because we feel that some of British Airways' qualities are going unnoticed. But that is part of the game. And if you cannot take that, go and do something else.

3 | L'Oréal: Achieving Success in Emerging Asian Markets

ALAIN EVRARD, *zone director Africa–Asia–Pacific*

How to win when you're starting from scratch

At the beginning of the 1990s, L'Oréal brands were strong in most regions of the world, including Europe and North and South America. But in the emerging Asian markets, the company's presence was limited to two subsidiaries in Hong Kong and Indonesia, as well as agents in other countries, for example, Thailand and Malaysia.

We decided we had to establish a major presence with our brands there because the markets were changing shape. The markets of developing countries tend to follow a certain pattern. At the outset, there is always a thin layer of people who want and can afford luxury goods, and buy higher-priced cosmetics such as Lancôme. Below that lies a very wide and unsophisticated mass market. But, as income per head starts moving over $2,000, the middle class begins to grow and have aspirations that are reflected in purchasing brands which offer quality and the right image. Many of the countries in South-East Asia, with the exceptions of Vietnam, Burma and Laos, have reached that point. For example, between 1989 and 1993 the markets for health and beauty products grew by 94 per cent in Indonesia, 93 per cent in Malaysia, 60 per cent in Taiwan and 90 per cent in Thailand.

The women in these countries increasingly want more sophisticated mass-market cosmetics. They have moved beyond using basic toiletries, shampoo and soap brands and, like women all over the world, want products to help them take better care of themselves. We realized that they increasingly fit the profile for the brands within the L'Oréal Paris signature, which are for women who are a little more affluent than average, are sensitive to style and fashion, believe in technology for beauty products, and have a modern attitude to self-service shopping.

Although we were already selling a small amount of haircare products in the area, we were basically starting from scratch. Is this a handicap? We don't think so. Our chairman, Lindsay Owen Jones, said recently that he strongly feels that it is never too late to capture a market if you have a better performing brand. It just has to be new, different and better.

The three critical factors in the success of L'Oréal brand development

We build our brands and base their success on three critical factors. First is performance, which comes from constant innovation through a deep commitment to research and development. For example, in 1995 the group spent 3 per cent of sales on research in cosmetology and dermatology, and registered over 270 patents. Second, communication of performance is essential, whether through advertising, point-of-sale material and sampling, or partnerships with groups such as retailers, hairdressers and journalists.

Finally, the third key element of success is the internationalization of our brands. Until the late 1960s, L'Oréal, which was founded in 1907 when Eugène Schueller invented the first synthetic hair dye, was mainly a French corporation. Then came considerable expansion in Europe and, following that, North and South America. In 1980 L'Oréal sales of cosmetics in the US market were about $100 million. By 1995 that had grown to $2 billion. Now almost 80 per cent of sales are outside France.

How the branding structure works

The name L'Oréal is both the corporation and a brand signature. The corporation, L'Oréal, had a turnover in 1996 of $11 billion. It is made up of a pharmaceutical division and four operating cosmetic divisions: consumer, perfumes and beauty, salon, and active cosmetics. These four divisions account for up to 80 per cent of the turnover.

Within each of the cosmetic divisions are several 'signatures' which are applied to a basket of brands and which appear prominently on the packaging. Each signature has its specific image and advertising. For example, in the consumer division, which is the largest and which contributes half of all cosmetic sales, the main signature is L'Oréal Paris. The brands include products in hair colouring (Excellence and Récital), skincare (Plénitude), haircare (Elsève) and make-up (Perfection). These are leading-edge products for people who care more about the way they look and will pay more. The positioning of L'Oréal Paris is French, technology, a bit elitist, and top of the mass market in terms of pricing. The slogan, 'L'Oréal, because I'm worth it', summarizes this specific positioning.

The second signature in the consumer division is Laboratoires Garnier, which contains portfolio brands like Synergie and Neutralia. These are more popular and accessible products based on the use of natural, mostly plant-based ingredients that are both gentle and safe, but without compromising performance. The next grouping is Gemey Paris and more recently, through acquisition, Maybelline New York and Jade, a well-known German brand. These are entry-level brands with a feeling of the 'girl next door'. There is also a range of mainly French brands under the 'Lascad' signature.

The perfume and beauty division, contributing almost 30 per cent of cosmetics sales, has in its portfolio international luxury brands like Lancôme, which covers skincare, make-up and fragrances, Biotherm for skincare and make-up, plus prestige fragrance brands such as Guy Laroche, Ralph Lauren, Helena Rubenstein and Paloma Picasso. Over 90 per cent of this division's sales are outside France.

The third division has brands aimed at professionals in salons, such as L'Oréal Professionel, Kérastase and Redken, and accounts for 13 per cent of sales of cosmetics.

The fourth division is involved with what we call the active cosmetics division, and has a portfolio of mainly European signatures such as Vichy, Phas and LaRoche-Posay which are usually sold through pharmacies. They contribute about 6 per cent to the cosmetics revenues.

Securing a prominent position through segmentation

This segmented approach to the brands gives the company a prominent position in the three main channels for distribution of cosmetics products: professionals in salons, mass market at different levels, and selective distribution channels such as department stores and perfumeries. It also means that innovation can filter down from the top end through to the mass-market brands, once ways to do so at lower costs are found.

Also, because the corporate name, L'Oréal, is not used on all the products, except within the L'Oréal Paris signature brands, we can sell not only the French way of life with signatures like L'Oréal Paris and Lancôme, but other cultures as well: the American way of life with Ralph Lauren at one end of the scale, and Maybelline New York at the other, Italian values with Armani and so forth.

This flexible approach means that there is no limit to marketing our brands consistently around the world: it is about the spirit, the image, the values of the way of life.

Each signature can function as its own business. This fosters the notion of internal competition, which we believe is vital to keep the company fit. It means as well that the advertising works harder and more effectively; since the consumer sees ads with a strong emphasis on the signature as well as the brand, the share of voice increases. And, because we have a certain vision of, for instance, the L'Oréal Paris woman, who will be the same in New York, Paris or Kuala Lumpur, it solves the key problem of what models we use for international advertising. It does not matter whether she is American, French or Chinese. She has to have something more than the average woman.

The only time this segmented strategy can present a few obstacles is in terms of corporate image, when we enter countries where we are relatively new. When it comes to hiring people in South-East Asia, for instance, we have to make them understand that they are joining not only a company manufacturing skincare which they may use, or for which they may have seen advertising, but one which is the number one cosmetics company in the world.

Anything we do can go global: the determinism of success

When a molecule is performing (and by molecule we mean a product molecular invention), we patent it and there is no good reason why we can't take it to the whole of the world.

To manage these brands we have to strike a delicate balance between harmonizing them internationally, and at the same time encouraging the entrepreneurial spirit in the individual countries. We do not force countries to take products, but we believe that the products we create can go global, and more often than not they do. It is what a former chairman called the 'determinism of success': when you have true performance in one market there is no reason you cannot do the same worldwide.

However, although we project the same brand-names and images in all markets, we do adapt products for different hair and skin needs in different countries, with the appropriate languages on the packaging. For example, hair colouring suitable for Asia can differ from that which will be successful in Denmark, although the active molecules are often the same. Similarly, with skincare products, we will sell more oil-free products in South-East Asia than in Scandinavia.

We use the local language on the packaging and adapt the international advertising, unless there are exceptional reasons for not doing so, such as legal constraints. For example, in Malaysia and Indonesia, it is forbidden to air TV ads with non-Malay/Indonesian models so we use well-known local models while the advertising execution remains the same.

Championing the brands: keeping the moral contract

Research carried out within Singapore highlights the central role of the brand for consumers in this region. Overall, the research showed that 97 per cent of the customers purchased a specific item because of the brand-name. The comparable figure for France is 60 per cent.

This underlines the fact that in emerging markets, where consumers are offered a wide range of local brands as well as counterfeits, international brands are widely trusted. We have to deliver. The level of performance is critical if we want to have a world brand and keep our credibility. We have to keep the moral contract between the brand and the consumers. We cannot compromise on performance. We have to be brand fanatics, championing both the advantages but also the obligations of the brand.

We also have to keep in mind that the brand challenge varies in different markets. India is a good example of how we have to think very carefully about our line of attack. The company has been in India for about five years, although it has been a fully-owned subsidiary for less than three years. The challenge in India is that one tends to think of it as a new market. But it is an incredibly old one, with deep-rooted traditions and consumption patterns that go back for generations. Because the economy has been so closed, India has been perceived as a virgin market where companies could sail in and sell their products, but that is simply not the case.

The Indians have had well-established indigenous products, from companies like Hindustan Lever, present on the local market for many years, although you would not recognize them in terms of their counterparts in London or Paris. Well-established consumption habits have been accompanied by a lack of competition, so there has been little incentive to be disloyal and try new brands, a fact which newcomers have to understand and deal with.

Haircare illustrates this. Everybody in the West knows what hair conditioner is used for. The question is which brand to buy. But in India women have been using hair oil for 2,000 years. It is a bigger market than shampoo. Why should they buy your conditioner, particularly when it is more expensive?

So our approach has been broadly the same as in other developing markets, in that we say to women, here is a modern, more efficient way of keeping and enhancing your beauty with products from Parisian laboratories. For instance, Indian women take good care of their faces, doing some sort of purifying at least once a month, so we developed a face mask within the Synergie line to fulfil that demand, which has been very successful. The Synergie line now has eight products, all faithful to the Synergie concept but tailored to the Indian market.

One interesting factor for L'Oréal in the Indian market is that France and French culture are relatively unknown because the background has been British. So part of the L'Oréal evangelism is to tell customers that there is another way of looking at beauty from a country well-known for its cosmetics. It adds to the pioneering feel of what we are doing.

The Asian challenge

The least international factor is distribution. No two countries have the same distribution pattern. In Asia, there are dynamic pharmacies (like Boots in the UK), there are supermarkets, and some department stores. So there are high traffic outlets suitable for L'Oréal Paris. One of our biggest challenges is to make sure that there is space for all the explanatory material that accompanies our products. You have to help people find their way through the ranges.

When we first launched hair colour in Thailand, we saw that half of cosmetics products were available through modern distribution channels, with the rest sold through a complicated maze of small shops. Also, the established competition like Procter & Gamble and Unilever had a very strong presence in that area. We took the decision to work through the big retailers because, even though we might lose sales, dealing with the small shops would have required a large infrastructure and might also have damaged the L'Oréal Paris image. This strategy proved to be the right thing to do: in skincare now, 75 per cent of sales are made through modern distribution channels. Over the next five to ten years that figure will rise.

Asia now accounts for about 6 per cent of cosmetics sales, a figure which has doubled in five years. The challenge is to increase that, to go step by step, aiming to be first in one market in one country, then the next, and so on. We consider ourselves challengers in Asia as a company, but if we are better we will achieve leadership. If a company just wants a financial battle it might be successful in the short term, but long term it will be beaten. We have to keep on growing by fighting our main competitors on their own fields.

A 'hair colour crusade' in Thailand: the strategy in action

How the brand strategy works can be seen from one of the first major forays we made into the Far East, in Thailand. We knew that historically the L'Oréal Paris success in Europe, South America and especially in the USA had begun with hair colouring, where we consider that we have the best technology, experience and expertise. However, the problem in Asia was that this market was small. Nevertheless, we believed we had to start there and so began what we called a 'hair colour crusade'.

We soon realized that it would be very difficult to develop an effective, long-term strategy to take advantage of this booming part of the world without our own organization, our own 'family', to give us feedback from the ground. So we appointed our first general manager in Thailand in 1992. We tried to hire people who could adapt to our business philosophy, and who could be, as we like to say at L'Oréal, both 'poet and peasant'. We also held a big press conference for the press, trade and VIPs. Our vision was that, whatever product line we started, it very quickly had to become number one. We needed victories. And a victory is market leadership.

The product we chose was an existing hair colourant called Imédia, well established in Europe but one for which we had developed a new formula for Asia. Instead of pushing basic products like shampoos and gels, we wanted to put all our resources behind a product that fitted in with the image of being technically advanced and reliable. You do not need ten to twenty products to get your name known. You invade the market with one brand and push all your energy behind it. So we were evangelists. We were determined that we would be successful and create the name L'Oréal Paris in Thailand and establish a modern hair colour market, so we could follow up hair colour with skincare and then make-up.

Because there was no existing international advertising, we developed new commercials for South-East Asia. We used a top European model with dark hair and found that the ad tested well. These ads were also the first time we strongly emphasized the L'Oréal Paris signature by putting it prominently at both the beginning and the end of the advertising. The ad was shot in Malaysia, developed in Japan, and had post-production done in Paris and Thailand for the Thai text. To show that good ideas are used internationally, this ad became the basis for others used around the world.

Like all our campaigns, it focused strongly on communicating performance. Our ads can be quite didactic, underlining the rational benefits and explaining how the product works. The key point for us was to get people to try the product and see its quality.

The result is that in Thailand, now the most important hair colouring market in South-East Asia, L'Oréal has been number one since 1995 and is the international preferred brand. This is despite the fact that the competition has been active there for ten to fifteen years. We are also launching a new, improved version called L'Oréal Imédia Excellence. We have based our television commercials on the international advertising for this new product using the actress Nastassja Kinski, except we have substituted a well-known Thai personality who is an actress, TV star and model. That ad has also tested well in Singapore and in other Asian markets.

We are also number one in hair colouring in Indonesia and the Philippines. We are only in third place in Singapore, however, because their hair colour is still sold from locked cupboards. We are having discussions to try and change that. Overall, the Asian market is now expanding very quickly: for instance, in South Korea, almost three-quarters of the women who use hair colouring have only done so in the last three years.

Innovative force from 'new' L'Oréal markets

We have had similar success in these markets with our L'Oréal skincare brand Plénitude, which is sold on the concept that it delays the effects of ageing. The range, consisting of about a dozen products, is sold in a 'boutique' display which is a powerful visual marketing tool, providing a lot of clear information about the various products. When we first launched Plénitude in Indonesia in 1991, TV ads were banned so we had to use print and sampling. When TV became possible, we had to re-do the international ad using Asian women because of legal requirements. And in the early days we had a few difficulties getting the pricing right. But the big jump came last year with the successful launch of Plénitude Excell A-3.

We launched the Plénitude range in Thailand in 1995 to build on our success with hair colour. If we had launched it too early we probably would have failed. We now lead the skincare market in Australia, New Zealand, Indonesia and Singapore, we are third in Thailand and Taiwan where we launched only in 1995. We are now working even more to respond to the very specific needs of Asian women, which are linked to particularly difficult environmental factors such as heat, humidity, pollution and sunlight. Four major projects are in hand, two of which are aimed at Asian women in the area of cleansing and care. What this means is that South-East Asia will increasingly become a source of innovation for worldwide development.

The essential make-up mix

Together with hair products and skincare, our third high-performing business area is make-up. We started with a test market in Malaysia, which was interesting and strategically difficult because we had to choose a single range for consumers with varying demands according to complexion, which can range from very pale to very dark.

First we had to identify the main product types which would meet market demand for the lipsticks, foundations and eye make-up, and then choose what we considered the strongest lines. We found that Malaysian women typically want products which are non-oily, anti-ultraviolet and offer protection against pollution, and are lightly perfumed or even perfume-free. Colour preference is for matte tones, although they also like red and orange shades. As with all markets, the wide range of items is constantly monitored.

We are now in first place in Malaysia and second in Singapore. Interestingly, our recently-acquired signature Maybelline New York is in first place in Singapore and second in Malaysia. As with skincare, partnership with retailers is crucial in order to have the most effective display. For example, we offer an exclusive display unit for the make-up range which was originally created for the US market and which is accessible, modular and designed to meet the needs of self-service.

Living the L'Oréal philosophy: the poet warrior

The important thing when starting up in a country is to put a good team together, send them to Paris so they can see the big company they are part of, and train them in the specific L'Oréal way of doing things. The culture is a key element. To start with, no matter what the nationality, the manager who starts the business has to live the culture from within, it cannot just be taught. We need someone who can explain every day why we do this or that, or why, for example, we decide at the last minute to change something that has been prepared for weeks.

Recruitment in any country is not only based on getting the best students from the universities. We are also interested in personalities and talents, in imaginative people who are both ambitious and generous and who can develop projects for markets which are becoming both more diverse and international. The human resources framework is very international, which allows for a permanent exchange of culture and abilities. It is a strategic decision to recruit and train managers locally to understand local issues and habits. Most of the managers in Asia are native Asians.

We also encourage people to stay with the company by putting great emphasis on experience and by helping to nurture both professional and personal growth for the long term.

Being committed to the long term means we have to help people to improve constantly but also accepting that sometimes they fail. We do not have it written in the form of a constitution but the right of error is officially accepted. What we are really passionate about is creating warriors for our brands. When we enter new countries, particularly in Asia, we feel we have a tremendous story to tell and excellent products to which people respond, which makes us ever more enthusiastic.

Because L'Oréal does not go into markets with huge budgets and cut-and-dried marketing plans that have been developed thousands of miles away, there is a sense of personal commitment to and involvement with the brands. There is a substantial element of local contribution to making sure the mix is right. Even more importantly, wherever the company is, we have to make sure we treat our employees with the same enthusiasm and respect with which we treat our brands.

4 | Levi Strauss: Focus on the Legend . . . and Record-breaking Global Sales

ROBERT HOLLOWAY, *vice president, global marketing*

Levi Strauss & Co. is the largest and most successful brand-name apparel business in the world. The company sells its distinctive clothing under the Levi's®, Dockers® and Slates® brands in more than sixty countries around the world.

In March 1996, *Forbes* magazine wrote: 'Levi jeans are not so much a product as an icon. Along with Coca-Cola, Gillette, McDonald's, rock music and TV sitcoms, they are a coveted symbol of the casual, unpretentious American lifestyle.'

Dating back to 1856, when Levi Strauss opened his first store, selling supplies to California gold rush miners, the Levi's brand has had a powerful heritage. The genesis and evolution of the original, authentic American blue jeans are central to the brand's global status as an American icon.

The Levi's brand has more than endured; it has flourished. In the early 1980s, however, both the brand and our company were on the ropes. The reason? In part it was because we had ceased to focus on our core youth market – the consumers who had made Levi Strauss & Co. and the Levi's brand what they had both become. Our job then was the same job we have today: we had to refocus and restructure to ensure that Levi Strauss & Co. would remain the largest and most successful brand-name apparel business in the world (with sales now exceeding US $7.1 billion).

In many respects, the challenges of the 1980s still exist today and the solutions we developed at that time are still our guiding principles. The ongoing challenge for Levi Strauss & Co. is twofold:

first, to remain relevant to a target audience that regenerates itself every four or five years; and second, to avoid the distractions of success.

The living brand: making the heritage relevant and motivating

Our strategy for success is deceptively simple. Worldwide, the target consumer for the Levi's brand are the fifteen- to nineteen-year-old young men who buy approximately 30 per cent of all jeans sold. The history of our business has borne out that if that core target is motivated by our brands, the other demographic categories, responsible for purchasing the remaining 70 per cent, will follow.

In essence, the Levi's brand has defined and continues to define what 'blue jeans' are, and our products are able to occupy that defining point because they are the original American blue jeans. It is an important point of distinction: only one manufacturer, one brand, can say it is the original, the 'genuine article'.

From its position of prominence in the marketplace, the Levi's brand stands for many things in the minds of target consumers: rebellion, youthfulness, quality, originality, excitement, fun – all the great things about being young. To put it another way, when we're successful with young consumers, the Levi's brand will live with young people through that crucial period when they 'find themselves'. And, more than that, the brand becomes an enduring point of identification for young consumers with that period in their lives. They choose the brand as a sort of uniform or symbol of youth; and, in Western cultures, as a symbol of independence and freedom – even defiance.

Consequently, for the success of the Levi's brand, it is essential that we understand what is cutting-edge in youth culture and remain aware of social, cultural and consumer trends. But, for products like ours, with a nearly 150-year history, it's equally important that we never forget our roots, that we don't begin to stand for fads and fashions that come and go. Paradoxically, as 'the original' we are expected and even required to be an extraordinary blend of forward-looking and traditional in the way we bring the Levi's brand to market.

Another important paradox about the Levi's brand is its individuality: it's a product built on a mass consumer audience of millions that allows you, the wearer, to be more yourself. The axioms 'know thyself' and 'to thine own self be true' are the cornerstones of the brand.

Related to that impulse towards genuine self-expression is a growing desire among consumers worldwide – a desire that the Levi's brand has effectively tapped into – for clothes and objects that have a genuineness and naturalness about them. It's a heritage that owes nothing to the marketer and everything to evolution and function.

The Levi's brand, and especially Levi's 501® jeans, have been successful for decades in large part because they feed those consumer desires for genuineness and self-expression. With minor variations, such as the addition of belt-loops and the Redtab™ device, Levi's 501s today are the product that has been worn by miners, cowboys and California farm-workers since the late 1800s. Its qualities have been memorably described by fashion designer Margaret Howell: '[They] are the original Levi jeans. The design is so right it never need alter, a timeless classic of clothes. Adaptable, like any well-designed object, you can wear them with almost anything. They are good-looking, well-made, functional and unobtrusive. What is more, they improve with age and increase in value with every wash.'

The features that make Levi's jeans different from other brands are almost quaint in their simplicity. The five trademarks that make Levi's 501 jeans unique date back to the mid-1800s and include the LS&CO. embossed buttons; the two horse patch above the right back pocket; the 'arcuate' design stitching on the back pockets (the oldest American trademark in constant use); the '501' lot number; and the Redtab device (introduced in 1936 to help salesmen count and identify Levi's jeans at rodeos).

As simple as they may seem, however, those five trademarks

tell consumers they are wearing original Levi's brand jeans. They represent more than a quality product; they represent the history, heritage and associations of our company. As a result, Levi Strauss & Co. protects the value of those simple features through a rigorous ongoing trademark protection effort. We also recognize the important role of our company historians in preserving the strength of our brands. The LS & CO. company archives make the history live again for the teams of employees who develop our advertising, Internet sites, retail stores and products.

History is only one element of the brand-building equation. The other part is adapting our history to a lifestyle that is relevant and interesting to today's consumers. A classic mistake brand managers frequently make is to become too obsessed with their own culture, talking to consumers in ways that are too remote from actual experience – preaching history. Consumers don't like it. But it's an easy mistake to make, particularly with a history as fascinating as ours. The bottom line is this: as marketers, we need to be sure we're talking to consumers, not just to ourselves.

For example, the historical symbolism of our 'two horse' label design trademark – a design that appears on the patch sewn on to every pair of Levi's 501 jeans – is widely known. It depicts a strength between two horses and a pair of 501 jeans. In fact, the jeans are always tougher than the horses trying to tear them apart, a fact confirmed in 1943 by a customer who tried the test with mules, one of whom expired from the effort.

It's a great story, of course, but will it sell jeans today? Will it build the associations that make for a strong brand with today's consumers? A better illustration of the product's strength was found to be far more excitingly expressed for our European core target market in an advertisement known as 'Truck' that appeared throughout Europe. Set in the 1950s, a young man in a battered truck comes upon a couple whose car has broken down on a dusty stretch of prairie road. He takes off his Levi's jeans. The sweet girl shrugs at her besuited, geeky boyfriend and climbs in alongside the Levi's guy, leaving the boyfriend to be towed behind on the strength of his rival's Levi's 501 jeans. The jeans as tow-rope are doing fine while, unfortunately for the geek, the bumper of his car dislodges, leaving him behind. No words. Great soundtrack. End frame. The ad's punch-line: 'Separates the men from the boys.'

Nurturing the brand: striking the right chords

The emotional chords any global brand needs to strike will have many similarities worldwide. It is how you hit them successfully in executional terms that ensures the brand's continuing success. But while the umbrella messages behind the brand positioning are universal, local interpretations of those themes drive the worldwide acceptance of the product. For example, in 1984, although all agencies were working to the same brief – to refocus the Levi's brand as the original, the authentic American blue jeans – the highly successful campaigns that resulted were very different around the world. It is how a company executes a strategy that both develops brand identity and recognizes regional or cultural differences that ensures any brand's continuing success.

Recognizing those differences, in the North American market, Levi's brand ad campaigns have been more product-led than in Europe where activity has been brand and fashion-oriented. In most Asia-Pacific markets, where the Levi's brand is a relative newcomer, advertising has borrowed from both the North American and European affiliates. In new and/or smaller markets our goal is to follow successful models from other regions until resources permit local creative strategies and campaigns.

In the USA in the mid-1980s, our 'US blues' ad campaign revolutionized apparel advertising and refocused and re-energized the Levi's brand. Abandoning the 1970s mod image and traditional cowboy themes, the campaign's 'slice of life' approach captured the individualistic essence of the brand. Paid fashion models and animated characters were replaced with real people filmed in urban settings. The ads captured the soul of Levi's 501 jeans. As far as American audiences were concerned, the Levi's brand had come home.

The 501 blues campaign highlights the difference between the US and European markets in terms of how the brand positioning has been developed over time. At the core, the themes are identical: authentic, original, youthful, rebellious, individual, and so on. The ways in which these themes are portrayed, however, are quite diverse. In Europe, Levi's 501 jeans are compulsory equipment for young consumers who care about the way they look. In Europe, the core of the jeans market, fifteen- to nineteen-year-old males, have been persuaded (for the moment) that 501 jeans are the right look and the only acceptable label.

In Europe, we developed a fascination, almost a reverence, for a mythical America of the past – the America that produced Dean and Presley, the '57 Chevrolet, *The Misfits* and a host of other heroes and cult objects. The ''50s look', suitably processed for the '80s and '90s, remains current, a look for which Levi's 501 jeans could legitimately claim to be an essential feature. The 1950s and later the '60s was a time when the Levi's brand meant jeans and jeans meant youth. It was a period of perhaps fifteen years that forever changed our industry and seeded the contemporary 'jeans world' of youth, sex, rebellion and heroism. Our European ad campaigns have re-evoked these associations and have given Levi's 501s jeans ownership of them.

It's a complex formula for developing a sophisticated global brand around what is essentially a simple product. There were, and are, two carefully integrated but essentially simple messages to European consumers: the rational ('We're the American original') and the emotional ('Wow! don't they look sexy'). By hitting the right note, sales for the Levi's brand went up 800 per cent.

The distraction of success: losing the focus

The challenge faced by companies with successful brands is to decide where to take the brand after it has become established in the minds of consumers. Perhaps the most common mistake when you become successful is to try to stamp your brand on everything.

Levi Strauss & Co. learned about that mistake the hard way. In the early 1970s, the company made the mistake of expanding beyond the core product lines it had manufactured for more than 100 years and began making and marketing a broad range of products under the Levi's brand. This expansion diluted the Levi's brand and its appeal to consumers.

At the time, my reaction as a brand manager echoed what our core target consumers were feeling: I had not joined Levi Strauss & Co. to market baby clothes or polyester leisure suits.

It often takes a calamity to focus a company's collective mind. When you're doing very well the temptation is to keep adding bits here and there. Ultimately you risk losing your core consumer. By the early 1980s, when LS&CO. was haemorrhaging money, it wasn't all due to competitive or distribution issues. We had lost focus and looked to blame all the problems on external forces.

It was at that moment of crisis that the top 100 managers of the company met to review the options. The decision was unanimous – the task of refocusing on our core strengths was essential. Courageously, a 'back to basics' decision was taken and our company's diversification strategy was reversed. Each region was reorganized as a single manufacturing and marketing entity and the company's management set about the task of putting Levi Strauss & Co. back into the *jeans* market in a single-minded way.

As well as focusing on denim and the Levis's brand, the decision was also taken to focus on image not volume. The high-image flagship product of the Levi's brand – 501 jeans – would lead the company's return to profitability. The refocusing was executed extremely well. As well as ruthlessly divesting LS&CO. of all non-core businesses, all our marketing programmes put the focus squarely back on jeans.

The process wasn't quick and it wasn't easy. By the early 1990s, however, the jeans market in the USA and around the world had been rejuvenated and, by 1996, denim was a high-interest fashion fabric again. More importantly, and dramatically of course, sales of Levi's 501 jeans increased massively and became a much larger proportion of Levi Strauss & Co.'s total denim sales.

LS&CO. brand architecture: flexible yet focused

As a result of our mid-'80s refocusing, we agreed who our core target consumer was – and will remain; what the Levi's brand stands for and what our core products are.

We've resolutely stood by those decisions. Our more recent initiatives have all been built around that central premise about who our consumers are, what they want and why. As a result, if we want to get into entirely new areas, we launch new brands – as we did with the Dockers brand in 1986 and the Slates brand in the USA in 1996. Why couldn't Dockers pants be carried under the Levi's brand? It's because they are intended for a different consumer. The core product is not jeans and the brand stands for something different. Similarly, our newest brand, Slates dress pants for men, are aimed at yet another target consumer audience. Each brand has its own core market, its own approach to building an identity and set of associations with its unique consumer base.

The acid wall approach to innovation: build the brand or burn

Within the parameters we have set for ourselves, LS&CO. is continually developing and innovating products for its Levi's, Dockers and Slates brands. We bring new products to market, develop new distribution strategies and marketing programmes, refine the internal processes we use to bring our brands to consumers. But whatever the area of our business or the nature of the innovation, all new ideas are judged according to two basic criteria: do they build the brand and do they build the business?

The launch of our Levi's 'Personal Pair'™ programme is a good example of innovation. The Personal Pair programme is a breakthrough technological development in the apparel industry – the first widespread mass customization program – where a consumer's measurements are taken and entered into a computer. This information is sent directly to one of our factories and personally fitted jeans are produced and delivered on a pair-by-pair basis within two weeks.

Since its introduction in 1995, the Personal Pair programme has greatly helped push the Levi's brand to develop a genuine one-on-one relationship with our target consumers. There's nothing else like it in the market today; like the Levi's brand, it's a genuine original. It is also a truly heartland Levi Strauss & Co. concept for the modern age.

The programme also is important for another reason: size, style and colour preference details of each consumer can be stored and accessed, giving the company a wealth of valuable information about each Personal Pair programme consumer. Since these individuals tend to be some of our most motivated and loyal Levi's brand consumers, our ability to know who they are and what they want most provides us with a powerful way to ensure their continued engagement with the Levi's brand today and in the future.

One general rule with the Levi's brand is that all innovations must be 'Levi's-like'. What that means is that innovations are pursued or rejected based on their compatibility with the core values and attributes of the brand. As an example, at one of our European affiliates, this involves something they call the 'acid wall test', a technique developed by Levi Strauss Europe marketing manager Lothar Schafer. The 'acid wall' is literally a wall of their facility on which are written all the values, attributes and core associations of the Levi's brand. In considering any new products or marketing programmes, the affiliate's marketing team convenes at that wall and, one by one, considers whether the innovations are consistent with the values of the brand. Had the acid wall test and its regional equivalents been there in the 1970s, I doubt polyester suits would have got very far!

You could perhaps say that in developing brand innovations we are too cautious and may miss some opportunities. We feel that caution is not only the result of our own recent history – where the brand was sometimes treated recklessly – but also the experience of other brands that come and go because their companies don't know how to nurture them properly. So, we may miss some opportunities or are slow to respond to others, but we would argue it's a good price to pay for the focus and integrity we have with our brands and our consumers.

During the history of LS & CO., we have learned that building the equity of the brand is paramount and, with an already strong brand, equity is linked to a complex list of associations in the minds of consumers. The moment you produce something that disturbs that set of associations – the soul of the brand – you're in trouble. One can only wonder about the future of the brands that forget that simple fact.

The framework for success: structural changes

The task of keeping the Levi's brand number one for a constantly evolving group of consumers is a challenging one. One of the reasons we continue to be successful is that, while we deliver a consistent brand globally, brand managers have the freedom to execute locally. When we talk to consumers about the brand we get very consistent feedback. However, if you look at the specific projects or executions or marketing programmes, you will see they are quite different. The reason for this is that while we deliver a global brand message we deliver it to people who are very different in markets which are very different.

Our goal is to ensure we deliver to consumers what the Levi's brand stands for – indeed, what it *must* stand for to remain successful. Our activities in both the United States and Europe have continued to succeed because entire regional teams have had the courage of their convictions. We know from experience that to try to achieve such powerful results out of our San Francisco world headquarters would be naïve and almost certainly doomed to failure. How can I or our global marketing team know all the trends, or the cultural, geographical and political issues? The challenges facing someone on the ground in India, for example, are totally different from those in a developed market such as Sweden.

Consequently, our approach at Levi Strauss & Co. is to retain the highest quality local management and give them a framework within which to develop the brand in their areas. This may result in quite dramatically different executions (Europeans and Americans are, for example, perplexed by the fifteen-second commercials we run in Japan), but as long as consumers are internalizing similar basic messages about the brand, the marketing programmes are working well, as diverse as they may be.

Occasionally, something 'clicks' with consumers worldwide but, as Nigel Bogle of Bartle Bogle Hegarty has said: 'Global campaigns are born not made.' You don't start out to conceive a global campaign. They just develop as you go along.

Gradually LS & CO. has moved from a local to a regional to a global company while maintaining the respective strengths we have learned during each phase of our existence. Back in the 1970s and early 1980s we were building the brand locality by locality and each brand manager could basically do what he or she wanted without fear of impact on other markets. They were isolated. TV channels didn't span borders. The Internet didn't exist. Ten years ago, on the other hand, it became clear that consumers were hearing messages about our brand on a region by region basis. We adjusted our brand strategy to the new rules of the game. Now, with the Internet and global media, the future of our brand really is being written on a genuinely global basis. We're still learning how to make this latest leap.

One thing is clear, however. Managing a brand globally is far more complex. In large part this has been, and will continue to be, because of technological developments. Our global websites (www.levi.com and www.dockers.com), for example, provide a host of opportunities that would have been unimaginable ten years ago. They also have implications for how the brand is managed in each market. Now, more than ever, the left hand really *does* need to know what the right hand is doing.

To help bring that about, in 1996 LS & CO. established a new global marketing group and charged the group with a tough assignment: be visionaries. What we mean by that in practice is that the global marketing group operates outside national and regional constraints to support our efforts to build and manage the brand by using the latest tools and techniques; global developments such as the Internet, the media, new sponsorship strategies, our Original Levi's Stores and revolutionary new brand equity measurement tools. The group also works to communicate and transfer best practices from local markets to global markets, bringing a new perspective to the individual and local businesses that previously didn't exist. Via benchmarking of marketing counterparts at other firms, Levi Strauss & Co. also benefits from other companies' experiences on a global basis.

We're still in the global marketing group's early days but the new organization feels like a step in the right direction for the future of our brands. The global marketing group's role is, fundamentally, to incubate new products and ideas, to look after them when fragile, in their infancy. LS&CO. believes this kind of nurturing is extremely important for the future of our brands. Sometimes off-the-wall leaps of faith are vital. Experimentation and failure are important and should be rewarded.

The majority of innovations, however, are done locally or regionally. That's because there is no way for a team in San Francisco to know what's hot in Bangalore, Rio or Jakarta at the moment. In fact, there are completely different product ranges in the four regions (Europe, Latin America, Asia Pacific, North America). The Levi's brand silverTab™ line, for example, is not available in Europe, and not surprisingly there's a quite different product mix between, say, arctic Norway and steamy Singapore. There are, of course, some global products too, chiefly our flagship Levi's 501 jeans.

As 'visionary' as the global marketing group may be, it nevertheless exists to support the local experts. It is vital for the success of any of our brands that our regional and local marketing teams remain strong.

Sites for culture not just clothes: keeping a tight grip on consumers

It bears repeating that the equity for the Levi's brand is driven by a youth mind-set. For LS&CO., it's a useful coincidence that the most obsessed users of the World Wide Web happen to be young. Our Levi's brand Internet site (www.levi.com) was first established in the autumn of 1995. Since that time, our evolving presence on the WWW is being driven by a strategy of using that mind-set as a springboard and to have a broad enough voice that it can be meaningful in all kinds of cultures. The site has been designed to be a cutting-edge resource that embraces and contributes to global youth culture.

More than that, today we're beginning to recognize the Web's potential as an entirely new means of communication. As a result, we're persuaded that it won't be possible simply to take a conventional marketing approach to the WWW by simply adapting efforts from traditional media. Rather, we're establishing an entirely new approach to marketing on the Internet – an approach that creates from scratch a new, logical, credible and entertaining extension of who we are for the new medium. We believe today that the Internet provides us with an entirely new global medium through which we can leverage our position as a leading-edge marketer and brand builder.

For instance, via the Internet we can deliver messages that are much more fully developed, deeper messages than are possible, say, with conventional print or television advertising. In addition, the Web allows all sorts of two-way interactions between the brand and its audience of target consumers. As a result, time spent on-line can be a richer, more multi-layered and more self-directed media experience than has ever before been possible.

We believe that www.levi.com is particularly important because the WWW is a world where the brand with the strongest existing relationships with consumers has the most to gain. We believe the Levi's brand occupies that advantageous position and we believe the Internet is a new way to solidify our relationships with our consumers by making an interaction with the brand available to them literally twenty-four hours a day. It's a powerful tool and we intend to use it.

But the Internet is not our only strategy for creating new links to our target consumers. We also control brand presentation through various forms of retail theatre at our Original Levi's Stores around the world.

Original Levi's Stores were first established in the mid-1980s either because no jeans stores existed in a country (as was the case in Poland) or because of concerns we had about the ways our brand was being presented in a particular market. We wanted to provide consumers with a genuine, compelling, Levi's brand experience. As other successful brands have done, we have used our Original Levi's Stores as a powerful presentation of the Levi's brand expressing the core values of the brand, its history and evolution. The Original Levi's Stores are also an invaluable test-bed for new ideas, such as powerful point-of-sale strategies related to our advertising campaigns.

Initially, of course, our traditional retailers were anxious about their business when Original Levi's Stores opened up nearby. Consistently, however, the opening of Original Levi's Stores has enhanced the business of other Levi's brand retailers as well as performing well for us. We're not so much competing with existing retailers as enhancing the overall strength of the market and the presentation of the brand.

Performance has been closely monitored so case histories have been available to reassure existing retailers in new locations. There are now about 1,000 Original Levi's Stores worldwide. They offer the optimal brand experience, selection and service. In some locations they are the only source of Levi's products. Our most dramatic launch was in Moscow where we completely sold out of stock the day the store opened.

Building for the future: opportunities and challenges

With the Levi's brand established as the definitive blue jean world-wide, LS&CO. is in the enviable position of being able to lead the market from the front, pioneering and then owning new looks, styles and fits in denim and initiating programmes in other fabrics. In a notoriously fickle and unsure global market, this proactive position has incalculable value when compared with the essentially reactive position of other brands.

There are, of course, always threats and challenges to that position. For the Levi's brand, the competition from designer denim at the top end of the market looks as if it is here to stay. Unlike the 1970s and '80s when designer jeans-makers were fly-by-night companies that disappeared as quickly as they appeared, today's designer competitors seem far sounder financially and are also promoting themselves well.

We also closely monitor our competition at the lower end of the marketplace. Particularly in the USA, retailers are consolidating and finding own denim labels highly profitable.

Whatever the future holds, we believe LS&CO. is structured and has evolved to be fit and ready for new opportunities. As a company, the quality of our people and their ideas is what gives us our competitive advantage. We also have strong beliefs as an organization about the way we should be working in a global marketplace. We were the first company, for example, to establish comprehensive global sourcing and operating guidelines to benefit the individuals who make our products, and to improve the quality of life in the communities in which they live.

And last but not least, we're a company that tends to take a long view of our success; we measure it in years and decades, not in financial quarters.

Do these things strengthen our brands? We think they make us a stronger company with a powerful, cohesive common vision of responsible commercial success. And that can't help but make us a more effective organization with better ideas about the growth and evolution of our brands. The strength of our brands has always been about the strength of our company's vision. The two can't be disengaged from each other.

For that reason, the Levi's brand has been and is likely to remain central to the lives of consumers around the world. From the overalls worn by California gold rush miners in the 1870s, to 1950s James Dean Hollywood denims, to the jeans that the baby-boomers rebelled in at Woodstock, to the 501 jeans they now look cool in, the Levi's brand has evolved to fit the times while remaining faithful to the bedrock values of our company's history.

As designer Bill Blass has recently noted, we have a flagship product that is the quintessential American fashion: 'Nothing any fashion designer has ever done has come close to having the influence of blue jeans. That Levi Strauss invention – one of the sexiest items a man or woman can wear – is the most significant contribution America has made to fashion.'

So, while the future of the Levi's brand is yet to be written, we can be justifiably confident that the enduring strength of the brand in the minds of consumers worldwide is the one asset above all others that will ensure the brand's continued success and our company's vitality. We will achieve the full measure of that potential success if we remember that we succeed because of our relationships with the consumers. Out ultimate goal – a goal we can never forget – is to keep our brands relevant to them.

| **Orient Overseas Container Line: Growth Reflecting the Rise of the Asia Pacific Economies**

C. C. TUNG, *chairman*

Of all the things that we could say about our company – its role in world trade, customer service, speed, efficiency, reliability – the one thing we have picked out to highlight in our corporate logo is: 'We take it personally'. That is at the heart of our brand.

An outsider looking at a company like ours may be sceptical when we say our brand and our commercial success rest on our 'people' value. Superficially, of course, they are right. All you see when you look at a container transportation company like ours is huge ocean-going ships (some of which are big enough to carry enough containers to stretch across the English Channel), stuffed full of products from cars to frozen fish, which are loaded and unloaded at vast freight terminals.

All of these cold, hard things are fundamental to our business. But we are convinced that it is our employees' dedication that makes the difference. That is the message of our corporate identity.

'The World is Square'

To understand how we came to this conclusion, you have to understand a little more about our industry and our company. Our mission is 'to be the most successful global container transportation company . . . providing the vital link to world trade'. That mission reflects the fundamental importance of the container to the global economy.

Without the container the global village would still be a concept, not a reality, because manufacturing would still be a local process. Car companies, for instance, would still have to insist that their components suppliers were located within 150 miles of their factory, as they once did.

Today, consumers enjoy cars, electronic goods, foods and garments from all around the globe because the container makes it possible to provide them at surprisingly low costs. Most people are astonished to discover that the cost of transporting a US$6,000 motorcycle from the Far East to America amounts to just $85, or that the cost of sending a bottle of whisky from Europe to the Far East adds just 10 cents to the price of a $35 bottle. That's why we say 'The World is Square' – because global trade as we know it would not exist without the square container.

If containerization has changed the world, the world of competition has changed our industry and our company. OOCL was the first Asian company to embrace containerization, and in doing so it helped to drive the development of the Asian economy. Without us, Asian companies such as Toyota and Sony would have found it harder to conquer world export markets. Back in those days, if you built a ship you could fill it with cargo. Nowadays, with every new ship launched you get more space than cargo. We are a mature industry. Load utilization rates have become critical. And we have to compete.

Some of our competitors have responded by creating lots of space on their vessels and offering it to customers at very low prices. We, on the other hand, are focusing on time-sensitive, specialized and quality-dependent products – products like refrigerated goods, garments and vehicle components that have to arrive at the right place, in the right condition and at the right time.

Achieving that requires great expertise. If a food product is to be edible at the end of its journey it must be kept within a tight range of temperatures and atmospheres, from the minute it leaves the farm or factory to the minute it is picked off a supermarket shelf. For most of that time it is in our hands and it is our responsibility. When a ship completes a thirty-five-day round trip to North

America and back it has only got a two-hour window – no matter what the weather conditions have been – to arrive at the port to meet waiting trains and trucks.

Over the last decade this last point – 'the right time' – has become particularly important because of the 'Just in Time' (JIT) movement. JIT created a complete change in customer requirements and expectations, and we had to change our business to meet them. We have had to move from a wholesale mentality to a retail mentality.

For example, companies like Boots and W H Smith are relaying scanned information from what goes through their tills back to their warehouses, and they are looking to us to help them maintain minimum stock at all times. That means we have to deliver less, more frequently. And that, in turn, means that instead of filling a ship with orders from a few customers, at any one time the ship may contain goods from between 500 and 1,000 different customers who ship small amounts frequently.

We have also had to extend our service to the store door. Before, an American importer may have ordered fifty containers of lounge chairs and put them into one warehouse and then re-despatched them, re-handling every one. That no longer happens. The importer now says: 'My store in such a city will order the following items from my supplier in Hong Kong. Please pack one container containing the following fifty orders.' Then, to avoid any warehousing, re-handling and unnecessary domestic trucking, items are shipped directly to that particular store. For that reason, we now look after containers on land as much we do on sea; the ocean link has become almost incidental. The intermodal links that connect A to B have become critical because they are the only way we can do a lot of 'store door' business.

To offer this kind of service we have to be good; nowadays, our customers are experiencing our brand virtues all the way from order to final delivery.

Becoming an information-intensive business

All these developments, however, mean that, for us, 'being good' has changed. Increasingly our industry is dominated not by the movement of physical goods but by information. With global alliances and fixed transportation structures now in place, every competitor has similar hardware, so it's the ability to manage the information that controls the movements of goods that is becoming critical. Our challenge is to find integrated and added value solutions for our customers. That means, increasingly, competitive edge lies on the software side.

It's like airlines. They all have the same aircraft, use the same airports, and meet the same safety regulations. So they compete on the softer side in customer service. The only difference is that our business is far more complex. We have far more destinations we can deliver to: we not only put you on and off the aeroplane, we remove the seat from the plane, put it on a car or truck, and deliver it to your home. What's more, we may be collecting many different items from many different sources to place into one single consolidated container. And, at every point along the way, information pops up and somebody down the road needs it.

So our business is really very complex. Ships, terminals, agents and truckers are linked with vast communication networks via satellite, computer and fax; clients now have access to up-to-the-minute information about their shipment; seamless intermodalism provides them with door-to-door service; and tracking and routing systems have become so exact that a two-week journey can be timed for arrival within fifteen minutes.

That is why we have been investing nearly $50 million in a state-of-the-art object-oriented computer system which will be the most advanced booking system in our industry. Effectively what it does is decentralize our computing, allowing marketing and operations staff to offer customers extremely rapid decisions and information while keeping an eye on their margins and their cost-effectiveness at the same time.

Nowadays, that's what the customer needs. Information. So we want each and every one of our staff to have that information at their fingertips so they can give it to our customers when they need it.

Making it personal

Even the best IT system is only a platform. It's people who actually deliver the service. Using the technologies of standardized containers and fast, accurate information, we believe it is only committed employees who can give customers a great experience of OOCL by tailor-making services to satisfy their individual business needs. What we need is a whole set of really experienced people who are able and willing to work together to deliver this service and information. In other words, the personal aspect is increasingly in demand. And to build a really strong company we need a strong set of corporate values.

Over the last five years, we have begun many initiatives designed to achieve this. We started a quality assurance process in 1990, and now that commitment to quality is embedded in our corporate identity. We say the five petals of our plum blossom logo represent the five components of our quality assurance process: customer satisfaction, management commitment, employee participation, quality partnership and continuous improvement. Our vessels carry the plum blossom on the funnel and bow symbolizing the strength of our company, and over the years it has been integrated within every facet of our organization. This commitment to quality is complete, so that, for instance, we will not use a trucker in the UK unless he is ISO certified.

This quality process was very painful at the beginning but it was also very useful. For example, initially when something did go wrong, we would say 'Right, we are committed to delivering it on time', so we would end up paying airfreight to the ship rather than miss the boat. We learned very fast that we couldn't afford to keep on doing this, so we had to fix our own organization, restructuring it so that such problems no longer happened.

Like IT, quality assurance is more of a platform than a guarantee of service. We want our slogan, 'We take it personally', eventually to become the norm in everything OOCL does worldwide. We want it to become a distinctive and unique attitude that differentiates OOCL from all other carriers. To help achieve this we have invested heavily in communications (we were the first shipping line to open up direct communications with our employees via the Internet) and we have organized special sessions to encourage all employees to think about the way they carry out their role. In particular, we are promoting a set of desired behaviours.

One of these is 'share information and encourage discussion'. For example, the first time we formulated a mission statement in 1987 we had some wise men put it together. The second time, in 1995, we asked our staff for their ideas, and a large proportion did have something to say.

We are also encouraging all our staff to develop our six core competencies, which are: customer focus, results orientation, teamwork, the drive to achieve, communication and innovation.

It is very important to stress, however, that we are not introducing a new culture. Our core values don't represent a programme that is here one year and gone the next. We are just reiterating and consolidating some of the work habits of our staff. At the same time, we cannot overestimate the importance of core values, in particular the people value. Our employees make the difference by 'taking it personally'.

How OOCL's identity emerged

If we feel clear about these things now, it wasn't always so. In the mid-1980s we had a severe financial crisis and it took two years of very hard work with 150 creditors successfully to restructure the company. During that time we went through a tremendous learning process, identifying what went wrong before and what we really needed to do from now on in order to set the company on the right course.

One of the reasons for our downfall was that we were not focused. We had been very diverse, operating in a whole host of businesses including oil drilling, hotels and travel agencies, and we did not know what we really wanted to be as a company. So we identified what we wanted to be – the best container business – and decided to focus on that. After two years of restructuring we realized that this wasn't enough. To survive you need to specialize. Then you can differentiate. And while we had succeeded as a wholesaler in container transportation, we really needed to aim for the retailers. That is how we differentiate. We will never be the biggest, nor do we want to be. But we do want to be the most profitable, and the one that people associate with quality.

We have had to change ourselves to keep up, but we have retained core brand values. In the old days, OOCL's senior managers were typically 'Asian' and middle-aged: reserved, shy and conservative. Now we have become more eager to learn, we have developed a truly international outlook, we have become more resourceful – wanting to make things happen – and we are keen to develop relationships with customers rather than strike one-time deals.

Our corporate identity has also developed in parallel – we have learned that it is a mistake not to believe in the importance of corporate branding. Before the Second World War we had the plum blossom as a sort of house flag on the chimney tops of our ships. But the logo was the script that was written on the side of the ship – first the Orient Overseas Line, then the Orient Overseas Container Line – and the two things were really treated separately.

Indeed, at that time we didn't really pay much attention to the logo other than to take the view that people needed to recognize the plum blossom and Orient Overseas. At that stage containerization was easy. Demand outstripped supply, and we were doing wholesale business where it was not important to build up a brand. Then we realized that Orient Overseas Container Line was a bit of a mouthful and we moved forward a little bit. Like FedEx we shortened our name, and started calling ourselves OOCL.

However, we still had many hybrids of the logo shape, and we didn't have a specialist dedicated to developing the brand-name. It was only after 1985 that we started standardizing the identity. At that time we felt it was really necessary to search within the organization to find out what we really stood for.

Now we have a clear identity. The plum blossom logo is for our parent company Orient Overseas International. The OOCL logo with the plum blossom in the second O is the Orient Overseas Container Line, which brings in about 95 per cent of our revenue. That is the identity we tend to promote – and on occasion it has required intervention at the most senior level to underline its importance. On one occasion, for example, an operational director decided to respray a ship a particular colour, using a certain kind of anti-rust paint. From a narrow cost point of view his decision was absolutely correct: it would need only three coats of paint. But it was totally inappropriate for the visual branding, undermining its positive, optimistic spirit. The captain of the ship objected and eventually it was C. H. Tung himself who decided that the brand image was more important, even if it did require five coats and cost more money.

There are other important aspects of the plum blossom. First, it has 'soft' values; we deliberately put a plum blossom on a massive ship of 50,000 tonnes of steel. Second, it says something about our character, our resilience. In the late 1980s we could have easily packed it in, and the brand would no longer exist. But in China the plum is a flower that blooms in the harshest conditions – in the winter, in the snow. Also there is a Chinese saying that 'You can break the saw but you cannot break the willow branch'. We like to think we have the same personality characteristic. Compared to cast iron we are resilient.

Developing the business

One benefit of having a clear focus is that we have a very good idea of where we need to invest. Over the last five years or so, hardly a month has gone by without some important development: ordering a new ship, opening a new sales office, or signing a deal with a third party trucking or railroad firm to secure intermodal links. We now have thirty liner services: half of them intercontinental and half intra-Asian. We have 144 sales outlets, including offices in Hong Kong, China, Macau, Japan, South Korea, Singapore, Indonesia, the Philippines, Thailand, USA, Canada, UK, Belgium, Germany, the Netherlands, France, and Australia. Many of them are relatively new – less than five years old.

With this infrastructure in place, and with our core values firmly established and as a driving force behind everything we do, we are in a good position to continue our strategy of selective growth. There are huge opportunities in China, a very complex market which we understand well. There are opportunities in targeting major customers we currently do not serve. We recently signed a contract with Volkswagen which has regular, high-volume shipments to Shanghai.

To achieve such gains we have reorganized our marketing and sales to be much more market-driven and customer focused. We now aim to offer most customers a single point of contact, and are determinedly developing our role as providers of solutions and not just lower-cost freight. In fact, increasingly we are training our sales people to function more as logistics consultants than standard service providers. We want them to meet the real needs of customers – not only their current needs but also their latent and future ones.

All of this is necessary if we are to avoid competing on price alone. In fact, transportation cost is a relatively small part of our major customers' total logistics expenditure, so we are increasingly trying to help them in other ways, such as reducing interest costs through minimum stocking, improving cash flow through speedy and error-free documentation, reducing customers' duty due to direct calling of suitable ports and multi-area consolidation/distribution. This is where our investment in quality, information technology, people and core values really shows through as direct customer benefits.

We have also realized that there is huge, untapped potential in smaller and medium-sized companies. We have long-term relationships with many global companies which are now household names: companies such as Ford and Michelin in cars; Sony and Philips in electronics; Acer, Gateway 2000, Hewlett-Packard and Dell in computing; Burton, Wal-Mart and Adidas in retail; United Distillers, Heineken, Bass and Guinness in wines and spirits; and Du Pont, Exxon and ICI in chemicals. Customers like these will always be of prime importance to OOCL: just 1.5 per cent of our total customer base accounts for approximately one-third of our turnover.

However, many thousands of smaller companies do not get the same sort of attention from us, and they tend to stay with us for a much shorter period of time. In fact, we recently undertook a study among our 21,000 smaller customers and discovered that, on average, they stay with us for only one year – a common figure for our industry. Improving customer retention among these smaller and medium-sized businesses could be one of our biggest opportunities for profit improvement.

By paying the smaller customers more attention, we have discovered three things. First, they are often surprised and delighted to be given this attention. Second, it is not uncommon for what we thought to be small accounts to turn out to be medium-sized opportunities after all. And third, many small customers grow rapidly – their long-term value can be extraordinarily high.

Pioneering the art of co-operation

Our customers' demands for integrated solutions, ever greater speed, quality and reliability have also prompted us to rethink our approach to business. Recently we formed a Global Alliance with four other major shipping companies; American President Lines, Malaysian International Shipping Corporation, Mitsui OSK Lines and Nedlloyd Lines. This is the first time that leading carriers from all the world's manufacturing powerhouse regions of the United States, Europe, Japan and South-East Asia have been brought together in one liner grouping.

The Global Alliance will enable us to offer new levels of customer service, and build on brand strengths. Those customers seeking more frequent deliveries of smaller orders may ask for a sailing three times a week rather than just once a week. To offer that we may need to have nine ships plying the route. It is much easier and cost efficient to do this if partners coordinate sailings and share ship space and terminals. For example, the Global Alliance now offers six weekly sailings between the West Coast of America and North and South Asia. We are also able to improve cost efficiencies by negotiating jointly with shipbuilders and forming joint consortia for the ordering of new ships. Having four big names in the industry behind such deals allows us to negotiate better terms.

One thing we are not doing is merging our marketing and sales function. And we are certainly not going to sacrifice our identity. While we cooperate on the operational side and seek to outcompete other alliance groupings in terms of service and cost structure, within the alliance we also compete as hard as ever for customers.

Promoting the brand

Now that we are clear about what we as a company stand for and we have built our brand internally first, we are in a strong position to communicate it more aggressively externally. The way we do this is by associating with events which give us a chance to explain better what we have to offer. For example, the Cirque de Soleil – a famous Montreal circus – came to us to ship their containers around the world because nobody else had the network. We had one batch of containers coming from Montreal and another from Strasbourg, and they were looped together, some coming through the Suez, some going trans-Pacific and others coming via Japan. But they had to arrive in Hong Kong on a precise day. Everything landed on time, and the big top was set up. We promoted that as an 'Amazing Journey with OOCL'.

Another example is our three-year sponsorship of the Asia Pacific Championship yacht race. The yachts are fully containerizable. They come from Sydney, the USA and from the UK – from everywhere. Everyone coordinates well, and there are no hitches. Of course, we are not like a big tobacco company throwing down $5–10 million to sponsor Formula One motor racing. But what we can offer is space on a ship, which is just an incidental cost to us. And by doing so we are able to show other people that we can perform amazing feats in transportation.

Say + look + do = reputation

This is the important thing. We have a saying which is 'Walk the talk'. As far as we are concerned, the brand-name is a combination of what we say, how we look and what we do. And what we do is the most important. If you look at the seal of GE, or FedEx or even ICI, they truly believe in their philosophy, they appreciate it, and they get their employees to practise it. Similarly, we could say what we like and have the prettiest logo but if we cannot deliver, forget it. To that extent, every employee is the guardian of the brand, particularly the last person you meet. That's why we believe the most important part of the organization is not our hardware, our ships or our containers, but ourselves: we cannot separate our culture and our brand at any time or in any place.

6 | McDonald's UK: Balancing the Global Local Demands of the Brand

JOHN HAWKES, *senior vice president*

In 1954 McDonald's™ founder Ray Kroc bought franchise rights to the embryonic chain from two McDonald brothers who operated a hamburger stand in California. By 1961, having acquired the full rights to the name, he had already licensed more than 200 McDonald's restaurants in the USA.

Now McDonald's, with sales of over $30 billion, operates over 21,000 restaurants in more than 101 countries, with a new restaurant opening every three hours somewhere in the world. Over the next few years the plan is to open 2,500 to 3,200 new restaurants, not only in existing markets but in new parts of the world.

Getting the McDonald's brand to travel to so many countries so successfully in such a relatively short time can be attributed to a number of factors. First, McDonald's is passionately committed to the brand's core functional attributes, which are about serving quality food, courteously, by friendly people in clean surroundings and at exceptional value for money. Second, we keep raising the bar on our own performance, reinventing ourselves to improve our restaurant operations and our purchasing, franchising, training and marketing skills. Getting it better is as much part of our culture as remaining focused on our core business.

There is another aspect to the way we operate that has helped us succeed in so many different countries. The brand is global and those core attributes are fundamental, but each market has autonomy in the way it delivers the vision. There is self-regulation. We hold the firm view that what is right for the brand and how we build it and maximize the commercial return in each market is best left to that market to decide, particularly as local conditions can vary so radically.

The evolution of the brand

When we first began international operations it was essential to emphasize those core functional attributes, because they were key to establishing McDonald's position in the marketplace. Our evolution in the UK illustrates how that process has worked, as well as showing how the brand strategy has to develop as markets mature. In 1974, when we opened our first restaurant in London, the idea of service, of eating 100 per cent pure beef hamburgers offered at excellent value for money, in clean surroundings, simply did not exist. The positioning of McDonald's as a restaurant which welcomed families, had high-chairs and did not mind if children made a noise, was new and different. Also, competition was very limited for the first five to six years.

By the early 1980s consumer research showed us that the perceived point of difference was narrowing, with the competition beginning to wise up and model their operational systems on us. Also, quick service restaurants (QSRs) were being seen as more of a pressured, utilitarian experience, not one that you could sit back and enjoy. So the brand went into evolutionary mode, to reassert its competitive edge and address some of the negative perceptions of the industry by focusing on our relationship with customers.

Then, from the late 1980s, as competition from companies like Burger King grew, the brand strategy began to move again, aiming at a positioning based on the unique role McDonald's plays in everyday British lives. After all, if you look at the total volume of hamburger restaurant meals consumed, McDonald's accounts for about three-quarters of them. Alternatively, in the USA, where the competition is more aggressive, heightened by price-cutting, market share is much lower.

The greatest potential weapon in our armoury in terms of building the brand for the future is to continue to reinforce that emotional connection. It is not through price discounting or short-term tactical promotional activity that we increase our brand equity. It is by building the long-term reputation of the brand through exceptional customer satisfaction and value.

That philosophy applies to other markets, where the challenge is to make McDonald's a multi-dimensional brand. As the company has grown, the brand has become bigger than the accumulation of the restaurants. Factors such as international travel and media globalization mean that more people know about our brand, or think they do. They are certainly visually aware of it, and even in countries where there are no McDonald's restaurants people still have an understanding of us. So now those functional and emotional aspects of the relationship are a lot closer together, even when we open a restaurant in a new market.

What we always have to keep in mind, however, is that although the world has moved on, particularly in terms of what people eat and how they use restaurants in general, the essence of our brand positioning, the family, and the importance of quality, service, cleanliness and value still hold.

Taking the brand to new markets

When a business is growing at such speed it is always difficult to identify defining moments in the brand's global progress. With hindsight, setting up in Russia in 1990 was probably one of these defining moments, because of the marketplace itself. McDonald's was already established in international markets around the world, but being one of the first Western brands moving into Russia in 1990, when so much change was taking place, made the brand seem truly global.

It took fourteen years from the original discussion until we finally opened the doors in Moscow. Before we were able to go ahead, we had to invest resources and integrate vertically through the local food industry, to make sure we had the quality of supplies we needed. We keep reminding ourselves what makes us successful.

We cannot just rush into new countries if it means we cannot achieve the level of quality and consistency our customers expect. It is much better to do the right thing and guarantee quality rather than to go for speed. And it works: the Moscow McDonald's is now one of the busiest in the world.

There is no pre-determined time scale for opening in new markets. It also took several years to develop in the UK. We needed to make sure prospective employees and suppliers had an understanding and acceptance of McDonald's culture, of what we were and what we required. The relationships with our suppliers are based on long-term commitment, so we have to build an infra-structure to support that. In order to achieve consistency, we need partners who not only understand us, but also live by our standards.

The strength of franchising

One of our greatest strengths has always been our approach to franchising. In some markets, up to 80 per cent of the restaurants are owned and operated by independent entrepreneurs. Almost by definition, if you are franchising to local people the delivery and interpretation of what might be seen as the culture of a US brand is automatically translated by local people, both in terms of what is delivered and the way it is delivered. The percentage of franchised restaurants may be lower in the UK, but our franchisees still bring a wealth of individual flair into the business. They come from a variety of different experiences and backgrounds, and they may well have been brought up in the local area of their restaurant, so they'll know it well. Franchisees typically sign up for twenty years, and because it is their livelihood they bring a great deal of dedication and energy to a restaurant's development.

Success in a new market comes largely from listening to the indigenous partners, franchisees, customers and suppliers. India is a good example. Along with our partners and suppliers, we have invested considerable resources in establishing operations, includ-ing the construction of restaurants, infrastructure, and developing employees and local suppliers. Our aim is to purchase products required for the restaurants locally; over several years, we have been working with Indian companies to develop products specifically for the restaurants, by sharing expertise, technology and equipment of the highest standard.

Our menus reflect the local cultural framework: McDonald's India offers products developed especially for the Indian market, especially vegetarian customers. It will serve only mutton, chicken, fish and vegetable products, not beef, pork or their by-products. Big Mac™ thus becomes Maharaja Mac™, which consists of two all-mutton patties, special sauce, lettuce, cheese, pickles and onions on a sesame seed bun. Israel has some kosher McDonald's restaurants, while Saudi Arabia has a restaurant which closes five times a day for Muslim prayer.

The fundamental essence of the menu is important to us. It needs to be limited, not only so it can be served efficiently, but also to keep the quality levels high. Most people around the world like our hamburgers, the French fries and Coca-Cola. Making small changes to account for local tastes is important. For instance, we make a pomme frite sauce for Belgium and Holland, and a special mayonnaise-based sauce that is unique to Iceland.

A part of the community

So the brand is global but it exists at the local level too. Whether you are in Moscow or Manchester, it is the experience you have when you go into a McDonald's restaurant that shapes what you think about the brand. And although our heritage is American, because we are locally managed we are not necessarily seen as an overtly American company outside the United States. We are part of the community because the employees and the customers they are serving are local. People tend to talk about their 'local' McDonald's.

The brand defines the culture

We conduct research to determine who our customers are, what they want and how they feel about us. They could probably be best described as a family, where the parents are anywhere up to thirty-five years, with children aged between three and seven.

We have always positioned ourselves as a family restaurant, but of course our appeal is very broad. Family members are individuals too, with teenagers and over thirty-fives being very important, and they can be marketed to in a different way. The restaurant, however, has to embrace all these different people and be relevant to their needs.

Once your core positioning is clearly established you can segment more easily without compromising it.

There is a very strong internal understanding of what the brand is and what is important to it, so there is a hands-on protection of core values. Every contact we have with a customer, even seemingly minor ones, can have an enormous impact on the brand. Every touch counts. It can be very easy to upset the balance of the elements that make up the total McDonald's experience.

We have a structured Operations hierarchy with people visiting the restaurants making continual checks and balances. This is not about furtively going in and observing from a distance, but about working with restaurant managers and franchisees to ensure everything is running as well as it can. However, we do use Mystery Shoppers to make sure levels of service and quality are kept up from the customers' point of view.

The 'have a nice day' syndrome is a misapprehension. We offer a personal, friendly service, and aim to have some kind of individual rapport with each of our costumers. Although consistency of service is, of course, important, we encourage our employees to add a little bit of their own personality – it's about engaging with the customer. The essence of what we do is consistent, but the rest is about tailoring it for local markets.

The promise we make through the brand is being delivered right now, to millions of people, and the emphasis on learning and improvement therefore is strong. Training is continuous throughout the company and in the restaurants this includes day-to-day coaching and technology-assisted learning programmes. Aspiring restaurant managers attend a two-week Advanced Operations and Management class at our Management Training Centre. Each year, instructors at Training Centres in the USA, Germany, the United Kingdom, Japan and Australia teach more than 5,000 students, including franchisees and corporate management, in twenty-two languages. And even people who join the company in a departmental function will usually undergo the basic training programme. As a trainee in most companies you would expect to begin work in a suit, behind a desk. Our graduate trainees start in crew uniform, in a restaurant, so they understand every aspect of the business.

Formal training about the business and operational procedures is underpinned by the cultural rub-off which keeps people very focused on the brand. We also never lose sight of our roots and once a year we hold what we call 'Founder's Day', usually in October on a Friday, when all office employees, including those in the corporate and regional offices, and many of the partners in our supplier companies, leave their desks, put on a crew uniform and work in a restaurant for the day. Remembering what business we are in is an important part of our culture.

The emphasis on developing people from within supports this. Employees may move around from one function to another to gain experience in all areas of the business. So someone who started in the restaurants may be seconded to another department as part of his or her career development programme. We also have people who move to different countries to support the development of new markets.

Global consistency, local autonomy

Within the corporate brand are trademarked products which could be thought of as sub-brands, like the Big Mac™, Happy Meal™ and Egg McMuffin™. These have to be consistent with the fundamental brand values of McDonald's.

There is sometimes a perception that, with our American heritage, we have a massive headquarters in the USA managing the business around the world. This is not the case. The management team in each country, whether there is an equity investment or local ownership, is relatively autonomous. That does not mean that employees go off and do their own thing. There is continuous communication between countries and regions, not so much for approval but for learning and sharing of best practice and to ensure consistency. We do have regional centres – for example, we have regional offices for Northern and Southern Europe – staffed by people who support, assist and facilitate the sharing of efficiencies, and make sure the wheel is not being reinvented each time we open in a new market. What is central is an understanding of the global brand.

We can, however, create new products for individual countries. There is no rule that an idea has to be able to travel to other markets, but by virtue of the networking and sharing of ideas, a lot of processes we have developed do travel well. For example, in the UK we took the lead in developing a modular building process which improved construction efficiencies enormously and it is now used in many other countries. Another way to network ideas is through our supplier-partners, who often export their products to McDonald's in other markets. Countries will test new products, new ideas, new promotional mechanics, and if they work in one market they can be adapted to work in others.

The 'not-invented-here' syndrome is a natural human characteristic. To minimize it, we credit those who innovate and then provide the encouragement and infrastructure to share. We do not worry about people taking ideas from other countries – on the contrary we do what we can to facilitate it. Rather than reinventing the wheel we seek to improve it. It is always important to remember how critical the local culture is, and that certain ideas simply will not travel. However, ultimately, there is more that is the same than is different.

We also have a senior vice president, responsible for an international team of marketing people who give guidance and help share ideas. The world is shrinking and with the advent of satellite communications and the Internet there is an increasing need to communicate more information, more quickly, about issues that arise in each country and how they may affect others. This is a vital part of managing the brand.

The power of the corporate identity

Our corporate identity, the Golden Arches, is very powerful and instantly recognized around the world. Because it is applied to so many different communication materials like stationery, packaging, signage, uniforms, literature and advertising, and by so many different people, it is important that it is used consistently.

Another misconception is that all of our restaurants are the same. This is not the case. To reinforce the brand identity, a single design for packaging is being developed, which will also save costs in production and distribution. However, our restaurant designers have broad scope in terms of the decor and furniture they use. Go into any McDonald's restaurant and the signage, the counter and the way the people serve customers will be consistent. But if you look at the architecture, the colour scheme, the fabrics and furnishings, the design, the artwork on the walls, you will find they can be very different and are often themed to the locality.

Communicating brand values at the global and local level

Apart from local marketing activity, television advertising often comes first when we enter a market, because it is the strongest communication medium. Then, as we grow and develop we will add to the media mix, whether it be radio, outdoor or press, in order to reach different audiences with different messages. Deciding the media is the last thing to do. The first task is to agree the objective and strategy, the issue we are trying to address. And then find the best way of communicating it.

Our advertising is usually produced locally. In the UK, for example, we produce our own advertising, although we have occasionally used international commercials where it was appropriate. Creating global advertising is not necessarily more cost-efficient, in terms of economies of scale, if the ads themselves are not as effective as those produced in the local market.

There are many different ways of communicating the same thing. In the USA a communication might be quite emotional, whereas in the UK the same sentiment will be communicated through humour. That is not to say, though, that a humorous commercial produced in the UK would not also strike a chord in another country.

In the UK we have occasionally adapted American ads – we may re-shoot them, or use the pictures with a different voice-over. There are no rules really, other than to be totally consistent with the brand values.

Sponsorship is another powerful vehicle for communication, whether at the global level, like the 1996 Olympic Games, the regional level, with the 1996 European football championship, 'Euro96', or at the local level. In the UK, we are the official restaurant of football's Premier League. A large proportion of the budget is directed at initiatives to encourage the involvement of families and young people. This sort of activity creates an excellent opportunity for our restaurants to become involved with the local community. It is also a way of keeping the brand alive and vital. So the management of the brand is very much in the detail. It has to work right the way down to the restaurants and bring the magic to life in the local community.

Strategic marketing alliances are another way to strengthen the brand. In 1996 we announced a ten-year alliance with the Walt Disney Corporation. McDonald's is Disney's promotional partner in the restaurant industry, giving us exclusive category marketing rights, linking our restaurants to Disney theatrical releases, theme parks and home video releases.

One of our most valuable assets, particularly in terms of our charitable and community activities, is Ronald McDonald™. He might visit a restaurant to do a magic show, and then go to a hospital and entertain the children's ward. He can also be a great teacher, for example on subjects like road safety, because children do listen to him. And he helps raise money for children's charities, including Ronald McDonald Houses™, which are homes-away-from-home for families of seriously ill children receiving treatment at nearby hospitals. At the end of 1996 there were 180 Houses in fifteen countries, accommodating 2,500 families every night.

Restaurant managers and franchisees often become involved with local charities and civic activities. The company has always had a strong corporate social responsibility stance, born out of founder Ray Kroc's desire to 'put something back' into the community. This has been adopted into the corporate culture, and community involvement and charitable fund-raising have become key features of local activity worldwide.

The brand as a living process

The challenges we face are different, market by market. The USA, for example, is dealing with issues which other countries can learn from. There are more and more opportunities for people to eat out, so it is a constant challenge for us to maintain market share. Our competition comes not just from other chains, so one of the ways we can grow is by making ourselves more convenient and taking the brand to where people congregate by using, for example, mobile restaurants. This approach is part of the objective to make the McDonald's brand and proposition available in more places. Unusual locations now include airports, hospitals, university campuses and military bases, among others. McDonald's food can also be found on aeroplanes, trains and ships.

There is a great deal of room for growth. Based on the populations of the countries where we currently operate, on a given day McDonald's still serves only 1 per cent of the population. In China, for example, there are only around sixty restaurants to serve 1.2 billion people!

It is fair to say that the business we are in is simple. But managing the brand is not a simple process. It might be relatively straightforward to sell one Big Mac to one customer. The skill lies in doing it well 20 million times a day, day in day out, around the world.

7 | Guinness Ireland: Broadening the Brand Franchise without Destroying the Mystique

TIM KELLY, *marketing director*

Ireland is, of course, Guinness' original and spiritual home market. As the brand's most mature market, it offers particular challenges that other less developed territories are yet to face. More Guinness is drunk per head in Ireland than anywhere else: one in every two pints sold is Guinness. And, despite having a population of only a twelfth of Great Britain's (5 million compared with 58.6 million), the Irish market's expenditure on the brand is nearly the same as Great Britain's. However, even in Ireland, Guinness faces competition from rival brands and is now fighting to secure future sales by increasing its appeal to a younger generation of drinkers.

In its home market, Guinness recently introduced a fresh approach. The company has tiered its brands, dividing different products into groups. 'National power brands' are Guinness and Budweiser and Carlsberg (which it brews locally under licence). These command high investment to support all aspects of the brand. Then there are 'strategic brands' (with potential to become power players) such as Kilkenny and Hudson Blue, and then there are the 'regional brands' such as Harp and Smithwicks, and they have strengths in particular areas such as Harp in Northern Ireland. The company's emphasis is to grow international business outside its most developed markets as well as expand its consumer base back home. It will have to achieve both if it is to achieve its goal: to move up from sixth position to become one of the top three beer brands in the world.

Two centuries in the making . . .

It may no longer be only an Irish business but, to many, Guinness is the quintessential Irish brand. It is a mixture of many elements: the product, the experience of drinking the product, and its history. Guinness' founder, Arthur Guinness, took over the brewery in Dublin's St James' Gate in 1759. At that time, Porter, a drink popular with the porters at Covent Garden and Billingsgate, was being exported by London brewers to Dublin and Guinness was brewing ale. Tackling the English brewers at their own game, Arthur Guinness turned his hand to 'porter' in the early 1790s. The decision led to the business becoming the largest porter and stout brewery of all time.

Today, the headquarters of Guinness plc is at Portman Square in London, where the company is listed on the London Stock Exchange. The announcement in May 1997 of the proposed merger with Grand Metropolitan, to be called GMG Brands, will create one of the largest food and drink companies in the world. At the time of writing, the merger still requires approval. Since its merger with United Distillers in 1986, Guinness has had two divisions: United Distillers, the spirits business with brands like Johnnie Walker and Gordon's Gin, and Guinness Brewing Worldwide (GBW) which handles all the beer business with brands like Guinness, Kilkenny, Harp, Red Stripe and Cruzcampo. GBW divides the world into six regions. There is Asia Pacific based in Singapore. Another is based in the United States and includes South America, Canada and the Caribbean. Ireland & Europe is based in Dublin. Then there is Great Britain, based at the Park Royal Brewery, London. The company has substantial business in Africa, and the final region is Spain, where the company bought Spain's largest brewer, Grupo Cruzcampo, in 1991. Each is headed by a regional managing director, and each is a profit centre as well as a geographic unit. Each regional managing director reports to the global managing director of GBW who, along with the managing director of United Distillers, sits on the board of Guinness plc.

Regional managing directors are autonomous but, like every global business, there is a very clear set of operating practices and targets. At GBW level, there are central staff covering the key functions such as technical, finance, personnel, marketing and public affairs. All are coordinated centrally and administered locally. So, there are the same reporting procedures and deadlines in every country. This is also important because we have people who are moving worldwide, so recruitment, employment terms and conditions and other organizational issues meet global standards. With marketing, however, GBW's role is quite different: by comparison it is quite decentralized. At Coca-Cola, central management is very strong, whereas, at Guinness, local markets have a lot of freedom and autonomy. Of course, with production there has to be a degree of uniformity, and purchasing is organized on a worldwide basis. Locally, however, there are differences in product, packaging, advertising and advertising agencies, although the core essence of Guinness is basically the same.

This structure used to be very different. Until four years ago, there were three regions: Ireland, Great Britain and International. The change was driven by the growing importance of international markets and their strong growth. Take the USA, for example, which although relatively new for Guinness is growing so rapidly it now needs its own local focus. Today, more and more decision-making is happening locally. The first US-specific TV advertising was recently shown; it was made in the USA and only for that market. Previously, the USA took everything from Dublin and London. Now it's a question of local expertise and achieving critical mass.

United Distillers has a similar structure with regional directors around the world, in local markets managing local business. But the nature of the spirits business is very different. More commonality exists. Take Johnnie Walker: it's made in one place, the graphics are the same worldwide and the advertising is the same worldwide. If a local marketing director wanted to 'break the rules', it would be discussed by head office in Hammersmith. The difference in approach comes down to the difference in product. Beer tends to be made locally; whisky is made in one place. Spirits are more of a luxury item; beer is an everyday purchase. Where spirits are purchased also differs significantly: for example, at duty-free outlets. And the quantities of each that are sold are very different. United Distillers' business is structured around local sales, marketing and distribution operations rather than manufacturing sites. As its business is bigger – UD is roughly twice the size of GBW – a different organizational model seems appropriate.

Beer is a relatively new business by comparison. The GBW structure offers a number of commercial benefits. Speed is one. Local understanding is another – we need those actually working in their market to understand that market better than anyone else. As a result, we tend to be able to recruit better people in the local market; we can offer them full freedom for that market.

'The wine of the country'

Defining the essence of the Guinness brand is something a lot of people have spent an awful lot of time doing, and we still have not found all the answers. There are some brands which you can discuss and everyone nods and knows what you are talking about. One of the difficulties of Guinness – and it is partly one of our own making – is that we have wrapped it up in a sort of language of complexity. This is complicated by the uniqueness of the product and the imagery and values which consumers attach to the brand. Marketing people have tended to cloak Guinness in jargon and unusual words. Guinness is a mainstream draught black beer for eighteen to thirty-five-year-olds. In Ireland it is an 'everyday drink'. Therefore it is the defining beer for the Irish market. In other markets it isn't. In Great Britain, for example, Guinness' share of the total beer market is in single figures and increasing, but it performs a different role, and its positioning is quite different. Here the positioning is everyday, everywhere, ubiquitous.

Now, there are a number of different elements to the brand which we map as a 'bullseye'. The core brand proposition at the centre sets Guinness as 'communion, power and exploration'.

Around this we have brand heritage, distinctiveness, complexity, naturalness, ubiquity, innovation and wit. Some of these are very similar across the brand worldwide. Others vary in significance according to the local market and consumers' perception. For example, the slogan 'Guinness is Good For You', which we used here in our advertising in the 1940s and 1950s, is still remembered in some markets. In Africa, for example, consumers have over the years attributed power to Guinness: an aphrodisiac, or a male reward. And of course we do have a heritage associated with the naturalness and benefit of the product. In Ireland, if you give blood you're given the option of a glass of Guinness, or a cup of tea, or coffee afterwards.

Then there are the physical properties of the pint: we call it 'the surge' – the way Guinness pours and settles and the ritual involved in that. This used to be peculiar and exclusive to Guinness. Now there are other brands coming in, like Kilkenny, which do it too. Even so, Guinness is still closely associated with that surge: the waiting, the anticipation. Also, Guinness is seen as natural – made from healthier ingredients to an original recipe. That's why some of the features on the packaging can be traced back to 1759 with the Arthur Guinness signature, and so on. It is seen as the original. Then there's the product, it's black – few products are only black, we 'own' the colour. We divide the emotional values of the brand into 'how it makes me feel' and 'what it says about me'. For example, individualistic, at ease with oneself, content, socially-bonded. Again, these vary market by market.

We don't push 'Irishness' in all markets around the world – in some, people may not have even heard of Ireland. However, in most there is at least a basic awareness of Irish culture: notably, Irish writers like James Joyce who memorably described Guinness as 'the wine of the country'. The greater challenge is the product itself, because it is at the root of the complexity which has tradition-ally surrounded the brand. It takes some getting used to if you've never tried it before. The colour is unusual compared to lager, and it has a more bitter taste.

People have explained the product and the marketing of it in terms of being complex, rewarding, deep, mysterious and so on. I believe too many people have been caught up with subtleties that may not exist. It is, after all, just a drink, a very different drink, but a drink none the less. It is usually drunk in pubs in draught format when people want to have a good time. People's needs in those situations are pretty straightforward and simple – they want to enjoy themselves. They don't want an intellectual game to be played to give them a reason to drink. There is a real risk in positioning a brand as too difficult or inaccessible. We need a more pragmatic approach.

Unravelling the mystery

Guinness has undergone two major shifts in branding and positioning in recent years. The first was in the 1970s. The second is taking place now and we call the strategy the 'Big Pint'.

In the 1970s, it would be fair to say Guinness was perceived as a cloth-cap brand. It was drunk by older people lower down the social scale, for example rural farmers, older men. Fifty-three per cent of beer drinkers were aged thirty-five or over; 63 per cent of Guinness drinkers fell into this bracket. At that time, the Irish beer market was divided into three neat categories: stout, ale and lager.

In the stout market – which at that time was in sharp decline – we had Guinness, in ales we had Smithwicks and in lager (a small but rapidly growing sector in the 1970s) Harp. Some things we did then had to change. There was a jaundiced trade view of Guinness as a company which was overall seen as caring less about its customers than its rivals. We were a typical company that had grown up successfully. As a company we had to reinvent ourselves to recognize new competition and a more demanding customer.

Guinness was failing to target the growing middle-class consumer group. And its consumer profile – predominantly male – did not reflect the growing importance of women in the market. So, in the 1980s, we developed a strategy to invest in revitalizing stout; this entailed new investment in the product, in production, the brand and its promotion. We reduced the serving temperature of the product and its quality was improved. There was a change in livery – colours were updated and packaging made more attractive, especially to women. Much of the marketing activity was designed to recruit younger people and move Guinness into outlets where it was not previously available. There was a marked difference between the old advertising focusing on the traditional male drinking market and the new.

The results were soon clear. By the 1980s, we had achieved a more upmarket consumer profile, more women drinkers and a growing share of new recruits to beer. There was real volume growth and Guinness recovered its share of all draught beer sales. At one point, stout had dropped to about 46 per cent of the total (Irish) beer market. After this initiative, it was brought back up to over 50 per cent. Successful companies can keep up to date and ahead of trends. Understanding the market and acting early is key and what Guinness managed to do was force change in the absence of a crisis.

In 1970, the majority of Guinness' total worldwide sales would have been sold in Ireland – between 70 and 80 per cent. This repositioning started in Ireland. It just wouldn't have been necessary or worthwhile elsewhere, because the sales volumes would have been so small. Since then, we have constantly worked to build on this. You can't stand still, even with an established brand. We are constantly working to improve our efficiencies, our processes, our marketing, our selling – everything. And we shall continue to do so.

Following the United Distillers–Guinness merger in 1986, there was a realization that if Guinness plc had a great global spirits business, we should fully develop our global beer business as well. Beer was already being exported, but what was required was a significant increase in resources to realize its potential. Activities were stepped up and, over the years since, as markets reach critical mass, local infrastructures have been established and local strategies set in place.

The 'Big Pint'

Today, however, we still face challenges. Research among Irish people shows tremendous loyalty towards the Guinness brand. But we must attract new, younger, drinkers if we are to grow Guinness in the longer term, and that is the essence of the challenge: to recruit new drinkers and retain current ones. Last year we switched from a local agency which had previously handled the business for many years, to London-based agency Howell Henry Chaldecott Lury & Partners. Together, we have developed the 'Big Pint' strategy. We never use those actual words, but the idea is all about size, substance, taste, texture, and worth – said in a way that is immediate, relevant and surprising but also with humour. Size matters. It's not mysterious, deep or complex. The 'Big Pint' and all the communication around it is based on the fact that Guinness is the world's biggest-selling pint. There's more to Guinness than other pints – more taste, more texture, more reward.

The thinking behind the 'Big Pint' is that Guinness is actually the biggest pint in the world. We can justify this because, as Guinness is nearly always sold in draught format, it is more often drunk as a pint than any other packaging format, which makes it the biggest-selling pint brand in the world. On its own, this says little. But explain it or show it in a way that's witty and says something about the product and brand – bigger taste, bigger density or texture – and it adds something to the brand. The next stage will be to explain the product in a new and engaging manner.

We have a reputation which requires us to keep our advertising up to date. We are always slightly nervous about a change in style; it is a delicate balance.

Because we want to secure the long-term health of the Guinness brand, we must constantly watch the market. This is why we are lowering the age profile of the brand. In hot drinks and soft drinks, as you buy into a brand and get older you don't tend to change your buying habits. But in Ireland, if you are a younger person you are likely to drink lager and be less brand-loyal. In the past, you might have moved into drinking stout as you get older, but that's not so much the case today. Young people are growing up in a world with many brand options, and they are more likely to stick to the brands they consume now as they age. We want to win over the younger drinkers. At the same time, we want to hold on to our older drinkers. They don't want themselves to be seen as drinking an older person's drink. We must make them feel good about drinking Guinness. We don't want to be so young we frighten them off.

Young people want a global brand image like Coke, Nike or Levi's. They want something for them. We used to talk about Guinness in the company as velvety, creamy, smooth, dark – the product language. These words mean little to an eighteen-year-old, who might even find them off-putting.

You could argue that it's 'old-fashioned' to have to wait for something – and Guinness is all about waiting: the 'Guinness Moment' as the pint is drawn and settles. They might say that in a Pepsi Max world the young want it now. But they'd be wrong. One of the great unique qualities of Guinness is the Guinness experience. The experience is the product. It is unique. Communicating this to younger drinkers is what we must now address. So the point of the 'Big Pint' is to use words and language that mean something to them. There are posters around using words like 'taste-tackler' – things that are amusing, or that instantly evoke an image, slightly funny, slightly tongue-in-cheek, but describing the product in a relevant way.

It's using our past but expressing it in a way that is relevant for today. We don't deny our heritage, nor do we want to. We are proud of it. We want to express it with relevance. When I first started here someone said to me 'Are you going to be a recruitment or a reassurance marketing director?' What he meant was, 'Are you going to hold on to existing customers or start recruiting new ones?' I don't believe it's an 'either/or' decision. If we recruited younger drinkers and upset older ones we'd struggle, and if we retained older drinkers and didn't win the young it would be the same. Our marketing effort is split across different age groups and targeted accordingly. We do hurling and opera sponsorship as well as music festivals. We walk a tightrope everyday between trying to attract someone in a language, a tone and with a message that's relevant to them without upsetting someone else.

Divide and conquer

One of the traps that anyone can fall into is following competitors. While new brands, like Murphys or Caffreys, have created a sense of freshness about them, we don't want to follow them. Part of the reason for our current change in strategy is to enable ourselves once more to take the lead and let them worry about how to respond.

We have also adopted a new approach to addressing our market. Now, we have 'need-states' – a world divided into different consumer needs. In the 1970s there was something drinkers light-heartedly referred to as the Holy Trinity: you started drinking Harp, you graduated to Smithwicks and then you went on to Guinness. Now the world is far more complicated than that.

Also, as market dynamics change – lager has grown at the expense of stout and ale, for example – we said rather than look at the market by sector, we would look at the total drinks market, the long alcoholic drinks market. And that's where 'need-states' come in. We've moved our market definition from Guinness being considered part of the stout market, to looking at Guinness as a proportion of the total drinks market with all the Guinness brands.

'Need-states' segment the market by consumer need. At one end, there's the need to enjoy yourself. At the other, the need to reward yourself after a busy day. There is easy sociability, everyday drinking, and there is the Friday night out, and so on. What we've got is different businesses in each need-state; each one can be quantified by volume share. We therefore can identify where we have too much of one and not enough of another, and then approach how to redress this if there is too much in a static box, too little in a growing one. We must stretch and pull our portfolio.

One of the differences in Ireland is that, unlike in other markets, we have a full range of brands aimed at different needs. We launched our first non-beer product last year: Hudson Blue, an ice cider. We have a market definition which is 'long alcoholic drinks'. This means more than just beer, and it enables us to look at the whole picture and introduce brands or packs to meet all needs. So we can cover the pitch rather than supply just one market.

To tackle the portion of the market which we don't have, we could launch Guinness either as different versions or in new packaging formats. But just how far could you stretch it? At the moment, it's only a black, draught product. Our cider is not, for example, branded as from the Guinness company, but some brand extensions have been launched. Guinness Draught Bitter is on sale in the UK and so is Guinness Extra Stout (a stronger, bottled version of traditional Guinness). But can it go only that far, or could Guinness be stretched to encompass something else? Brand stretching has seen more casualties than successes, so before we embark on any change we would have to be very confident.

Could we ever apply the same qualities Guinness has to other products? If we were to use all things consistent with the Guinness brand and do it in the right way, maybe. However, you won't succeed unless you make an effort, and in making an effort, sometimes you will fail. You have got to try several things several times to move, and all companies I am sure would like to be more innovative.

We have learned many lessons from NPD. We are far more conscious now of consumer needs, and we are becoming more innovative. Today, we do a large amount of research, and relationships with our consumers are worked on very, very hard. Many US companies are saying 'stick to core competencies – single products, single brands'. We believe there is more growth in the Guinness brand than anywhere. There are no plans to change the product.

Spreading the word

Our priority now is to grow volume in different markets. One way we are doing this internationally is with the help of the Irish pubs. The Guinness Irish Pub concept helps publicans and entrepreneurs around the world establish 'authentic' Irish pubs. Guinness is well placed to offer professional advice on how to re-create genuine Irish pub culture. There are four key elements: pub design and ambience; friendly, efficient staff; the unique appeal of Irish food; drink and Irish music – sometimes it's live, always it's there. It is a very good way of seeding interest and growing demand. When looking at a brand-new market, we must consider a number of options. Do we export? Or do we set up a plant? A few Irish pubs serving Guinness in the right way with the right music, Irish food and Irish style is a wonderful way of developing the market. It is also the perfect environment for consumers to sample a perfect pint of Guinness.

The whole Irish phenomenon has arisen over the past decade or so. Irish culture now has international appeal. The Irish pub plays a central role in this. Irish pub culture is unique. The Irish drink in pubs more than anywhere in the world. I don't know of any other European Union summit where John Major took time out to visit a local bar. But when they were in Dublin, John Major and Kenneth Clarke slipped off to the pub for a quiet pint of Guinness. What better way to present a new concept – Guinness – than in the context of the Irish pub? Imagine it arriving, by can, in a Chinese shop. Or a local bar in Peru simply starts serving it without any understanding. Remember, you need to try it a few times before you become a regular consumer.

We don't have direct investment in any of our pubs and it's not a franchising arrangement. We *do* put a lot of emphasis on quality. We have people employed worldwide who are pub retail experts, and they help to build up the relationships and build pub business. We help ensure best practice, exchange information and put the people with the money in touch with the suppliers. You can buy a bespoke kit for an Irish pub made here in a variety of designs.

Many leave here in a lorry, are unpacked, assembled and built at the other end. We are the facilitators.

The Irish pub concept is not necessarily a first step towards a global strategy for the Guinness brand. Walk into some and they are playing local, not traditional Irish music. Walk into others and you can find local musicians playing Irish music who could be mistaken for an Irish band. The point is the format allows local consumers to interpret and participate in the values it embodies.

There is, however, an emerging need to have greater uniformity for the Guinness brand around the world. In time, I think we will find more common elements – it will happen naturally. With the overall objective to grow the Guinness brand worldwide, we must develop both the home core market and new developing markets with high potential. You have got to allow freedom if these developing markets are to fulfil their potential. Even so, there is a set strategy for developing new markets: there is no need to reinvent the wheel every time.

Walking the tightrope

The Guinness brand and Guinness the company are so closely entwined in Ireland that we have to be acutely conscious of public reaction to what we do. Ireland remains a big source of volume and profit. Guinness plc has profits of about £970 million a year; United Distillers accounts for around 60 per cent of this, GBW around 40 per cent. In the Irish market we are challenged by new brands all the time. Like all businesses, there is globalization. What would once have been a local brewery in Cork is now owned by Heineken, which owns Murphy; Beamish is owned by Scottish Courage; Bass has a site in Belfast. Growing competition has meant we spend more time monitoring our product, both against our own standards and against the competition in terms of quality, taste and colour. There is an obsession, almost a missionary zeal, within the company about quality – achieving a uniform product at a particular standard – and every employee is encouraged to play a role in this. It's not just ensuring it leaves the brewery in perfect condition but that it should also be perfect when the consumer drinks it in the pub.

There is an obsessive quality in Ireland about beer. It's important here. You still hear all these stories about Guinness on the west coast not tasting as good as Guinness on the east coast because it has travelled further. And people do move from pub to pub because they say, 'I prefer it over there', or 'This is a bad day from this one'. Whether it really does taste better in Ireland than anywhere else, however, it's hard to say. Many have tried to prove it, with inconclusive results. I think it's perhaps that you enjoy yourself more when you are drinking it here.

This universal interest in Guinness is a critical factor. Our major challenge is keeping up to date, as it has been every decade since 1759. You have to work very hard at this, and not be a follower of fashion. Because markets and lead times are so short, things happen and change more quickly. We believe if you understand today, tomorrow will follow. We don't worry about five or ten years down the line, in that respect. But we do need to ensure we connect with our consumers and really understand what they are doing today and why, and why not. It is a fundamental belief. Understanding the consumer is not just an issue for the marketing department, it is an issue across the entire company.

Brand positioning, essence and relevance go beyond marketing. There is involvement and interest throughout the company. Employees ring me up and say, 'I saw that', 'I liked it', 'I didn't like it' in a way I've never experienced in previous roles. There is a special concern for quality among everyone who encounters the brand.

Custody of the brand has to sit somewhere – and that's in the marketing department. Ultimately, however, the true custodian is the consumer. In Ireland, the brand is as significant as Coke in the US or Carlsberg in Denmark – it's the national brand as well as Ireland's favourite drink. The level of attention our consumers pay to every detail is remarkable. Sometimes it makes us cautious, but we are very, very close to our market and our consumers as a company, not just as a department.

Recently, we did some work looking at companies which optimize consumer marketing. Those who do are those who are closest to the consumer. These companies include Tesco, Nike, Levi Strauss, Pepsi, Mars. Tesco, for example, has consumer panels which meet every week to say what they want and what they don't want. That sort of approach is deeply impressive. We've improved as a result. The managing director frequently consults consumer groups. In fact, he and others are now offering insights, comments and understanding of marketing in a way they would never have done previously. Marketing within Guinness has often clouded itself in secrecy and jargon, and this is an effort to break it down.

Last year we ran some ads which some of our employees didn't like. They felt frustrated because they felt they couldn't tell us. But everyone has a voice and a right to be heard. Obviously, you can't be so democratic, or afraid, that you are solely ruled by that. But people should feel confident they can tell you, that you will listen and, where applicable, that you will take it on board. If I were to draw one lesson from all of this it would be: know your consumers. And ensure you listen.

8 | Rentokil Initial: Building a Strong Corporate Brand for Growth and Diversity

SIR CLIVE THOMPSON, *chief executive*

When I arrived at Rentokil as chief executive in 1982, one of the first major decisions I had to make was on our branding strategy. We considered the two main schools of thought on branding. The first was that pioneered by companies such as Procter & Gamble: you have an individual brand representing a product category, and product categories that are sufficiently large to be able to justify advertising and promotional support at such a level that it makes a noise in the marketplace; where you have a number of well-known brands from a deliberately recessive parent company.

The second is that other group of companies which believe there are enormous benefits in having a relatively limited number of product/service categories covered by a single brand-name. Even if each individual activity is relatively small, you get the cumulative benefits of the brand and leverage from one activity to another. The downside is potential dilution of the impact of the brand, because it acts as an umbrella rather than being sharp and focused on the single activity.

In 1982 at Rentokil the approach to branding was inconsistent. While Rentokil was the name of the company, there were, in addition, a whole variety of individual brands, and the name 'Rentokil' was not commonly used throughout. This was probably the result of individual operating brands being perceived as stronger, and because managers of subsidiaries liked being independent and to develop their own brands. The second trend was a shortening of Rentokil, with the rather unfortunate word 'Rento' being associated with all sorts of different activities like Rento-Clean and Rento-Secure.

My view on joining Rentokil was that the activities we were likely to develop in industrial and commercial services were relatively small niche markets – ones where major advertising appropriation would not be affordable.

Another issue we had to debate was whether we could take a brand which had an excellent reputation for pest control, and stretch it to areas where, at first sight, customers might not feel comfortable.

We chose to go with a single brand-name and banned any subdivision of the brand. We felt that although we would be selling all our activities through separate sales and service operations, we could get a spin-off from satisfied customers for other areas of the business. We also felt we could develop the brand internationally.

My view is that to some extent you can take almost any brand, almost any name and, if the commitment is deep enough and the application is over a sufficiently long period of time, you will get to where you want to be.

Origins of the brand

Rentokil has come a long way from its roots. Back in 1920, a Professor Lefroy developed a chemical called 'endocil' for use in killing deathwatch beetles in Westminster Hall. He wanted to create a name for the generic chemical which he could register, and played around with letters until he came up with 'Rentokil'.

At around the same time a company called British Ratin emerged, which produced a rat poison called 'Ratin'. Just after the Second World War it acquired Rentokil. I like to think of the board of the newly combined company sitting down and having deep discussions about which of these two fine names they would use for the company. I suspect they made the right decision by a short head.

By the early 1980s, Rentokil was a relatively low-profile pest control and wood preservative specialist. Over the last fifteen years, through a combination of organic growth and acquisition, Rentokil Initial (as it was renamed in 1996) has become a blue-chip multinational with 140,000 employees in forty countries, and sales of £3 billion. When it was floated on the London Stock Exchange in 1969 it was capitalized at £12.5 million. That figure today is approximately £6.5 billion.

We operate in a range of services under the brand headings of Hygiene and Cleaning Services; Distribution and Plant Services; Personnel Services; Pest Control; Property Services and Security. We see ourselves very much as an industrial and commercial service company, with our markets driven by outsourcing of blue-collar activities on the one hand, and on the other by the demand by employers for an improved and/or sustained environment for their employees.

A virtuous circle

Our objective has been to create a virtuous circle. We provide a quality of service in industrial and commercial activities under the same brand-name, so that a customer satisfied with one Rentokil Initial service is potentially a satisfied customer for another. We give one operation the customer list from another, so that a Rentokil Initial sales person for pest control, for example, has a list of Rentokil Initial customers for tropical plants.

Although it was considered somewhat odd at the time, one of the reasons we moved into tropical plants was in fact to help put the brand in front of decision-makers. Our service people maintaining the plants go in through the front door and are visible to the customer. This contrasts with pest control where no one really notices unless we fail.

Over time, we have carefully developed and extended the brand by focusing on our core competence. We see this as our ability to carry out high quality services on other people's premises through well-recruited, well-trained and motivated staff. We focus on industrial commercial services as distinct from domestic and residential services. However, and this might seem like a contradiction, having decided we want to enter an activity, we don't always consider as a prime requirement whether the brand-name is perfectly applicable. We would like it to be, and if we work hard, we can often persuade ourselves that it is.

Having said that, even we have to admit that there are some areas where the name 'Rentokil' clearly would not be applicable, such as funeral services or homes for the elderly. Still, that in itself would not have stopped us going into those areas had we chosen to. It would just have been more difficult. For example, we bid for several major catering businesses, Sutcliffe and Gardner Merchant specifically, a few years ago. Although our name would certainly not at first sight have been appropriate here, this consideration was secondary to it being the right activity in terms of our core competence.

I have often said that the name 'Rentokil' is not the most favourable – Initial has many advantages over it. The word 'Initial' is a positive one – an individual's signature of approval – and it means first. Rentokil conjures up immediate negatives, but we work to transcend that by emphasizing what the brand represents. The brand stands for honesty, reliability, consistency, integrity and technical leadership.

Brand expansion

One of the main reasons we acquired the much larger BET services group in April 1996, for £2.2 billion, was to incorporate the Initial brand within our activities. Initial was a strong textile services company acquired by BET in the early 1980s, and was allowed to develop as the subsidiary's management considered appropriate. The Initial brand offered strong prospects for international growth along the lines on which we developed Rentokil. Initial would stand alongside Rentokil as a brand, and ultimately as an international brand.

The company is called 'Rentokil Initial' to make it quite clear to the observer that these two great brands, Rentokil and Initial, come from the house of Rentokil Initial. The house of Rentokil

Initial will have the same personality but it will be slightly amended according to the service activity involved, because we have also split our activities between the two brands.

Ideally, we would like to have the one brand, but the spread of activities is so great now, that to try and extend a single brand over too many businesses does risk diluting the impact and weakening the power of the original brand. And as I said before, the name 'Rentokil' isn't one that lends itself well to some activities. For example, we have bought a number of security companies and in some of the American states we would have a problem registering the name 'Rentokil' for security services, for obvious reasons. In cases like these, we will be able to use 'Initial' instead.

Having acquired over 200 companies in the last ten years or so, many of which have had strong local, national or even regional brands, we have had extensive experience of changing brand-names to Rentokil. The arguments that are put forward by the employees of those companies usually concentrate on the problems they feel they will have in the marketplace if they eliminate the original brand-name. But, in practice, most of the problems are in the minds of the employees. It is more a concern about losing independence – a perception of being submerged beneath a larger company, of being a division of a company rather than a company in its own right.

We have had to face the same challenges in picking up the Initial brand, which is a relatively small part of B E T, and saying that certain companies will now be called Initial and others will be called Rentokil. In the case of Rentokil employees, their reaction was to wonder why they had to adopt the name 'Initial' when Rentokil had won the battle. So we put out the message that this was a new company that nobody had been part of for more than a few months. We were all equal and no one had an inside track. Rentokil employees might have thought this was unfair, but former B E T employees thought it entirely fair.

Central control, local implementation

Corporate strategy is set and controlled by the centre, although the head office is lean and has few of the usual staff functions like marketing and personnel. We decide which activities we wish to be involved in, where, and what are the development priorities. There is no doubt that the corporate, marketing and thereby brand strategy has to be one and the same, and be centred round a focus on customers.

We operate through an extensive network of about 1,200 branches. A typical branch consists of between forty and seventy people and is run as a profit centre. The fact that each branch might have only several hundred customers encourages attention to detail in terms of quality and customer relationships, but also of cost control.

Above branch level, area managers cover four to five branches, and they in turn report to the general managers of their divisions, such as healthcare or pest control. Those general managers are answerable to the national managing directors, who report to the regional managing directors, who answer to headquarters. We have the same structure and the same organization covering each activity, wherever we are in the world.

We have fairly tight central control over presentation. In terms of an individual activity like pest control, security, tropical plants or textile services, we have marketing people who are close to the general managers of each division in each country. So the tactical promotion or advertising support of any individual service activity is done within the country and within that division, although those tactics have to conform to the presentational demands and integrity of the brand. There is therefore central strategic control, but within this narrow framework there is room for broad tactical enterprise.

Because of the nature of our markets and because we have a sharp concentration on cost control, we tend to use promotional techniques such as direct marketing which are entirely appropriate and moreover can be justified financially in the short term. There is no central advertising budget because if headquarters was seen to be splashing money around, people elsewhere in the organization would ask why. Also, unlike consumer products companies, we are not working through a distributive channel where you are not directly in contact with the end consumer, and where it can be hard to correct misapprehensions of the brand. Most of our contact is through direct mail or face-to-face so we can talk to our customers direct.

In any industry there are two requirements to achieve action: a decision and its implementation. In the oil industry, for example, the quality of a decision, such as where you put a refinery or a judgement as to what the price of crude oil will be in five years' time, has an enormous impact on the organization. The quality of the implementation has only to be reasonable to be acceptable.

In a business like ours, on the other hand, decisions are relatively simple. If you get them wrong, the results are grey rather than black and white. Implementation, however, is crucial. It determines success. What is important in our business are the people, the speed and the determination with which you carry out that implementation. That is why Rentokil Initial is such a disciplined and systematic organization. One of our greatest strengths is the quality of our implementation.

We have to keep a careful eye on the many ideas suggested by our employees. If someone comes up with a bright idea – and it is the people at the customer interface who have bright ideas, not people like me sitting in ivory towers – we evaluate whether it is potentially applicable around the world. We won't go any further if it isn't. We prefer to be technical leaders, operate to 85 per cent of the market opportunity and manage it properly.

However, sometimes our very culture can make this hard to control. People who work for Rentokil Initial are straightforward and action-oriented and they like recognition. Also, because we move people around, we are a closely-linked international company. For example, someone in Australia has a great idea about tropical plant maintenance and is allowed to test it, then he tells others around the world about it, who pick up the idea before it has been centrally agreed that it should be implemented on a broader scale.

The problem is that you don't know how long it can take to establish if something is a good idea or not, and it varies for different activities and different countries.

Getting the brand to travel

As we developed the brand internationally through the 1980s, we did not impose brand regulations as thoroughly as we should have done. What began to happen was similar to what happens to many companies as they develop internationally. There was an interpretation of how the brand should be projected in the individual countries, and it was very much in terms of the fashion or culture or sheer belief of the individuals who were running the businesses at that time. So, by the mid-1980s, we had to decide which way to go. One way was to understand and adapt our services and branding to the local culture, fashions, creeds and so on. The other was to be quite dogmatic and agree on the benefits of international branding in terms of consistent presentation of the brand throughout the world, even though that might not be ideal in terms of the local market.

We chose the second route of international branding and we devised strict rules about how to present the brand. Before we acquired Initial our colours were red and white. So all our customers saw Rentokil people getting out of vans which looked the same everywhere in the world: white with the name 'Rentokil' in red, and the Royal Warrant, which is a strong part of our corporate identity. We decided that all our services would be presented both in terms of marketing and technical aspects in the same way, irrespective of the country in which we operated.

We do not allow any modifications. As a result, we accept that we may only appeal to 85 to 90 per cent of the market. But we see the benefits of consistency worldwide, including the ability to transfer people from country to country.

There are benefits also for a number of our customers, many of whom are international, such as general managers of hotels and hospitality outlets who, if they have used Rentokil in one country can expect Rentokil to operate in the same way in another country. Also, it means we know that if we have a problem in one country, we can probably resolve it quite swiftly because we have handled it elsewhere. We have found that these are great advantages, therefore we are not prepared to amend the presentation of the brand or the technical presentation of the product. We see ourselves very much as a McDonald's or Coca-Cola. We hope there will be a large proportion of the market which will welcome this approach.

Geographically we describe ourselves not as 'global' but as 'international'. Global to me means operating in every country in the world. We specifically set out to operate in the major developed economies of the world, which are represented by the three economic groupings of North America, Europe and Asia Pacific, because the demands for our services only really exist in developed or fast developing economies. Although many of our services are hygiene-related and standards of hygiene are often very poor in developing countries, they still come way down their list of priorities.

Cultural unity

There are two things which business schools usually associate with a company's success: strategy and culture. We believe that our culture is more mid-Atlantic than British, and certainly not American. It is somewhere in between. We applaud and recognize success and do not tolerate failure. We recognize and reward the individual. We have been able to superimpose our culture upon European, North American and South-East Asian countries, where local cultures can be very different.

We have of course faced certain challenges. Some of our major problems culturally have been in continental Europe, where there are probably more cultures than in any other part of the world and where, perhaps for historic reasons, people adhere strongly to their culture. In North America, on the other hand, there is an enormous need for success. Our experience is that North Americans are more than happy to accept the challenging targets and budgets we set but, if they fail to achieve them, they simply ignore the targets and declare to themselves, their friends and their colleagues that they are a success and that the targets were irrelevant. Whereas in Asia, the issue of pride is so important that people are very wary of accepting targets which are in any way challenging for fear of failure. For them, being seen to achieve success is very important and they are not prepared to change the rules.

To say we have handled all these issues without difficulty would be wrong. It varies according to the prevailing circumstances in a certain business at a certain time. But I think, by and large, we have been successful at bringing people together by transferring people from country to country, particularly at middle management levels. It would be surprising if you were able to tell the difference between Rentokil people from different countries, apart from the way they look physically. There is definitely a Rentokil, and now a Rentokil Initial, way.

Rentokil Initial is quite a military organization in many ways. In other companies, discussion of decisions can play a big role, and if people don't agree with something they often don't wholeheartedly buy into it. At Rentokil Initial, if the organization has decided to do something, people will do it to the best of their abilities. If they can't buy into that culture they don't stay, or simply don't join us in the first place.

We frequently say there are two ways of joining Rentokil Initial. One is to join as a graduate in your early twenties, and be trained around the world in different activities. The other is to be acquired. The latter brings cultural challenges, of course. But our success results from employees knowing the Rentokil Initial way.

A branded future

We will continue to think long and hard about what we are good at and concentrate on a relatively few number of activities. We don't in any way see ourselves as being a conglomerate, because we can transfer our know-how in terms of management and culture from activity to activity in the same way, with the only difference being technical aspects. The customer base is essentially the same, and the styles and management controls are the same, so we are a single company in practice, providing a variety of products or services.

We are probably unusual in that most service companies have not really concentrated on branding, or attempting to leverage more than one service under an umbrella brand. Similarly there are no companies comparable to Rentokil Initial: operating in a number of service markets and in many geographical areas. Comparison of performance is difficult. We therefore benchmark ourselves against ourselves, branch by branch, country by country, activity by activity. The competition varies enormously, from large companies in some activities, to very small ones in others. Pick up any Yellow Pages and you will see from ten to hundreds of competing companies in different areas. But the reason there are few credible competitors is probably because the industrial commercial service industry is relatively new.

That will change, however. I believe that the service industry will consolidate and grow, so there will be a number of major international players in the next fifteen to twenty years, very much in the way manufacturers of consumer products grew from the 1920s through to the 1950s.

Concentrating on branding has definitely been of major benefit to us for two reasons. First there is that virtuous circle of delivering high-quality service and then building a reputation, and using that reputation to move into other areas. Second, there is the leverage of the brand which acts as reassurance to customers that those other services will be delivered with the same quality as the original service they received.

We see our future as becoming progressively more international while concentrating on growth in the three key geographical regions we have identified. Our goal over the next few years is for the brand to have the same recognition, the same strength and the same image wherever we operate.

9 | Hewlett-Packard: Keeping the Brand Vision Alive

JOS BRENKEL, *director of Personal Systems Group,*
European Marketing Centre, Hewlett-Packard

In 1937 two twenty-six-year-old engineers called David Packard and William Hewlett started working together in a one-car garage in Palo Alto, California. At first they made just about any sort of electrical equipment to survive, producing products such as bowling alley sensors and a shock machine for weight reduction. Their first big sale was of eight audio oscillators, which were electronic test instruments, to Walt Disney Studios to use in developing the movie *Fantasia*. In 1939, the Hewlett-Packard company was born.

As the company grew, so did the views of the founders about what the company was for. It was not just about making money, although that was essential to survive and grow. What the company was in essence, they felt, was a group of people who were assembled to do something collectively which they could not do individually. In that way they could make a unique contribution to society. By 1957, they had formalized these ideas into a set of corporate objectives, organizational values and effective strategies and practices called the 'HP Way', which is about profit and growth, but equally about customers, employees, good management and citizenship.

Brand values

The 'HP Way' is still the cornerstone of the way we operate today, although we are now a $38.4 billion global company which designs, manufactures and services electronic products and systems for measurement, computing and communication. The corporate culture has been defined by the corporate objectives and values, and reflects the company's basic character and personality. That in turn has defined what the brand stands for: reliability and quality, being somewhat conservative, no matter where it is in the world or what business it is in. The values we have established are the bedrock of the organization, our bible if you like. They encompass trusting and respecting individuals; focusing on a high level of achievement and contribution; conducting business with uncompromising integrity; achieving common objectives through teamwork; encouraging flexibility and innovation.

That brand image is strong not because of rigid rules imposed from the top. It has more to do with the fact that the brand, with its roots in test and measurement, has always been associated with reliability and quality, whether from instrumentation, to the first hand-held calculator through to medical equipment, computers and printers. Unlike Sony, for example, as an organization we have not gone out of our way to create one brand, because we are a very decentralized company. But the perception of what we stand for, across what is a wide range of products, is very consistent and has arisen from both culture and behaviour. We have had over fifty years to build up values based on our people, customer support and service, the products, innovation and active citizenship.

If Hewlett-Packard were a person, our research shows that he or she, as in some of the categories like printers, would be a reliable friend, someone you know you can ask to do something, and it will be done really well. And if he makes a mistake, he will do everything he can to fix that. He is someone who will probably be quite conservative when it comes to dress, middle to upper class, neither very rich nor very poor; also, someone who is innovative in his or her thinking but not exceptionally creative. In contrast, our research has shown that an Apple person would wear very modern dress, be very creative, with lots of ideas, but would not necessarily bring all those ideas into being. An Apple person probably talks before he thinks.

Keeping the global/local balance

We are a global company that tries to maintain a good mix between what needs to be centralized and what needs to be localized. Centralization means cost saving. Localization means being closer to your customer. Our entrepreneurial flexibility is fostered by the decentralized business units which have a fair degree of autonomy. The marketing structure is relatively fluid, with marketing being done by product divisions, by marketing centres such as the European Marketing Centre in Grenoble, and by channel marketing people. However, because wholesalers often take more than one product, there is an increasing stress on taking an integrated approach that cuts across product lines. So the regional marketing centres act as a bridge between specific product markets and their resellers and the Hewlett-Packard product divisions, as well as devising pan-regional activities.

There is also a corporate marketing communications network at headquarters and in the regions, which puts together guidelines and training to make sure we have the same look and feel in marketing. However, added complexity comes from the fact that we work through so many distribution channels. For example, if a business unit does an advertisement for a product, and the channel partner does one for it as well, there can be a problem because the unit is advertising to create awareness and preference and build the brand, while the channel partner is aiming for traffic and sales. As a result, there is a danger that Hewlett-Packard will be perceived as two different companies. We have to make sure that the money invested in the campaign by both parties goes in the right direction, which means carrying the corporate guidelines into the channel. We have an advantage here in that we are used to working across divisions, so we need to treat the resellers like another division of the company.

Where we do have stringent rules is regarding the logo, which is made up of a lozenge with the letters 'hp' inside, and the words 'Hewlett-Packard' alongside the lozenge. This system has been in operation since 1989, when our then worldwide marketing director, Richard Alberding, decided that some fairly fundamental changes had to be made because of the inconsistencies around the world, with parts of the company using different colours and different typefaces. He hired a design agency which came up with a much more systematic approach to the logo, creating a grid-like model which could cover all situations where the logo might be used, from packaging and literature to business cards, as well as modifying the logo itself for only the eighth time in its history. The modular design means there is some flexibility on how to apply it.

These new mandatory rules admittedly came as a bit of a shock to what is such an entrepreneurial culture, but, with training, people began to see the advantages of a system with templates allowing speed and cost saving, and where there was still room for creativity. With hindsight, this can be seen as the start of our becoming more conscious of our trademark as a brand.

Where we have not been centrally driven is in terms of corporate branding. For instance, we have never done corporate advertising and probably never will. There are a number of reasons for that. The philosophy of our co-founder Dave Packard was 'just be'. In other words, don't advertise your values, just live them.

Also, we have the example of IBM, which told people year in and year out that it made big mainframe computers. But that set its feet in concrete and made it difficult for IBM to encompass new offerings, which is dangerous in such a fast-moving market like high technology.

What we have increasingly realized, however, is the crucial role that branding and brand management should play in an industry noted more for being technology- than marketing-driven. A few years ago, therefore, we set up a worldwide brand equity taskforce, made up of representatives from across the businesses, which has been investigating just what the brand stands for, and how far it can stretch. This has been spurred on by our move into developing products for the home, where, although we are well-established in printers, we have had to begin to understand how easily the perception of the brand can move to other products like home PCs or digital cameras, or whether it might need some adjustments.

Staying nimble

We feel that one of our greatest advantages over the past fifty years has been our ability to move into new areas. For example, we were first known for instrumentation. That was followed over the years by a range of new products, such as mini-computers, calculators and touch-screen personal computers. Then we developed our business in workstations, then printers. We have become one of the world's biggest medical equipment suppliers. We are now one of the leading brands in home PCs, and plan to extend the consumer side with a raft of new consumer devices such as those for digital imaging. Tomorrow it will be something else. So if we positioned ourselves strongly within an individual product category, it could hinder us when we want to move into some of the new product areas that technology will create in the future. And we will be going into all sorts of new places. Innovation is crucial: each year we spend about 7 per cent of our net revenue on R & D, and more than half the company's audit in 1996 was for products introduced during the previous two years.

We like to stay flexible. We were considered late in entering the PC market, both for professional and personal users. In fact, we entered the market for consumer PCs in only 1995 with a multimedia range called Pavilion. We are now in the top five personal PC companies, while we are in the top three in terms of the large corporate PC arena. We feel we have the resources and patience to get things right even if we enter a market like PCs later than the competition.

We decided to enter the home PC market for a number of reasons. Home PCs are one of the fastest-growing segments, and one where we felt we could exploit our reputation for reliability and quality and the good-will people feel towards the brand because of their experience with our printers. Also, because the home is where new technologies like multi-media go first these days, we realized we needed to be active in domestic technologies so we can be ready to feed those technologies into the business sector. In addition, it would give us economies of scale across all our activities.

Redefining the brand

There are big challenges to face in the home PC market. First, you have to create a brand personality that consumers can associate with. The Hewlett-Packard brand-name is strong in professional and business markets, where the emphasis is on product features and technology. When you move into the home, however, you have to begin to build up brand awareness in the consumer's mind. The big problem is that in terms of branding, the home PC market overall is still relatively immature. What image do people have of Compaq or Packard-Bell, for example? There have been exceptions: Apple was good at exploiting its image of youth and creativity. And Intel has been very successful at branding itself in the consumer's mind with its 'Intel inside' campaign. But most high-technology companies are not that good at branding. Many people still view PCs the way they think about their refrigerators – as relatively undifferentiated appliances.

However, as the market moves more to sophisticated multi-media PCs, and then to communication-oriented PCs, the scene will be more and more controlled by large retailers carrying, at the most, four or five brands from highly competent suppliers, with strong brand images and close relationships with Intel and Microsoft, and who are able to manufacture and support 'mass customized' products on a global basis.

So the brand equity taskforce has had to examine all the issues surrounding our brand and where it needs to go. One of its first steps was to document the core values that make up our brand equity. A branding consultancy was hired a year or so back to look at all the volumes of research that had been carried out by our marketing people. That meant trawling through over ninety different research projects to see what was consistent in terms of the brand values that went with the Hewlett-Packard logo and whether, if you were starting afresh, you would choose those brand values for positioning the brand in the home.

Hewlett-Packard as mentor

It was found that the core values were basically good ones. People said to leave the logo alone, that its assurance of trust, quality and reliability should be constant, no matter how flashy we might make the product design or packaging. So we have decided that we should build on the positioning of being seen as people who can sort you out better than anyone else – as a mentor.

Of course, you have to be careful that you don't move a whole corporation based on a few focus groups. But the findings help to show us that as we move more into the home, if we want to crack new markets we have to adapt without moving 180 degrees away from what we do now. We want to build on that aura of professional expertise in a more positive sense, and one that stays perfectly in tune with our business-to-business stance. So it is more tweaking than outright changing, shifting from the perception that we are an understated leader to one of being a more pro-active leader.

Adding sparkle to the brand image

We do need to give the brand image a lift for domestic markets. Brand mapping has shown us that we need to consider adding some new values that will allow us to become more established with consumers. So we have been considering what sort of adaptations we have to make to Hewlett-Packard's core values.

One approach is to adapt our marketing techniques and learn from consumer goods companies, including hiring people with consumer marketing experience.

Partnering is another route: the printer business has entered into a number of joint promotions with companies such as Disney to run their interactive software on a new home colour printer. That creates a powerful combination of brand values, since such partnerships bring a sense of adventure, of liveliness and fun in terms of good, clean, family fun. In time, as we build up volumes for the

PCs, partnerships with consumer goods companies could be the way to strengthen brand awareness and enable Hewlett-Packard to become more established in the home. We have to change our way of thinking and learn to associate our brand with children and families, and not with business customers. Design is also important. We probably need to move from being seen as functional and practical to being seen as appealing and practical.

Advertising is another way to add a sense of colour to our positioning. We have run two executions for the Pavilion in the United States which have also travelled to the UK, and which illustrate what we are trying to do. One centres on sibling rivalry. A teenage boy steals his sister's diary, and then she catches him playing shadow guitar in his bedroom, wearing some very strange boxer shorts. She takes a Polaroid picture of him, runs downstairs, and enters it into the Pavilion through the photo scanner. When she demands her diary back, and he refuses to give it, she sends the photo to a girl he likes. Then his father comes in and sees the photo on the screen and wonders what is going on. The advertising is about humour and family, but it also shows the product features.

In another execution, an unfit, overweight man is running a marathon and is last in at nine hours, twenty-three minutes and fifty-six seconds. Someone takes a picture of him, which he takes home, scans into the Pavilion, and changes the nine hours to two hours. This is also about humour, showing that the HP Pavilion allows you to be creative and do what you want to do.

Sponsorship will help broaden awareness among a much bigger mass audience. In the UK, for example, we sponsor Tottenham Hotspur football club. We are also involved in Formula One motor racing. In one of the largest sponsorship deals we have ever done, we have become the official IT hardware and maintenance supplier to the organizing committee of the 1998 World Cup in France. We will be providing more than seventy-five products lines, including PCs and servers, storage devices, notebook and palmtop computers, laser and inkjet printers, scanners and some medical and chemical-measurement equipment. Virtually every piece of computer hardware will have the Hewlett-Packard brand on it. It is estimated that up to 37 billion viewers around the world will watch the tournament.

Creating power brands

A brand is something that has values beyond what the product does and it is customers who bestow the brand attributes, who buy it and recommend it. It takes time to create real brands. What we have in Hewlett-Packard are probably only two power or sub-brands, the LaserJet and DeskJet range of printers. But even here the Hewlett-Packard name adds value: store testing has shown that if the mother brand-name were removed from the range, we could lose up to half our sales.

What we do have are strong product names, like Vectra in professional PCs and the 'Jets'. As well as DeskJet and LaserJet, there are DesignJet large-format plotters and printers, ScanJet scanners, OfficeJet printer–fax–copiers, and CopyJet colour printer–copiers. These are not yet brands, although their ranges have a family name and feel. There are some inconsistencies, which is not surprising given our history of decentralized organization. The scale is huge: in fact we have 24,000 product names and numbers!

We have examined whether there are any issues arising from being seen either as HP or Hewlett-Packard. We found that half of the respondents in a survey know us as HP and half as Hewlett-Packard, but, surprisingly, there is no conflict. People seem to feel comfortable with either. So we currently have no intention of settling on just HP or Hewlett-Packard.

The HP Way

The pace of change in this industry means that we have to restructure constantly to deal with market challenges. We are always looking at our customer base, our channels, at products coming through and asking ourselves how can we get closer to our customers. We always have to be on our toes so that when we decide to move, we move quickly. That is the personality of the company. We constantly challenge ourselves to see if we can do something better even if there is nothing wrong. And that means we have to hire people who like change, but who understand that change must never affect product quality, or compromise our core values. So Hewlett-Packard hires a certain sort of person, one who can fit in with our culture. There is definitely a recognizable HP person. No matter where you go, in whichever country, HP people are the same both in appearances and in the way they react. Even the offices look the same, both inside and out. We once hired a manager for Italy who could not speak Italian because he did not need to. What could almost be called an ideology creates a corporate glue, because to succeed in Hewlett-Packard you have to buy into the values set out in the HP Way. Our co-founder Bill Hewlett defined that as 'the policies and actions that flow from the belief that men and women want to do a good job, a creative job, and that if they are provided the proper environment they will do so'.

Nevertheless, trying to cement together this very diverse company, with its 112,000 employees, can still be a challenge. One way is through our extensive Intranet system, which is beginning to act as a central nervous system. We also promote a consistent look to our Website, which has over 40,000 pages. However, the process of achieving consistency is not always straightforward. Before we could get the Website design rules finalized, Germany had to get its site up and running in time for an important fair. We let them create their site with the promise that they would conform to the guidelines as soon as they were out. But in the meantime, Taiwan and Australia had copied Germany's approach. So we have to stay on our corporate toes, although there is a lot of self-policing too. This is important as it is very easy to dilute the brand identity if it becomes fragmented.

Each individual business unit benchmarks itself against others in its field. In the personal products group we frequently benchmark ourselves against Compaq, whereas the printer division will benchmark itself against companies like Canon. It is interesting that there is no one company to benchmark ourselves against as a whole. If we did have a common competitor, that would be one of the biggest risks we could face. But we do not.

The impact of the Internet

The information explosion is going to change the way every person lives and works. Consider how quickly the Internet has made an impact. Companies now put their Website address on their ads, whether they are for washing powder or cars, so how you brand yourself through the Net will become critically important.

Our goal is to be at the forefront of this by becoming known as the leading systems integrator. Lewis Platt, the chairman of Hewlett-Packard, has said that increasingly customers are saying to him that they need help managing the chaos of so many diverse products and systems. This has resulted from the fragmentation of the high-technology industry over the years into horizontal layer of specialist companies, compared to previous times which were characterized by big, vertically-integrated giants like IBM. This proliferation of products and systems can make gluing IT systems together a corporate nightmare.

Hewlett-Packard is one of the few companies with a rich enough ecology of technologies and products to be able to help companies tie it all together. But gaining recognition means we have to work on our image as a highly branded integrator, the prime contractor who can tie the systems together, whether it is systems in large corporations or providing a small business with an instant office. The core computing strategy will be a practical approach in helping companies reach beyond their corporate environments, to create IT solutions that encompass business partners, suppliers, remote workers and customers. This will also serve as an internal unifying force, since all divisions will be looking in the same direction. So even if we do not do corporate advertising, because the different parts of the company will be focusing on this 'bundling' objective, we will be speaking with one voice.

Hewlett-Packard wants to be a brand that is going to be very well known in every sense. Currently, if you asked a child what Sony means to them, you would probably be given some sort of image. That is not the case yet with Hewlett-Packard. Over time we want that to change. But that does not mean radically changing the personality. What we want is for that personality to be known by more people in more environments.

10 | Cadbury Ltd: Harnessing the Strengths of the Corporate Brand

ALAN PALMER, *marketing director*

In the UK, Cadbury enjoys a 30 per cent share of all chocolate sales and a 50 per cent share of moulded chocolate bars, and the Cadbury brand is believed to be worth an estimated £1.3 billion in the UK, compared with Coca-Cola (UK only) at £1.2 billion and Walkers at £500 million. The company's chocolate products span a range of sub-categories headed by its so-called 'CDM Mega Brand' moulded chocolate bars: Cadbury Dairy Milk, Fruit & Nut and Whole Nut. Other categories include chocolate assortments, such as Milk Tray; 'countlines', such as Wispa, Time Out and Crunchie; and bagged chocolates, such as Buttons. Cadbury has also developed sub-brands for particular occasions, such as Cadbury Creme Egg – a product available only between New Year and Easter each year.

Cadbury has become the largest single product brand in Britain. However, its horizons have broadened in recent years. Although it is determined to retain its UK market dominance and continue to develop the market through product innovation, it also aims to develop its international business significantly. Cadbury is already one of the top world chocolate businesses, alongside Ferrero, Hershey, Mars, Nestlé and Philip Morris.

A flair for indulgence born from a Quaker heritage

Cadbury is a consumer brand which is directly shaped and coloured by the history of its parent company. The essence of the brand can be defined as 'Cadbury-ness', and it has been built over more than a hundred years. Father John Cadbury and, later, the brothers George and Richard, set up business in Birmingham in 1824, originally dealing in tea and coffee. The family were Quakers who, like many of their contemporaries, established their own commercial enterprises because of restrictions they faced in terms of education, and career. The brothers developed an interest in cocoa, initially as a beverage although they subsequently developed the manufacturing of chocolate confectionery in 1847. The social ideals of the Cadbury family created an environment and a corporate integrity that has provided the platform for a highly successful business and consumer brand. These values are difficult to distil individually, but collectively they represent care for employees, consumers and the family. Such social concerns have consistently shaped how our staff, our business partners and our consumers view us.

Cadbury had to compete in the nineteenth century with several hundred other confectionery companies – including Rowntree and Fry – and its early success was attributable to many management qualities and insights more familiar to today's business environment. Sales and marketing (although not described as such then) were in place at an early stage, as ledgers illustrate. In 1905, for example, the 'Introducers Department' spent £41,694 and 10 shillings, of which £20,000 went on advertising and signwriting; and, from the remainder, £15 and 4 shillings on customer urns! Many of today's Cadbury brands can trace their history back to 1905 when Cadbury Dairy Milk was first launched.

It is worth noting that much of the early development of the business and its product range was done under the umbrella of the Cadbury brand, with products identified by descriptive names such as Dairy Milk chocolate, Milk Tray assorted, Drinking Chocolate prefaced by the Cadbury logo, which first appeared in block letter form, and subsequently the Cadbury script, from 1928. Other Cadbury brand icons, such as the colour purple and the glass and a half of milk device date from a similar era. The combination of these icons evokes a very powerful consumer association with Cadbury's chocolate.

Over subsequent years, a focus on building strong, consumer-relevant values evolved. Coupons were introduced in 1906, gifts in the 1930s, even a Children's Club which was specifically designed to restore customer loyalty after the end of the Second World War. Once rationing ended, the chocolate market grew rapidly and sales of Cadbury, the market leader, exploded.

There can be no question that the arrival of commercial television, and its ability to capture the attention of a mass audience, became an important milestone in the development of the confectionery market, and more specifically the chocolate brands. With a history of brand communication from posters, the colour and black-and-white press, and the cinema, suddenly it became possible to add new dimensions to the sub-brands, to the extent that they developed even stronger identities than that of the Cadbury brand. Famous advertising campaigns for Dairy Milk ('award yourself a CDM'), Fruit & Nut (Fruit & Nutcase), Flake ('Only the crumbliest . . .') and Milk Tray (Man in Black) started to define how people viewed the brands from both an emotional and a rational perspective.

The medium defined the message. However, it also offered opportunities to any of the bigger brands in the market to break through and create a strong identity. Cadbury, which enjoyed a clear market leadership in the 1960s and early 1970s, found its position increasingly threatened as some new entrants, such as Rowntree's Yorkie, achieved spectacular success through the strength of their powerful advertising and product positioning. The nuclear family, in the 1960s and 1970s, sat in front of the television revelling in its novelty, and absorbing the information that was beamed at them. How much things change!

Commercial TV also enabled the company to segment its market, leading to the development of a larger number of new products which established brand ubiquity in the minds of consumers. The company's reputation for the quality of its products, and the product benefits communicated within its advertising and related marketing activities, have made a significant contribution to the Cadbury brand. Today, as the only surviving company to put its name as an umbrella across its entire portfolio, Cadbury has a unique competitive and discriminating advantage. From the consumer's perspective, Cadbury = chocolate = Cadbury, is a truism which we sought to strengthen by creating a feeling of 'Cadburyness' in much of the imagery and activity built into the brand programmes.

The 'master brand' approach

Our clear market positioning has come about through a combined process of evolution and managed change. Two factors in particular have shaped our thinking in recent years. One has been the issue of corporate versus consumer branding; the other has been diversification. Throughout the 1960s, Cadbury diversified into a number of food sectors – cocoa beverages, chocolate biscuits and others – all marketed by Cadbury Foods.

The merger of Cadbury Brothers with Schweppes in 1969 to create Cadbury Schweppes Plc brought a significant increase in the food brand range; to accommodate them a stand-alone division, Cadbury Typhoo, was created. Inevitably, the development of that business generated new brands, such as Marvel, Smash, Soya Choice and others, that were marketed under the house brand of Cadbury. Research at the time endorsed this strategy, as consumers fed back the view that Cadbury provided quality reassurance. At that time it appeared to give the business the appropriate critical mass necessary to deal with the fast consolidating retail grocery market.

During the 1980s, particularly the early to mid-'80s, the development of corporate brands became a particularly fashionable theme for a variety of reasons. Among food companies particularly, a series of contested takeovers, and the emerging trend of seeking to capture some of the value of the brand equity on the balance sheet, were sufficient justification. For others, media inflation was beginning to undermine the traditional support that had sustained brand portfolios, and thus it had appeared to be a legitimate economy of scale to try to motivate the consumer at the umbrella brand level. But for many it proved to be a leap too far. The logic of binding a corporate message on to consumer brand communication – often seeking to contemporize the corporate brand more than the individual portfolio brands – does seem, with the benefit of hindsight, to be a little thin.

By the start of the 1980s, there were growing concerns that the dilution of investment in the Cadbury brand, and the growth of some competitor chocolate franchises, needed to be addressed. A detailed overhaul was undertaken of all the aspects of the brand portfolio, the quality of the product range and, of course, the communication strategy. It was clear that the gold standards for the company's leading brand Dairy Milk needed to be re-established, and all the elements of packaging, pricing and product quality were interrogated. The advertising agency Foote Cone and Belding (FCB) developed a television campaign that ran from 1980 to 1982 called 'This is Cadbury', which set out to reinforce many of the core chocolate values embodied in the brand. The agency used techniques developed by Oxford Scientific Films to create stunning close-up imagery of 'chunks' and 'pouring milk'. It provided a new platform for the business, enabling the challenges – particularly from Rowntree's Yorkie – to be sloughed off. It gave a renewed sense of direction.

In 1986, the foods business Cadbury Typhoo Ltd was sold off to its management team and relaunched as Premier Brands. It is now part of Hillsdown Holdings. This proved to be the critical opportunity to remove the Cadbury name from a variety of previously Cadbury branded products that were not chocolate (such as Smash and Marvel). At a stroke the business refocused the Cadbury name back behind its core: chocolate confectionery, cocoa-based beverages and chocolate biscuits. Since that time, an active programme of franchising the Cadbury brand rather than organic development has taken the brand across a unique range of chocolate-based products in diverse categories from chilled desserts, through to frozen cakes and ice creams, instant beverages and even a liqueur.

The Cadbury brand is both the product brand and the corporate brand. At issue was to what extent we should communicate it as one or the other. Like any organization, we identified both corporate and consumer values. Corporate values were rational: quality and reputation. By the mid-1980s, we were running communications activities about the success of Cadbury Schweppes as an organization in addition to the brands themselves. In a fiercely competitive marketplace, you cannot afford to be complacent. We realized we had to refocus all our activities to ensure that we communicated in a consumer-relevant way. We refocused on the emotional values associated with the Cadbury name – associations with the family, children, fun and warmth. We evolved the 'working concept' of 'Cadburyness' and sought to increase the prominence of the Cadbury name, and its umbrella role for a diverse confectionery portfolio. The challenge was how to maintain a bridge between the desired corporate brand values and the essential warmth and vitality that is fundamental to successful growth.

It is interesting to contrast some of the successes and shortcomings of the initiatives in support of 'Cadburyness'. The biggest single frustration in the whole matter was the seeming inability to generate advertising of stature and effectiveness for the Cadbury Dairy Milk brand at the heart of this whole business. It had long been felt that the relationship between the brand 'Cadbury' and the brand 'Dairy Milk' was that they were one and the same. As a consequence, copy strategy and development always fell over the burden of trying to carry the aspirations and values of the broad-scale consumer brand Cadbury, at the same time as giving the diverse pack options with the Dairy Milk brand a sense of identity and role. Almost two decades of effort, with a number of agencies, and the brains and motivation of the business had generated advertising campaigns that registered only as acceptable on the advertising record.

A new model for the Cadbury brand and its relationship with the component brands in the portfolio was assembled, and it set out to establish a clear distinction between the Cadbury master brand, and the sub-brands that made up the portfolio.

The relationship between Cadbury, the master brand, and the Dairy Milk brand is clearly a dynamic one, where the values pass back and forth as if they were the blood supply between the heart and brain of a body. However, the relationship between Dairy Milk and the other sub-brands is more delicate. Hitherto it is a matter of record that the 'brands' alongside Dairy Milk, such as Fruit & Nut and Wholenut, were distinctive brands, but inspection today suggests that they are products of commercial television advertising, and are thus beneficiaries of strong advertising properties, as their buyer/consumer base overlaps heavily with Dairy Milk. It was therefore legitimate to create a Cadbury's Dairy Milk (CDM) megabrand, comprising the core Dairy Milk brand with its pure milk chocolate delivery, and added to that, Fruit & Nut and Wholenut (offering the taste and eating enjoyment of Dairy Milk but with added ingredients). It was a statement of the obvious maybe, but it explained many of the other dynamics of these sub-brands in very logical terms. The critical mass of the CDM megabrand placed it firmly at the front of the triumvirate of brands that define the chocolate confectionery market. These are CDM megabrand, Kit-Kat, and Mars Bar.

Today, Cadbury is the largest food brand in the British Isles linked by a single product, in this case chocolate. Consumers spend over £1.3 billion a year on brands bearing the Cadbury name. Cadbury Dairy Milk is the biggest brand in the chocolate market, both by volume and value; UK sales alone now exceed £230 million a year. The 'master brand' strategy has played a crucial role in achieving all of this, by re-establishing the Cadbury name centre-stage. This has not just been a cosmetic application of the Cadbury trademark on to any product containing chocolate. All recipes, including those for franchised products, are developed under the direction of Cadbury technical managers and seek to retain the essential (and unique) taste characteristics of Cadbury's Chocolate. This entire exercise is an example of how important it is for a business periodically to go back to its roots and to make sure the core elements responsible for its success are not being frittered away. Today, our sector leadership is the largest it has been in twenty years.

Fine-targeting a mass market

Confectionery enjoys between 98 and 99 per cent market penetration in the UK today. Total UK confectionery sales total
around £4.9 billion. Chocolate accounts for around 70 per cent of
this. Our audience is clearly mass market, but it is not a static one.
Both chocolate and sugar sweets sales are steadily increasing by
around 5 and 4 per cent a year. And the dynamics of the market
are continually changing and evolving over time. One trend evident
over the past decade, for example, has been that more confectionery
is being bought by housewives as a larder item. Today, impulse
purchases account for between 50 and 60 per cent of all confectionery sales. Another development has been the growth in purchases
made for a particular occasion – Christmas and Easter, for example.
We now have quite a specific map of the consumer market which
sets out clusters of purchasing decisions. This ranges from snacking
to hunger satisfaction, 'gifting' – be it a formal gift or an informal,
small 'thank you' – to personal indulgence. Inevitably, some of
these compete with other product sectors. In 'gifting', we compete
with records, wine and flowers; in snacking we compete with soft
drinks and crisps.

Today's chocolate market is therefore both sophisticated in
brand make-up and complex in terms of consumer motivation.
Purchase and consumption of chocolate is a balance of rational and
emotional responses to the product. All confectionery brands carry
an enormous mantle of emotional values. There are no models, but
universal truths: such as the fact that people love chocolate and can
anticipate the gratification they'll experience eating it. To a degree,
science has tried to analyse the reasons for this and a number of
theories have been put forward. But at the end of the day, it's about
liking the taste and ease of access to the product.

The pattern of consumption is similar between boys and girls, but
women have an exceptionally strong influence, purchasing nearly
two-thirds of all confectionery, both for their own consumption
and on behalf of the family. There is, however, a degree of life-stage
influence on consumption in developed markets. The over-forties,

for example, are influenced by different motivators than sixteen-to twenty-four-year-olds. Older consumers relate more to the traditions and the heritage of the brand and adopt a more thoughtful, planned approach to purchase. Younger consumers are more likely to impulse buy and purchase a broader repertoire of products.

Our marketing activities focus heavily on this latter age group. Our major challenge is to ensure that today's teens remain loyal to Cadbury into their forties, and beyond. That's why we have to support the Cadbury brand. It is easy to be seduced into the notion that commitment to a single product, like Fuse, carries equal weight to Cadbury. It does not.

Manufacturing marketing solutions

Strategically, our business has faced a number of important challenges and opportunities. First, the icons that Cadbury has established – chocolate and purple, the Cadbury logo and the glass and a half – were potent motivators but only if their individual strengths could be harnessed together. Second, functionally and psychologically, the role that chocolate plays for consumers is incredibly complex. Liberating these desires through advertising and brand development is difficult.

These challenges are set against a complex media environment with ever-increasing clutter – as more and more messages compete for consumers' attention – and media inflation. Once centre-stage in the early days of TV advertising, food and confectionery brands now find themselves overwhelmed with an increasing volume of marketing spend from financial services, retail and utilities. The differential between the UK's biggest TV spending brand, British Telecom which spends more than £90 million a year on TV advertising, and the biggest spending single confectionery brand, whose annual TV budget is a mere £4.5 million, says it all.

Cadbury took the view that there had to be a new approach. To increase the prominence of the Cadbury name, and its umbrella role for the diverse confectionery portfolio, the Cadbury endorsement was strengthened within the portfolio, using 'presence marketing' and sponsorship along with a unified endorsement strategy on packaging to provide visibility and saliency for the Cadbury trademark to complement the more targeted and specific communication that paid-for advertising could provide.

In the packaging arena, the Cadbury swatch was developed to bond the range of Countline brands more closely to the core moulded block range with a purple swatch and the Cadbury script. All the brand advertising was adapted to carry a 'tear strip' in purple, with the Cadbury logo in the end-frame corner.

A 'presence marketing' programme was devised to establish the Cadbury brand in a range of high-profile locations: volume leisure sites such as Alton Towers and the Natural History Museum, travel terminals such as airports and the Channel Tunnel, and shopping malls. The combination of an attractive location and a retailing unit provided a self-financing vehicle to draw consumers closer to the Cadbury brand. A charitable/cause-related association with Save the Children Fund set out to underpin some of the core values of social concern. When linked to sponsorship of the Cadbury Pantomime Season, which reached over 2.5 million people each year, and the Cadbury Strollerthon, involving over 20,000 charity walkers every year, this package of activities started to add texture and a more tangible bond to the brand. Meanwhile, the development of Cadbury World, the visitor attraction on the Bournville factory site, represented a hugely important piece to the jigsaw. With over half a million visitors each year, it provides an enduring bond between the visitor and Cadbury that is fundamentally stronger and more enduring than any advertising or promotional impact could be.

We also developed a more creative approach to using traditional UK media. An ideal opportunity arose with the chance to sponsor Britain's most popular soap opera, *Coronation Street* on ITV. The series celebrated its thirty-five years at the top of the British TV ratings. The association seemed logical – the coming together of two of the nation's favourites. With our £10 million sponsorship of *Coronation Street* – British TV's largest broadcast sponsorship to date – we have developed a range of marketing and promotional activities to support our association with the nation's best-loved soap.

Research confirms the effectiveness of this strategy. Seventy-one per cent of the population are aware of the association; viewers perceive it to be 'enjoyable' and 'appropriate' for Cadbury, and image enhancements for our brand have included improved perceptions of 'quality' and 'better taste' (source: Millward Brown/RSGB/Laser 1996). It has never been more important for food brands to cultivate a position of saliency, trust and relevance to their consumers.

Brand extensions

Ten years ago, I would have said the UK confectionery market was showing signs of saturation, and that the full portfolio was established. Yet, in the last decade we've seen the launch of many new brands. The market is unique in that it is still dominated by a very large number of brands that have been around for more than sixty years. The reason for this is the confectionery industry's skill in making their brands appear consistently relevant to today. Since the 1970s, one or two manufacturers have been able to develop new brands so effectively that today they are among the top twenty or thirty of all brands. As our understanding of the consumer map has expanded, we have filled in the gaps identified with new products which complement the existing portfolio. We have catered for snacking, for example, with the decline of formal meals. New product development is not only an engine for our own growth, it is an engine for industry growth.

Cadbury has launched many new brands over the past decade, driven by both technology and the developed understanding of consumer needs. Time Out was the result of unique technology which enabled flake to be put on to wafer. Whispa Gold was the result of a development which allowed aerated chocolate and caramel. Fuse, although not produced by a unique process, was a brand-new combination of ingredients. This resulted in Cadbury achieving a programme of NPD that was materially more successful than any of its competitors.

The road to new product development is littered, however, with projects that have failed. Few can remember such Cadbury brands from the 1970s: Aztec, Welcome, Rumba, Amazing Raisin. They failed not because they didn't taste nice, but because they weren't distinctive enough. It was, perhaps, a reflection that our understanding of the sector was limited. People like confectionery and are prepared to try new products. The issue is whether the new product is sufficiently distinctive to be quickly taken into a consumer's regular eating repertoire.

Typically, we have a major new product launch every two years, with a number of smaller limited edition lines rolled out annually. Also, we reintroduce old favourites periodically – for example, Freddo the Chocolate Frog. It usually takes between two and five years of a product being on the market for us to make a decision about whether or not it has worked. We are in this for the long term, and make our decisions accordingly. It would be wrong to assume that the detail of such a programme or a 'grand scheme' was all pre-planned from the outset. It was only once a pattern had been established that the business was able quickly to adopt mechanisms to fast-track success, aided by a growing level of credibility among customers. To a degree, successful new products force the launch of their own successors, as the annual sales peaks are lapped in the next year.

Around the world

Perhaps not surprisingly, the major markets that Cadbury first developed were related to British colonial influence in the 1920s and 1930s, and to patterns not far removed from the UK position. Only since the 1980s have the leading British confectionery companies really moved towards having international status. One turning point was when Nestlé bought Rowntree. Cadbury also undertook a programme of acquisition and green-field development. Today, Cadbury is an international business with managed operations in twenty-four countries and products distributed in more than 160. Our largest market is the UK. As a world player we are one of the top confectionery companies. Our aim is to ensure we remain in and move up the premier league in this fast-moving world business.

Developing markets are a significant growth area. Local manufacturing recently began in Russia, China and Poland; we continue to invest in new factories in other countries, including India and Argentina. We have a series of power-bases for our chocolate business around the world, but the UK remains our most important market with Ireland, Canada and Australia also strong. In Britain, average consumption of chocolate per head of the population is 8kg a year, not as much as Switzerland (10kg), but still high. Other developed markets range from Ireland, Austria and Benelux (8kg) to Australia (6kg), USA (5kg) and Japan (2kg). Clearly, there is a challenge, introducing a new confectionery brand to a developing market. For a start, consumer motivation can vary markedly. A typical pattern in developed countries, for example, is the growing emphasis on 'gifting' and indulging. In developing markets, the role of confectionery is different. In India, for example, there is no gift sector as such. For economic and climactic reasons the brands of confectionery sold tend to be more biscuit-based or sugar sweets.

We still believe it is possible for consumers in these developing markets to buy into the values of 'Cadburyness'. It is our intention that they bond closely with the Cadbury brand and what it stands for, so we are now converging the style and tone of our advertising and marketing communications, worldwide.

The 'Cadbury Master Brand' positioning was developed with a group of senior marketing directors representing our major companies around the world in the spring of 1995 and the 'master brand' commercial will now be adapted for other established and newer developing markets.

Inspiring indulgence

Much has been written about the declining influence of food, beverage and household brands in a more value-conscious, consumer-educated environment. Almost in the same breath, you hear talk of an emerging 'new order' of retailers, goods and services that supply food and drink packaged for the needs of today's society. These new trade-marked entities have, in many cases, yet to build the more permanent superstructures that we associate with established brands, differentiation, consumer loyalty, and imagery. They change hands with remarkable frequency, and are often submerged into the corporate hierarchy or identity of their new owners. Meanwhile, own label is a growing challenge in many sectors – although less so in confectionery where own label sales are only 6 per cent. While own label's strongest categories are in block chocolate and seasonal offerings from the grocery multiples, this is unlikely to undermine our market.

Corporate surveys undertaken by Taylor Nelson on our behalf in 1990 and 1995, have proved insightful. When consumers were asked to name spontaneously the most favoured food and drink manufacturers and retailers in the country, the number one and two positions were occupied by Heinz and Cadbury. Perhaps more surprisingly, the demographic group of fourteen- to seventeen-year-olds also endorsed the same two organizations at the top of their list, although the positions were reversed, with Cadbury at number one.

It is probably no accident that those branded entities that have survived and prospered under a single company's ownership owe their success to deep-rooted management competencies and considered investment over time in the core values of their products. We believe Cadbury is a classic example of this: its identity and pre-eminent position in the UK chocolate market have become a springboard for the development of a worldwide brand.

It has never been more important for food brand manufacturers to enjoy a position of saliency, trust and relevance to today's consumers. More parochial and within each competitive set, the tasks of sustaining category leadership and clear water ahead of our competitors require both strategic clarity and executional excellence.

11 | VTech: From Vision to Culture

ALLAN WONG, *chairman and CEO*

VTech was created with the idea of using the latest technology available to produce high-quality, innovative brand-name products that were better than anything else on the market. It would be accurate to say that everything we have done and continue to do to the present day serves this philosophy. This vision is the creative and driving force behind the company. Even when we were a modestly successful but still small manufacturer of single-chip microprocessor video games, we were driven to offer something better with every successive generation of products. The impetus is partly due to the nature of our business. Ideas and technology do not remain uncopied for long, so you must continue to produce innovative products to stay in the market and be competitive. The other force behind the company's drive is less concrete but perhaps more important, because it deals with spirit, motivation and aspiration. My colleague and I founded VTech with a passion for electronics and the determination to excel. The VTech's company personality was therefore forged in an entrepreneurial spirit and with a belief in technology. Through the years, the products have changed a lot, but the underlying vision has not.

When the company was established in 1976, the name VTech was shorthand for 'video technology'. Looking back, however, the name VTech was prescient, for it can also stand for 'vision and technology'. We make an effort to give consumers products no one else has, or which they are unable to make as well as we can. This is the reason why we have kept ourselves at the leading edge of technological advances for our core businesses. VTech is really about 'vision and technology'.

Innovation and creativity mean we place a lot of emphasis on R & D, generating an average of sixty new products a year using proprietary technology. VTech invests an average of 4 per cent of the group's annual turnover in research and development facilities. Our innovation extends not only to technology and new product ideas and features, but also to how a product can be manufactured at a lower cost and with higher reliability. All this combined has contributed to our progress and allowed us to stay one step ahead of our competition.

Borrowing the best across core businesses

One component of VTech's rapid growth has been the considerable cross-fertilization across our core businesses: electronic learning games, telecommunications and computer systems. Some companies may have expertise in one technology or maybe two, but few possess all three of the technologies for these sectors. This gives us a real advantage.

For instance, numerous VTech electronic learning toys incorporate technology that has arisen from our computer division, thus making them very sophisticated. Typically, toy companies do not have such unhampered and immediate direct access to computer technology, so they employ outside consultants or form joint ventures with computer manufacturers. The problem with this arrangement is that it cannot guarantee good results. VTech is able to draw on technological advances and expertise very easily without going outside.

The same application of cross-fertilization exists between the telecommunications division and our other divisions. A very successful product of this process is the VTech Tropez 900DX cordless phone. Integration capabilities made it possible for us to produce this unit cost effectively, passing the cost savings on to the market. Our customers receive all the benefits and power of a 900MHz cordless phone at a very attractive and competitive price.

Leveraging brand recognition

End-users of our products are blissfully unaware of the efficiency, cost-effectiveness and advanced-technology-at-our-fingertips advantages brought about by VTech's strong cross-fertilization, but they do experience its benefits in terms of performance and price. Moreover, if our end-users have children, they probably already know that our products deliver what they promise. A whole generation of children and parents now know VTech. Our first product was one of the first toys on the market to incorporate microchip technology, producing an interactive game for children. Consumers loved it. Since then parents have been looking to us for entertaining and educational toys and they buy them for their quality, originality, dependability and safety.

This recognition is of great benefit for our other core businesses when it comes to the trade. We can go to see buyers about our telecommunication products and if they don't know who VTech is, our marketing people can talk about VTech's educational toys. Chances are, however, if the buyers have young children they are already well disposed towards VTech. This crossover is also true of end-customers. After all, we sell 14 million pieces of electronic educational toys every year, and the parents who buy them are from the baby-boom generation and comprise the largest demographic segment of our customer profile. These same people are those most apt to buy our cordless phones.

Sharpening the brand focus

This is not to say we are sitting pretty. The success of VTech's electronic toys, and the solid reputation this has helped us build, are things we think serve us well in positioning the company as a whole. Our reputation rests on totally safe, high-quality products, particularly those designed for children. If you look at the dominant names in the industry of our core businesses, VTech can be seen as a relative newcomer and so we need to continue to build our brand and what it stands for. Some of the most entrenched brands in the toy industry have been around for generations. Electronic toys entered the market only in the last twenty-five years or so, and comprise only 2 per cent of the entire toy market. There is a tremendous potential for growth here, and an exciting window of opportunity for VTech. We currently have a dominant market share in the USA and Europe in electronic toys: over 60 per cent. This puts our brand in a very visible and favourable light in this high-growth market.

Courting customers with brand strengths

This is one of the reasons why we are paying more attention to branding, and focusing on brand identity as a competitive advantage. When we first set up VTech, the market was small and we could beat everyone else with our innovations. However, as the market has become bigger there are also more competitors. It becomes harder to stand out and be seen as appreciably better than everybody else. As the gap between us and other companies narrows and the market grows larger, we will rely increasingly on brand recognition to differentiate VTech from 'me too' competitors.

Our game plan is to build brand recognition, bolstered by our reputation for trustworthiness and reliability, not only with end-users but also with the buyers in the middle of the process. We want to strengthen all of our relationships and have people associate the VTech brand with first-class quality and performance. We want our buyers and business partners to regard VTech as their most reliable supplier. And we would like our end-users to perceive VTech as honest, reliable and innovative, with top-notch customer service.

One mistake that companies make is to focus too much on costs and too little on nurturing and investing in the brand. This has been perhaps one of the greatest weaknesses of companies in the region. Many Hong Kong companies do not place sufficient emphasis on brand-building. Instead, they focus on tangible things like cost and product function. To many Hong Kong companies 'brands' are intangible; they do not yield immediate results, and hence people, being pragmatic by nature, do not pay much attention to them. But as markets become bigger and competition gets fiercer, the company that develops its branding will be a winner.

We have recognized the importance of our brand as a competitive advantage for a number of years. In this respect, VTech has been atypical in Hong Kong. We may not have done it in as coordinated a way as we would have liked, but we are now assigning a very high priority to branding as a factor for future competitive advantage.

This has to be done without actually losing sight of innovation, reliability and value, of products exceeding customer expectation – those things that comprise our vision and core values. It goes without saying that we need good products in order to compete. No matter how great our brand is, if our products are inferior they don't stand a chance.

Another strong rationale for our branding thrust is the fact that we are competing in more mature markets such as Europe and the USA. In these regions, we have an excellent opportunity to build our presence the way companies like Fisher Price have. We are much younger than Fisher Price and some of the other major names in the toy business, but our market outlook is very positive, so building our brand strength will be an important way to beat our competitors, which we are determined to do over the next few years.

The role of the corporate brand

In tandem with our focus on brand-building is the strategic positioning of our corporate brand. In the past we did not exploit the strength of the corporate brand and had in its place what could be called a multiple brand strategy. For example, we believed that different product ranges in telecommunications and computers would be better off with different brand-names, because we felt that VTech was strongly associated with more 'low-tech' toy products. We felt that using the VTech name on sophisticated personal computers or telecommunication products might affect customers' perceptions.

However, five years ago we began to rethink this and changed our strategy, focusing on VTech as a monolithic brand. At the crux of our change of mind lay the growing realization that our brand values – innovation, quality, reliability – do not actually have to be product-related. In fact, these characteristics are 'givens' even before an idea reaches a VTech drawing-board; they are part of the fabric of the organization. These qualities therefore can be applied to any product, whether it is high-tech or low-tech.

If our brand represented only one product type, then we couldn't have made VTech monolithic. By having a range of products and investing in strengthening the core values of the brand, however, we have greater brand elasticity and are able to transfer the VTech name across our full range. We have therefore shifted what were distinct product brand-names to the corporate brand.

However, we intend to keep using product line-names. For instance, under the VTech category of educational toys we have four basic line-names – Pre-computer, Talking Whiz Kid, Smart Start and Alphabet Desk – although there could be more over time. There are a number of benefits to this structure of corporate brand- and line-names. First, there are strong commercial benefits to be reaped from leveraging the corporate brand-name across all individual line product promotions. This tactic also lessens confusion in the market. Previously, when we used product brand-names alongside VTech, it meant that we had to try much harder to explain the relationship. Using VTech as the main brand now makes things much simpler, especially at the trade level. On the end-user level, this approach strengthens the brand-name in the minds of opinion-makers. Parents may read about us in the business pages, and then go home and see their children using VTech products. It leaves a solid impression.

Finally, there is another potentially long-term benefit for putting the VTech brand centre stage, so to speak. There are currently around 15 million children playing with VTech products. Those who are aged between six and twelve will be growing up with VTech. As they become teenagers, we will have an opportunity to create products that will appeal to them, in part through brand recognition. One of the reasons why a company like Fisher Price, for example, has better brand recognition is that several generations have grown up with its products – when children become parents themselves, buying Fisher Price is a natural choice. Since VTech is a younger company, we cannot make as large a claim but, given our market dominance, looking ahead we can see where we want to be. We have already come a long way: in the USA, for instance, results from focus group studies of people with children in the target age group for our toys give VTech 70 per cent brand recognition compared to 96 per cent for Fisher Price. We have an excellent opportunity to enjoy the same high level of brand recognition in a few years' time.

In our major markets we promote the brand and the products quite heavily. In terms of print advertising, the magazines people read have not changed much. However, there have been tremendous changes in television, which is why we are reconfiguring our strategy so that we can use this medium most effectively, facing the challenges of cable and satellite, the Internet and so on. Having said this, however, the importance of word-of-mouth as one of the most effective means for brand promotion cannot be underestimated. For example, the Little Tikes company has a very low promotional budget, and yet it has a name that is almost as well recognized as Fisher Price. It comes full circle, then, essentially to product substance and customer satisfaction. In view of this, the 14 million people who buy our products every year are our best brand promoters, ambassadors and advocates.

Developing the design

Visual branding is also something that speaks to the customer. At VTech, we try to make sure products are inviting and user-friendly. In fact, our products are designed in such a way to encourage interaction between the parent and child. In this way, parents use the toy to play with their children to the greater enjoyment of both.

Designing electronic toys so that they attract parents as well as children is perhaps one of our greatest challenges in this sector. Ninety per cent of purchase decisions are made by parents, so they also have to like and understand what they see. This also holds true for our promotions – box designs and in-store displays are essential components of the success of a product. Our research shows that 60 per cent of purchase decisions are made in-store. The customer will come in wanting something educational – a traditional toy or an electronic-type product – or they may initially decide to buy a Nintendo. They see our product and decide to buy it as well. Point-of-sale impact of our designs is therefore crucial and we always keep in mind that the person who chooses is not necessarily the child.

Currently, we are considering another aspect of our visual branding: how similar a design should be across the various product lines. For instance, there is a 'family' resemblance across three particular lines: the electronic learning aids (age six to twelve years), electronic preschool (age two to six years) and the electronic infant–toddler products. At the same time, the three lines are still distinct from each other. The debate is about how far to go in giving the products a similar appearance. We have to be careful not to stifle the creative spirit of our designers by imposing strict guidelines.

We are now making a major effort to impose our corporate identity on all our products as we have not done this enough in the past. Based on our thinking at the time, our aim was to sell products and this basically meant promoting what the product did. For example, the name of a product like Talking Whiz Kid was more prominently displayed and better promoted than the name

VTech. As a result, Talking Whiz Kid became the better known name.

This situation is not that harmful in the short term, but in the long term it is no way to build a corporate identity. We have amended this by having more distinct brand positioning on packaging and on products. And in our television advertisements we show the VTech logo for the final five seconds.

We have found that the brand equity we do have is a valuable foundation upon which to build. We have a good twenty-year track record and a following of customers and business partners who have confidence in our brand and what it stands for. While we have made inroads into brand awareness and recognition, the essence of the matter is that VTech is competing against high-growth and very competitive industries. Our branding efforts must continue to augment and leverage our strengths for the group's future growth and continued success.

Translating vision to culture

Our brand values are not just associated with our products; they are also contiguous with our corporate culture. If we were to describe VTech as a person, it would be someone with these qualities: creativity, possessing high integrity and reliability, with more substance than meets the eye. You might say that our corporate personality fosters our corporate culture internally and externally; it imbues all our enterprises and our conduct in business and society.

Perhaps because of this, VTech is involved in advising, mentoring and educating through schools, universities, business and industry organizations, and government agencies. We like to undertake joint projects with Hong Kong's institutions of higher learning, helping students to understand the industry. We participate in government and industry panels and organizations, offering what knowledge we can to help policy-makers make decisions for the continued vitality of Hong Kong's business environment. Our support of education also extends to other countries in which we do business. We donate our products to schools and are committed to educational charity work.

We see our involvement and activities in these areas as good business practice and good corporate citizenship. Our role in working with the university exposes us to students who might consider working for an organization like VTech when they graduate. When we donate products to schools there is a business incentive, but we also have a sense of social responsibility and feel it is simply the right thing to do.

This responsibility is something we feel very strongly when it comes to our employees. We feel that our success is attributable to the high quality of our staff. We put a great deal of effort into human resources development and ensuring the well-being of our employees, including those at our prime manufacturing facility in Dongguan in southern China. We strongly believe that if our employees are happy, they will do a better job. In our Dongguan manufacturing complex, we have invested in providing standard conditions in terms of the quality of the working environment, living standards, dining and recreational facilities, and training. We continue to offer comprehensive development programmes and training courses, covering topics such as computers, languages, accounting and technology. To outstanding performers we offer a Hong Kong training programme so that, over time, our staff in China will acquire Hong Kong management style and methodology. We decided when we moved our manufacturing operations to China to use the resources there that we were also going to give something back.

We don't want to give the impression that we are not profit-driven. We are a company where the bottom line is still the most important thing, but we feel that it is equally important to do all other things correctly. The people who work for us benefit, our products benefit, and the company as a whole advances. While our Chinese employees are making 14 million toys a year to help educate children in the USA and Europe, at the same time we also offer venues to educate themselves. Quality begins with the people in an organization and successful organizations nurture the culture that enables them to succeed. Our attitude is that, within our capability and adhering to the highest ethical standards and business practices, we seek to achieve success for ourselves and this success can also be used to benefit society. With this approach, we are consistent in our corporate values, within and without, which is as it should be.

A passion for R & D

We are still growing and learning. We try to learn from our mistakes and take each of our successes to a new height. In the evolution of VTech, we study the successes of other players in the industry and learn from them. Look at a company like Hewlett-Packard. It stands for innovation, integrity, performing beyond people's expectations; everything we also strive to stand for. Hewlett-Packard has put a lot of emphasis on hiring good people. When the company was set up it established itself near Stanford University and was built around hiring Stanford's brightest graduates. Its emphasis on good research and development has been instrumental to its success.

We are also deeply committed to research and development, and our R & D department is one of the strongest in the region. We have not needed to locate our R & D facility right next to a university as Hewlett-Packard did in order to get the best people, because nothing in Hong Kong is that far away. We do, however, have a product development group of 100 people in Kowloon Tong in Hong Kong next to the City University. We also have a group in China of about 300 people from Chinese universities which provides support to the Hong Kong group.

We work on the basis that some regions have particular technological strengths and offer the best fresh ideas, so we recruit people from individual markets and technology clusters to provide us with the latest market information, technologies, and what's going on in general. Sourcing the best talent from areas with expertise and excellence results in a world-class, world-quality team of experts – the best minds working for us in one of our most vital areas, contributing to the organization's growth. We have our telecommunications R & D team in the UK and Canada, our computer people are in Silicon Valley in the USA, our educational electronics are in Europe and the USA. We have also recruited engineers from China's top universities. In our industry, product cycles are getting shorter and shorter, so we need good engineering teams to turn out new products and ideas quickly. We have found that recruiting from China has been a very good solution to rounding out our teams of engineers. The way our R & D departments are structured enables VTech to tap ideas from all over the world and bring state-of-the-art innovations back to Hong Kong.

R & D is the life-blood of innovation and creativity. It has been through R & D that we have been able to be pioneers, helping our company gain overseas market share and recognition. One of our earlier successes, introducing voice synthesizers into our line of electronic, interactive educational toys, set a new trend in the marketplace and placed us at the cutting edge of this technology.

Building the brand

If you put together our emphasis on research and development, our vision, our values, and our culture, we feel we are in a strong position to benefit from the tremendous growth potential in this dynamic industry. We have set our sights on what we should tackle over the next few years. High on our list of priorities is to strengthen our brand – it is still not as developed as we would like. Strong focus on technology and products is on-going. The product is still key – quality is the number one objective. We need to have better products than anyone else. However, for the time being we will stay with our core businesses; product extensions are something we can consider longer term. At this point in time VTech is not like Coca-Cola where you can apply your brand to other products and people will still buy them. We are still at an earlier stage in development.

As the chief executive and chairman of VTech, I have the ultimate responsibility for guardianship of the brand. I also have the advantage of having been one of the company's founders, so I see the corporate brand and what it stands for from the point of view of someone who has seen a vision realized and embodied successively in our products.

Basically, one question needs to be answered in all corporate promotion or corporate identity development – does it represent the company's vision? Will it further the themes of quality, integrity, high technology, innovation and creativity that the company was built on from inception? In VTech, as with any organization, issues must be managed at both macro- and micro-level to be effective, including brand management. Individual marketing departments are responsible for promoting products in their market segments and within brand guidelines. My responsibility is to see that the overall integrity of the corporate brand and all our orchestrated efforts stay true to the vision.

12 | London International Group: The Benefits of Globalizing a Brand in a Fragmented Marketplace

NICK HODGES, *chief executive*

London International Group plc (LIG) makes around one-fifth of the 3.6 billion condoms sold each year. Today, LIG continues to re-name and re-package local products which are added to its portfolio through acquisition, and it is entering developing markets. It has approximately a 22 per cent share of the world branded condoms market; its nearest rival, Ansell, stands at 12 per cent. Durex condoms represents around one-third of LIG's business – the group's other core brands include Regent medical gloves and Marigold household and industrial gloves.

Latest financial figures show a steady improvement in profits. Much will depend, however, on the success of LIG's attempts to raise its condom profile in America, where it trails in second position, and the sustained growth of Regent medical gloves. The company's recent acquisition of Aladan, a leading US examination glove and condom manufacturer, coupled with its focus on a single condom brand, Durex, and continued technological innovation are expected to boost earnings and market share.

Brand – or bust

The day I was appointed chief executive of LIG, in September 1993, we posted a profits warning. We were in trouble and needed time to assess what to do. Three months later, we came back with our plan: to concentrate on core parts of the business and refocus on the Durex brand. We refinanced the business with a one-for-one disaster rights issue in July 1994. Those who bought then have so far more than doubled their money. Today, we have a very profitable business which is cash positive. We set a three-year term for recovery of the business and, in the third year of that, we are on track.

The origin of the Durex brand-name is Du-rability, Re-liability and Ex-cellence. It was registered in 1929 by the London Rubber Company. LRC was founded in 1915 selling barbers' sundries and 'protectives' imported from Germany and sold from the back room. Until comparatively recently, Durex has been a British brand with some exports – and I put the stress on 'exports' rather than saying we were a 'multinational business'. The brand was distributed by export managers and developed a presence in quite a few territories, mostly in colonial countries. Only since we actively started acquiring international businesses – from 1987 onwards – did we truly start to 'go international'. Even then, we didn't immediately brand the products Durex. In some countries we had Durex products, in others we had acquired local brands. Only since 1994 have we actively worked to globalize Durex as a single brand.

The change in strategy was a result of the state of group business. LIG had diversified throughout the 1980s. The then management was convinced that growth in condoms was minimal, as the business had been in decline before the AIDS crisis. The Pill was gaining market share, and our traditional surgical gloves business was still to develop. Diversification was a 1980's vogue, so we moved into areas many at the time thought surprising (and they were subsequently proven right): photoprocessing and fine china. We bought Royal Worcester and Spode, which bore little relationship to our core business. Eventually, we got out of china – but only after we tried to buy Wedgwood and were stopped by the Monopolies Commission.

However, LIG continued to invest extensively in photoprocessing. By 1989, we were one of the largest photoprocessors in the UK with a substantial mail-order presence in Europe. Photoprocessing, however, was a cash-eater, requiring new technology every year. And from 1989 to 1993, the business progressively declined from being profitable to haemorrhaging cash. Management tried to protect the business by squeezing core activities to the limit. In 1993, not only was photoprocessing losing money but all our other businesses were being stretched – in profit terms – to the very limit. We were considerably in debt. If we hadn't taken action, we wouldn't have been able to refinance the company and we would certainly have gone bankrupt. Diversification had led to management losing sight of the core business – the Durex brand and Biogel surgical gloves – and the heritage of the company. It was clear to me that we had two superb businesses: condoms and surgical gloves. They were interlinked because the technology was basically the same, but they were very different markets. I was always convinced both could provide long-term growth for the company and profit growth for our shareholders. The question was: how?

Before 1994, LIG's condom business had a very fragmented range – with different names in different territories for the same product, and different packaging for the same product, and even different products for the same sub-brand name. The net result was a diluted effect on the brand because while Durex was recognizable in a number of countries, there was cross-over, confusion and duplication. With no opportunity for global advertising and marketing, there was no opportunity for enhancing the brand.

During 1993 and 1994, we put together a plan to globalize the Durex brand, cutting costs by closing smaller factories, moving production to the East and automating production in the West. In May 1994 we agreed our goals: to increase our share of the world condom market; to be the quality leader; to achieve a single brand-name which was instantly recognized in all trade sectors, globally; to have common advertising and PR messages, lower costs, central control of logistics; to improve margins and profitability in the major cash contributors of the group. It was a single-minded strategy: to focus on the Durex brand and make it global.

World ambitions, local sensitivities

At the time, while we were in most territories, we had not adequately supported the Durex brand. LIG's markets were being run by local barons, with no thought to global strategy. We decided to globalize by expanding geographically, and by acquiring other brands such as Mister in Malaysia and Androtex in Spain.

Internally, a number of people had loyalties to existing local brand-names, so they had to be convinced of our strategy. We had to adopt a whole new system: instead of local factories supplying only local products, we had to globalize sourcing and streamline packaging, so that while we might have different artwork on local packs, Durex was instantly recognizable on all of them. We also had to rationalize our sub-brands to make them as comparable as possible in all the countries. Fetherlite, for instance, must be the same product variant around the world, not thin in one territory and ribbed in another.

Although LIG had a central marketing department pre-dating my appointment, it was somewhat toothless. From the time we said we would globalize the brand we gave it the power to ensure that all marketing strategies from every country were centrally approved. Today we have a situation of global-led strategy and local interpretation and implementation.

To ensure visual consistency and consistency of tone and message, we produced branding guidelines for internal use and for use by external suppliers. The Durex brand has rational and emotional values; our positioning is designed to communicate quality, reliability and safety and the brand's unique selling proposition: sensitivity *and* protection. The emphasis varies by market: in developed countries we talk more about the sensual experience; in less developed, stricter countries, we address the need for protection. The tone in all communication has to be positive. Consumer research underlines the fact that people do not respond positively to AIDS-driven gloom and doom.

We also specify what information and guidance should be carried on all packs and on leaflets within, so as to educate consumers on the benefits and limitations of the product and comply fully with local regulations. We give local managers full details and back-up information to support product and corporate claims.

Another important element of the globalization process was the introduction of the Durex Seal of Quality – a trademark used for external branding although use varies by market. When re-branding local brands – such as Hatu in Italy, Sheik in the United States or London in Germany – we implement a three-step plan. Step one sees the Durex Seal of Quality on the front of all non-Durex branded packs. Step two links the local brand to Durex on the front of the pack. Step three positions Durex as the parent brand, Durex Sheik, for example.

Considerable efforts have been made to ensure the Durex brand does not become a generic; for example, we refer not to sales of 'Durex', but 'Durex condoms'.

However, we can't decide to roll out a brand globally and just do it. Local attitudes, approaches and sensitivities must all be taken into account. While eventually all our brands will have the Durex name, they will retain different external designs; for instance, in Middle East markets we're not allowed to show women on pack. In some countries birth control is taboo. Other companies face similar challenges. You always see the corny expression, 'Think globally, act locally'; well, even big brands must take local action.

Then there are the attitudes of local managers. We are moving as fast as possible but are very aware of the danger of damaging a strong, local brand. Frequently the biggest resistance is from our own territory managers rather than members of the public who, if the re-branding is conducted properly, don't even notice. Take Rowntree's Smarties: the packs are now clearly branded Nestlé with no sign of Rowntree at all.

Italy is one of the world's largest branded condom markets. In Hatu we already have the leading brand, with approximately 55 per cent market share, and a brand heritage older than Durex. Over the last eighteen months, through working with MTV Europe and global PR initiatives, and the launch of a new premium sub-brand,

Tutto, the first branded condom to carry Durex in the Italian market, we have moved subtly to link Durex with Hatu.

One aspect of the Durex brand positioning is that sex is fun. Of course, we have to judge how much to play this up (or down) depending on the particular territory. In Western countries we can promote the safer-sex message through humour, but Eastern cultures are more restrained. Malaysia forbids condom advertising, for example. Indonesia, the world's largest Muslim population outside the Middle East, allows advertising, but cautiously. With a population of 200 million, AIDS has the potential to become a major problem in Indonesia. So, with government agreement, US-funded AIDS education and condom distribution programmes are now being implemented by LIG and local non-governmental organizations, initially in the high-risk areas of Java and Surabaya, now elsewhere as well. It is a blend of both commercial initiative and social marketing.

The impact of AIDS

AIDS really came into the public arena in the UK between 1987 and 1988. It was being talked about before then, but it was not until the government's high-profile AIDS-awareness advertising that it became a national issue. We realized from the start that we needed to understand what was going on; how the HIV virus was spread and how its spread could be reduced. We therefore invested in our own clinical research to get the support data which would enable us to say, 'Use condoms because they are effective barriers for disease control'.

A significant hurdle was the ban on condom advertising on UK television, although this ban was quickly lifted. The first major education initiative came from the government with its 'Iceberg' and 'Tombstone' advertisements in newspapers. Although they involved a 'use a condom' message, these early advertisements focused on doom-laden imagery and scare tactics – an approach we were not keen to take. Our first TV campaign ran in 1987 using the theme song 'The Power of Love'. In 1989/90, we cooperated with the Health Education Authority which made the 'Mrs Dawson' campaign featuring a female worker in our condom factory. This coincided with visits by MPs to condom production lines. The aim was to familiarize the public with the condom and to become used to discussing safer sex.

We also moved quickly to participate in the government's All-Party Parliamentary Group on AIDS, set up in 1986, and we have sponsored the committee's activities ever since. The committee ensures that HIV remains on Parliament's agenda, bridging the gap between statutory and voluntary sectors and providing a forum for the exchange of information.

Our strategy towards AIDS was honed in the UK and rolled out in other markets as the Durex brand was developed internationally. While education has always been a part of our branding and marketing activity, AIDS forced us to place an increased emphasis on gathering data and disseminating facts. Our educational materials and pamphlets became more sophisticated.

We have used clinical trials to clarify our protection message. We have to be able to discuss the respective risks and benefits of condoms when used in different ways. There are often restrictions on what we can say in our advertising, but we are addressing it now in our in-pack literature. We have also developed our own globally applicable pack health warning. Although we can't spell it all out, we can offer best-use advice. It's a difficult, highly sensitive issue.

Cashing in on corporate conscience

From the corporate perspective, we are trying to grow LIG's share of the condom market and grow condoms' share of the entire birth control market. We see ourselves as one of the major educators with an obligation to inform people of the limitations of the product, as well as to explain the product's benefits and correct usage throughout the world. We have enhanced our brand-name considerably by spending money on education programmes, literature, sponsorship and so on. The whole methodology is to educate people that a condom is a life-saving device, and a healthcare product.

We work with local GPs and healthcare workers to get across the message of why, when and how condoms should be used. In the UK we produce 'Practice Makes Perfect', a sexual health resource for medical professionals. In other markets, we rely on third-party endorsement and work with external experts to offer best practice guidelines and information. Another example is 'Condoms across the Curriculum' which is 'supported by an education grant from LIG'. The book suggests schools projects and exercises which can familiarize pupils with the existence and importance of condoms – rubber production in Malaysia in a geography class, for example; advertising jingles for condoms in a music or marketing class. We also produce a booklet called 'The Ins and Outs of Sex Teaching' for those who teach healthcare professionals.

International initiatives range from sponsorship participation at international conferences on AIDS, including the biannual World AIDS Conference, and campaigns such as the 'Europe Against AIDS' programme, to more practical activities in developing markets. With MTV, we have promoted safer sex in over seventy-seven countries worldwide, addressing key issues of importance to the young: sexually-transmitted diseases and unwanted pregnancy.

India is potentially the single biggest condom market in the world. The spread of HIV is alarming, and if population growth is unchecked, estimates suggest it will exceed China in the early twenty-first century. There has been no active promotion of family planning or use of condoms for healthcare for years. Our response is proactive marketing and the promotion of healthcare and condoms. We have a joint venture in India where our local brand, Kohinoor, dominates the relatively small market. Since the 1980s, when TV controls were relaxed, we have been able to market our product more aggressively, but we are up against religious beliefs, lack of education and overwhelming economic factors. Eighty per cent of India's population is rural and so, during the past two years, we have started to take the safer-sex message to them, employing professionals to go into small villages to advise on birth control, AIDS and sexually-transmitted diseases. We hope the success of such initiatives will persuade the government to invest further in family welfare and AIDS programmes.

Inevitably, these activities have a benefit to us and to our shareholders; however, I believe we still have a corporate responsibility to become involved in education programmes. There is clearly a major problem in many countries where birth control is still unavailable or condoms are yet to be accepted. I'd tell any government minister it is his or her duty to promote products like ours. The more education campaigning we put in, the more people we can convert to using our product.

Quality is the key issue, here. Durex must be seen as the highest quality condom in the world. We make significant investment in research to ensure all our products are made to the highest regulatory standards and are acceptable anywhere. We work closely with regulators to advise on quality guidelines and are actively involved in revising international condom quality through our representation on national, pan-national and international standards committees. All of this gives us an advantage over our competitors. As we have said in a number of recent publicity campaigns: 'If it doesn't have Durex in the pack, it's not Durex in the box.' We don't produce own label.

During the last two years we have also begun to supply unbranded product to government and non-government agencies for distribution in developing countries. The fact remains, once we get people using condoms, whether free or not, they will start to demand branded products.

Staying ahead of the game

Of course, there will be a growth of own brands in other markets, as markets develop – where you have a credible pharmacy chain, for example. Boots launched own brand condoms in the UK in 1996, and at the same time we re-launched Durex. The facelift involved dynamic new products and packs designed to be more modern and up to date. We identified three distinct stages of condom usage in the market, and targeted each accordingly. We created sub-brands for each, for example, Safe Play for younger adults and Select, a variety pack including ribbed, coloured condoms and flavoured condoms (such as 'Ice Mint' and 'Tangerine Dream') and square foil packaging to enhance quality.

Own brands will be the ultimate test for the Durex brand and I'm very comfortable about that. They may take a small share of the market, but they may help expand the market, too. The worldwide condom market continues to grow at around 2 to 3 per cent a year – quite slowly when you think the Pill is probably in decline and you still have a large number of people at risk, having casual sex without using a condom. This is because the condom is still not widely seen as the preferred product to use: it has to be at hand, at the right time. And that's where I think a good brand-name and wider acceptance is going to help.

Our advertising is designed to create new usage; in other words, to make the sexual act with a condom more exciting than it is without one. Achieving this is always going to be a challenge, because using condoms you start from second base, so to speak. The new products we are bringing into the market (the polyurethane condom, for example) should help tempt new users and expand the market.

Rival brands have always posed a threat in certain markets, but the greatest threat came when Durex was seen as a tired brand, and when newer brands, such as Mates, were seen as more fashionable. Durex is now positioned as the upbeat brand, and we feel prepared to fight anyone. Since 1993, we have tried to make Durex appeal more to younger users while still remaining relevant to and trusted by older users. We have achieved this by segmenting the market. Evidence suggests that if we can pick up the young, we keep them as they age. Our strength used to be in the older age bracket: twenty-five and upwards. What I'm hoping is that our new marketing and positioning will ensure we are seen as the right choice when people start out, and that we also get endorsement from mother to daughter, father to son in later years. The ability to pick and choose different products in the range as users get older – for greater sensitivity, for more security and so on – is essential. To encourage people to move through the range we use leaflets, packaging, advertising and PR to explain the differences.

The positioning of the product has shifted. In the early days, condoms were only ever bought at the barber or pharmacy. But throughout the 1980s, in developed markets, condoms shifted towards being a fast-moving consumer good (FMCG) as increasingly they were sold in grocery stores and supermarkets. Because of the importance of research to all our activities, and partly in response to AIDS, we felt it was important to position condoms as a rational purchase. Our approach was to position them as a clinical product. This also moved Durex away, once and for all, from condoms' once seedy image. Despite the increased public debate, many people still had a little smirk about them, and advertisements still showed people embarrassed by the product. We started saying, 'This is just a standard medical product'; in the most extreme case it might save your life; it can stop you catching a sexually-transmitted disease; it can prevent unwanted pregnancy; and it's for sale over the counter.

Clearly, condoms are now under intense regulatory controls around the world. At the same time, business is being driven by clinical endorsement of the product. In the past, doctors and nurses rarely endorsed condoms, instead they advised people to use the Pill. Today, however, we are seeing increased endorsement from GPs and healthcare professionals around the world. In addition, in-store promotional activities related to new products communicate that using a condom is more acceptable – we have to encourage people to think of using condoms as second nature. As fun.

Room for growth

At an international level, competition has altered very little – the market remains fragmented; there is no other global branded player. There is tremendous advantage in having a global brand-name in a deeply fragmented market. In Italy and Spain Durex is up against Artsana; in Germany – Mappa; in France – Prophyltex; in Scandinavia – RFSU; and in North America – Carter Wallace and Ansell. A single brand-name and a single message communicated across all markets poses a significant problem for local brands. They face the weight of our local advertising and international campaigns, too. This is important for us. Unlike other global brands – such as the big Proctor & Gamble brands – our market remains relatively small worldwide, so we can't possibly afford to advertise in every single country. We therefore have a broad swathe of PR and advertising which covers a single brand. I am confident it will work well.

In the past, well before my time, there were widespread ventures which tried using the Durex brand-name. We still have Durex-branded spermicidal lubricants. My personal opinion, however, is that I see a very clear message for condoms and closely-related products. I would be very wary of trying to make it a wider range. There may be obvious possibilities for brand extension – such as pregnancy-testing kits – but I believe the time is not yet right. We must ensure there is absolutely no confusion or dilution of the Durex name. Durex must be synonymous with being the best condom in the world. Besides, there are other more immediate challenges.

The biggest conversation about brands today is no longer about taking on local labels and own brands. It's about what to do when we have a low-price product and a high-price brand and whether we can put Durex on the low-price product. Or, when there are pharmacy and mass market differentials, whether we can sell the same brand at different prices in those two outlets. In that situation, we have kept the Durex name, but have used different sub-brands. This is a feature in many markets – especially larger and more developed ones where our traditional sector remains pharmacy. But mass market grocery outlets are growing in most cases, taking up to a quarter of the market, often at a much lower price.

I won't be satisfied until we have good awareness of the brand in as many countries as possible. We are already a leader in forty countries and in another twenty or thirty we are number two. We are on an aggressive acquisitions strategy and I am determined Durex will be the sole condom brand for the group. I will be happy when I have achieved good brand recognition in every country where we sell. But product innovation and sustained investment in research and development is also important. By ensuring our product gets better and better, we raise the standards for everyone else. This gives us an edge.

Also, we continue to develop new products. We launched the polyurethane condom because it has a number of attractions, being non-latex, odourless, colourless and made from a material that is twice as strong, allowing a much thinner film to be used to increase sensitivity. It is another way of bringing new users into the market. We think it will be a niche, certainly for the foreseeable future, although I think non-latex condoms will have 10 per cent of the market in ten years' time, which is why we are continuing to work to improve it.

I am a great believer in single brands where you are a single distributor. I admire Coca-Cola. I think Procter & Gamble still does a magnificent job. I admire these companies both because of their confidence – it's not misplaced, but correct – which leads them to do more for branding and sales of product, and because they are strong enough to withstand the retail pressure which comes from own brands. Wherever there are very strong brands, the retail own brand has tremendous trouble trying to take them on. Kellogg is another strong company which defends its brands and basically says, 'Nothing else is as good'. That's my position on Durex for condoms. I want the world to hear the message: 'Durex is the best – you can go and buy a cheaper one, but it isn't as good.'*

* Durex, Durex Seal of Quality, Regent, Biogel, Marigold, Fetherlite, Mister, Androtex, London, Hatu, Tutto, Kohinoor, Safe Play, Sheik and Select are all trademarks of London International Group plc and are registered in the countries of use.

13 | Mandarin Oriental Hotel Group: Delivering the Eastern Promise Worldwide

ROBERT E. RILEY, *managing director*

Mandarin Oriental Hotel Group is an international hotel investment and management group which operates a dozen deluxe and first-class hotels, principally in the Asia Pacific region, employing 6,600 staff in twelve countries. The business generates most of its income from the Hong Kong hotel market which has enjoyed a significant recovery since mid-1995 following a period of static growth. Its flagship hotel is Mandarin Oriental, Hong Kong, which opened in 1963 – originally as 'The Mandarin' – as a deluxe hotel catering for the growing number of business and leisure travellers visiting the island.

In the early 1970s, additional Mandarin Hotels were built in Jakarta and Manila, the Excelsior Hotel was built in Hong Kong and the Oriental, Bangkok, was acquired. In 1974, to accommodate this expansion, Mandarin International Hotels Ltd was formed as an umbrella hotel management company. In 1985, in anticipation of further expansion, the company restructured its management company under the brand Mandarin Oriental and adopted the fan logo. During that decade a further three deluxe hotels were added in Macau, Singapore and San Francisco. Thus far during the 1990s, a further four deluxe hotels have been added in Indonesia, Hawaii, London and Kuala Lumpur. Mandarin Oriental International Ltd is now a publicly listed company with net assets of $1.3 billion.

The group's focus is to continue to expand its deluxe hotel portfolio while meeting the interests of guests, staff and shareholders. Mandarin Oriental defines its mission as 'to completely delight and satisfy' its guests. Near obsession with building and maintaining a corporate culture to achieve this mission significantly contributes to the reinforcement on a daily basis of the Mandarin Oriental brand.

Aiming above customers' expectations

Mandarin Oriental had a wonderful brand long before I came to the group in 1988. As is often the case with a business like ours, a group of core individuals was committed to deliver a service, as opposed simply to satisfy customers – there is a difference. They delivered a service that rapidly became recognized as something extraordinary. Mandarin Oriental, Hong Kong, was rated the 'Best Hotel in the World' by *Forbes* magazine in 1967. And from then on it enjoyed growing recognition. A brand is a promise, and our promise is never to say 'no' to a guest. Guests can rely on the fact that if they ask for something that's humanly possible to deliver, we'll do it, and that we do not have regimented parameters beyond which we will not step.

There are many good companies represented in our markets. Our total commitment to our guests distinguishes us and keeps us competitive. All of our training programmes are designed to ensure everyone takes personal responsibility for whatever a guest needs. Our Mandarin Oriental mission is not only to give guests a great service, but also to delight them with our ability to anticipate their needs. And it's a surprise for them: we aim to do something for them that they need, before they even know that they need it.

This mission is underpinned by some basic guiding principles. We strive to understand client and guest needs by listening to their requirements and responding appropriately. We are committed to working together as colleagues – with an emphasis on sharing responsibility, accountability and recognition through teamwork. By treating each other with mutual respect and trust, every employee contributes to the group's overall success more productively than if each worked in isolation. We actively promote a climate of enthusiasm, working to create a caring, motivating and rewarding environment. We work hard to be the best – an innovative leader in the hotel industry – and, as a result, we seek the same standards from our suppliers. We are committed to growth and delivering shareholder value, to internal and external relationships that match our high service standards in terms of integrity and fair play, and to act responsibly, for example, in environmental improvement.

There are some simple illustrations of this which are duplicated day in, day out, as a matter of course. When a guest asks for an international newspaper, somebody will go out and get it, instead of saying where it can be bought down the street. If a guest arrives with a broken piece of luggage, it's repaired without anybody making a big deal out of it. Even if a passer-by is having a problem, our staff respond. In one particular case, a lady was struggling outside with a sick child, the doorman jumped into a cab and took them to hospital. These things continue to surprise guests. Recently, a housekeeper in Thailand found $40,000 in cash and turned it in. This value system filters down to all areas of interaction between staff and non-staff: it's a basic response to human beings whether they are our paying guests, or not. Because, often, you just can't tell the difference.

The Mandarin Oriental brand is all about human values – people who really care. It's more than being a caring company. Like British Airways, it's about personal interaction. This is a difference that really matters – it's about care, concern and delight.

Learn to live the brand

To ensure we live the brand, one of the first things we must do is to attract the best people.

We are committed to 'modelling' – leading by example. If I see a piece of rubbish lying on the hotel floor, I will pick it up, put it in my pocket and keep right on going, rather than pick it up and hand it to somebody, or tell somebody else to do it. When a member of management sees an ashtray in an elevator bank overloaded, he cleans it, and takes it out with him. We do it because we want the staff to see the importance attached to even the smallest matter. Of course I could tell somebody to sort it out, but doing it myself adds to the modelling effect and stresses the fact that we all should take responsibility for anything that needs doing.

Senior managers try to get all management – everyone, in fact – to appreciate that often the folks with the lowest job in the hierarchy have the most important job. They're the ones who are with the guests continually. Housekeepers, doormen, waiters are constantly with guests, they certainly see more of them than I do. The doorman probably has 3,000 interactions with guests every day.

So, although they are trained to do a specific function, our people are trained beyond that, too. Again, we use this word 'delight' a lot. Because it's a better word than 'serve'. 'Isn't it wonderful to see a guest squeal with delight?', someone once said and that's how we came up with the word. We all have our specific functions, but the central issue is that the guests are there for an experience. They will come back because of a real, positive, personal interaction with our staff. All of us are the people that they look to for security and comfort.

Building pride in the brand through recognition and development

Mandarin Oriental operates a highly visible modulized staff training programme. Whenever employees complete a module, a star goes up by their name on the training board.

It's a creative development programme. If someone wants to move from being a waiter to a head waiter, say, he has to complete a certain number of modules before he is eligible for promotion. When people get gold stars by their names, it's a highly visible way for us to acknowledge their achievement.

Building on this, we're introducing a 'you made a difference' campaign. Whenever somebody does something important, we give them a certificate straight away. Instant, personal recognition is extremely important. I write at least half a dozen letters a week to individual staff members, thanking them for doing something special for a guest.

Being a laundry attendant is a pretty tough job, and so is washing dishes. How do we keep these people motivated when they've been doing the same job for the past thirty years, so that they really get their tableware clean and out there in time for the other staff to get them back on the tables? We must recognize their efforts. We must pay them well (we offer among the highest rates in the industry). And then, for appropriate positions, we must find ways of making them reach upwards – through incentive compensation. We all respond positively to stroking. We're fortunate in that we have different hotels and different cultures, therefore we can use a lot of what we call 'cross exposure' – motivational trips. For instance, Giovanni Valenti, an Italian concierge at Mandarin Oriental, Hong Kong, who's been with us for twenty years, recently spent time at the Mandarin Oriental Hyde Park in London. We had inherited a lot of Italian business there, and we did it because we wanted to show Hyde Park's Italian guests that they were important, and so is Giovanni Valenti. He had a wonderful time sharing experiences with his new London colleagues.

Also, we send people to night schools and summer schools for further education and career development. We also send a number of staff on courses at Cornell or INSEAD, and each year we try to have at least one general manager go on either Stanford's or Harvard's executive business program. In the past many of our general managers did not have university degrees, and it was quite difficult for us to get them in the program. However, because of their past performances in the program, these universities now welcome our people.

World standards, local needs

Many Western guests – particularly Americans – are very comfortable with service staff being personally familiar with them. In contrast, European guests and, to a greater extent, people in Asia, prefer to be recognized for their status and position. So you have to find the right balance. I was at Mandarin Oriental, San Francisco, recently, having lunch with the general manager, and a waiter that I knew came up and said, 'Hello, Mr Riley, how are you?' He then reached across the table and shook my hand, adding, 'Good to see you back.' The general manager turned to me and remarked that this behaviour is typical in America. And I love it. But a senior waiter wouldn't be comfortable behaving the same way with many of the guests at Mandarin Oriental, Hong Kong.

It's not always easy in Eastern cultures to ensure people get the right balance of personal interaction. So we devote time to helping our people understand the effect of eye contact, and that sometimes it doesn't hurt to touch a guest affectionately. At the same time, cultural differences have an impact. Eastern guests have different expectations from Western guests which must be respected.

Back in the mid-1980s it was easy to talk about the service levels of Asian hotels. There weren't many international groups operating in Asia. Labour was inexpensive, therefore staff were plentiful and so was service. But now it's different. Labour costs are no longer so inexpensive. We experience a lot of competition for good staff from white-collar industries such as insurance and banking. In these white-collar service industries, young people don't have to work shifts or weekends. So we have more challenges with recruitment, training and retention than we used to. We still attract dedicated and talented people, but there's just much more competition for them.

Then, of course, there are many other hotel companies here, who are also doing a fine job. Standards are very high everywhere. There are lots of good hotels in American cities, too. We have to approach the market differently. We try to focus our activities. Using the word 'delight' helps us concentrate on personal inter-action. It's now the core theme of our marketing and advertising activities. The mission to delight is our brand. That's the Mandarin Oriental promise.

Meeting changing service needs

We've been going through a transition. When we first started here in Hong Kong, we knew exactly what we needed to do; we based this knowledge on past experience in other markets, primarily the UK and Europe. But the increasing numbers of people travelling here and the rise of affluence in Asia means that Asians had their own ideas about what they were looking for in hotels. We have to accept that 'the traveller' is changing, which is why we continually update our image.

In the late 1980s, we asked customers (and non-customers) what they thought of us. They thought we offered excellent services. However, they also thought that we were 'formal', and if you wanted to take that over to the negative, 'stuffy'. We've had to recognize that the travelling public has become younger, and that more Asians are travelling. We've had to adapt to this. Again the word 'delight' came up. We've worked very hard to overcome what was perceived as a stuffy image. We've tried to engage and interact and never to say 'no', to present ourselves as offering everything you want. The consistent offer is essential.

Today, the challenge is to become more accessible, while at the same time preserving our traditional customer base. And we're doing it with considerable success. In the past three years we have totally revamped eighteen of our restaurants to compete with free-standing restaurants in the local marketplace. We don't want them to be seen only as 'hotel restaurants'. And we've done that, at times, without the total enthusiasm of our more traditional loyalists. I'm pleased to report, however, that in most cases we have been able to keep these loyalists, who now acknowledge that some of the changes were the right thing for us to have done in the current market environment.

Our guests are made up of a variety of different groups, from 'traditionalists', older more conservative travellers, to 'achievers' who are younger, assertive and ambitious. Our customer mix depends on where our hotels are located, so we constantly have to balance the interests of each group.

In the late 1980s, we dropped the requirement for jacket and tie in several of our restaurants and bars. Before then, we had Europeans walking in wearing expensive designer casual outfits and Asians with open-neck shirts and we couldn't serve them. So dropping the jacket and tie requirement made sense. When you come down to it, very few Asians wear a jacket and tie when they're travelling. They live in hot climates. It was important therefore to modify the code while at the same time maintaining the degree of decorum our clientele expected.

Also, we've refitted our restaurants and bars to appeal to a younger clientele. In Asia, the image and the positioning of your hotel is highly dependent upon the perceptions of the local market. The recommendations of local people are vital for customers deciding where to stay. If you have younger achievers coming into your hotel for food and entertainment and they find it fun, they'll recommend your hotel. If they find us stiff, there's a whole market that's not going to be recommended to us. All of these were profound changes for a very traditional European-influenced hotel company.

Sometimes, we've made mistakes in promoting our brand. When I arrived at Mandarin Oriental, our advertising campaign was based on 'the legend'. If you think about it, calling something a legend today seems rather old-fashioned and arrogant. Also, we had an advertising campaign where we focused on the negative side of travel: restless flights, long days of meetings. The idea we wanted to portray was that, after all this hassle, it's always lovely to come home to the warmth of Mandarin Oriental. The problem was that we weren't really promoting the reasons why you should choose Mandarin Oriental first, or what it was that made Mandarin Oriental really special.

Today, the creative strategy is about moments of personal delight based on customers' experiences. Customers regularly contact us and recount details of their stay. 'I found paradise at the Oriental Spa, Bangkok. I never thought I'd feel this good,' one wrote. 'We now understand why your hotel has received all these awards. Your staff are like angels,' another said. We came to realize we should be proud of what we are doing, and that what we talked about should have real consumer appeal. The refocusing on our mission to delight placed the emphasis on interaction and involvement with our customers. That is what we believe to be our unique selling point.

Our latest advertising campaign is much cleaner, fresher and more vibrant than previous attempts: it reflects the vibrancy of all the new things that we're doing with our hotels.

A monolithic approach to branding

Mandarin Oriental is our brand for our deluxe hotels. Our symbol – the fan – is always accompanied by our name. The fan encapsulates service in an elegant, incredibly refined way. It is about achieving the right temperature – being comfortable. It can be either a basic comfort or the height of indulgence. The eleven-point fan symbol is particularly effective because many Asian cultures have an interest in symbols. That's why all of our hotels around the world adopt it. The fan logo links all of our hotels, even if they all, for one reason or another, cannot carry the Mandarin Oriental name. However, for decorative purposes, each hotel has the flexibility to design a variation on the symbol that's relevant to them. Some have been based on locally produced antiques. In London, for example, we worked with Sotheby's and Christie's to find the right design. In Hawaii, where their bamboo fans did not convey the required image, a local florist designed one for us using local flowers. This kind of originality gives life to our identity – it's not a rigid, static thing.

If it were possible, every luxury hotel we operate would carry the Mandarin Oriental name. It's not surprising that there are a number of hotels throughout Asia named either 'Mandarin' or 'Oriental'. In the mid-1980s, we joined the two names for two reasons. The first was to link our two flagship properties, The Mandarin in Hong Kong and The Oriental, Bangkok, both then and now recognized as among the best in the world. The second reason was that the joint name, together with the fan logo, is a separately identifiable brand-name which could be protected. And we legally protect the brand aggressively.

So now, whenever it's legally permissible, our hotels will be called 'Mandarin Oriental'. And where for historical purposes, such as The Oriental, Bangkok, and Hotel Majapahit, Surabaya, we use the historical name, the use of the fan logo and other references to Mandarin Oriental make it clear that the hotel is part of our group.

In some cases, we've been able to combine both the strength of our brand and the benefit of the historical name. In Hawaii we now have Kahala Mandarin Oriental, Hawaii. Actually, if we had our way it would be called Mandarin Oriental Kahala. Our partner, who initiated the purchase and invited us in has a sentimental attachment to the name 'Kahala'. Since we did not want to lose the deal over the name, we agreed to have Kahala precede Mandarin Oriental. Also, since the local community and many frequent guests knew the hotel as 'the Kahala', substantial benefit was gained by keeping that reference.

In 1996, we bought the Hyde Park Hotel in London, now known as The Mandarin Oriental Hyde Park. Again, combining the strength of the brand with the benefits of past associations. Because we own it, one hundred per cent, Mandarin Oriental is the most important name it could have. We will always put the Mandarin Oriental name on a hotel if it's at all possible. If we bought the Ritz in Paris, I'd call it the Mandarin Oriental Ritz Paris because I think it's important for the brand.

However, wherever we put the brand-name we have to assume that we are able to deliver on the promises the brand stands for: to delight and never to say 'no'. Although, because of differences in local cultures, a guest will get a different style of service in San Francisco, Hong Kong and London, we can still focus on the important areas to make sure we delight our guests in those areas. What we have found is that, as long as you're within the luxury segment, your guests will understand that there's a difference in style in different parts of the world. Their loyalty to the brand is solid, and they are prepared to adapt their expectations depending on the local culture of the place in which they are staying.

This becomes particularly challenging when we make an acquisition like the Hyde Park Hotel. With such an established hotel, you can't expect regular guests to understand your brand offering overnight, but you can gear up the hotel to act immediately on the change. We closed the Hyde Park deal very quickly and, within thirty-five minutes of signing, we were in the hotel introducing ourselves to the staff and assuming its management. That was on a Friday and I came back the following Tuesday to present our mission statement to them. I presented the concept to all the staff and personally gave each a personal copy of the statement and our fan pin. As a result, I have been able to meet each one of them. It takes time, but it is vital if they are to buy into the new concept.

Interestingly, the general manager at the Hyde Park recently told me of a guest's letter of complaint. This guest had been staying at the Hyde Park for many years, and he wrote with a long list of things that were wrong with his latest visit. In the last paragraph he said: 'I've been putting up with all these things for many years, but now that Mandarin Oriental is managing it, I expect better.' He said it tongue-in-cheek, but our involvement immediately raised his expectations.

Learning by example

You cannot help but admire and try to emulate those organizations which know how to develop really motivated staff. Take a company like General Electric, which is consistently recognized as one of the best performing companies in the world. GE attracts good people, keeps them and makes sure they're motivated, and they are aggressive and gung-ho for each other. At the same time, they're tough businessmen and they understand their brands, too.

Then there are those who successfully change or improve their brand, like British Airways. What's encouraging there is that there's hope for everyone – that you can change if you've got sufficient belief and will. We're close to British Airways and we've invited their training company to talk to us about what they do; it's all about putting people first, because you have to. People talk about satisfying the customer, but what this invariably stems from is satisfying your staff. As senior management, that's our job – we must ensure that our staff have the resources, the training, the motivation and the appreciation, so that when they're out there, on the front line, it flows through to the guest.

The brand starts from within and then moves outwards. As part of our induction programme, along with the presentation of the mission statement, we give everybody a fan-shaped pin to wear. It's a symbol of our commitment to our mission. It's not compulsory to wear it, but most people do.

Avoid the pitfalls of uncontrolled growth

We have to be very deliberate when planning for growth. We are a niche player, but there are a number of ways in which the company can build profit without necessarily having to dilute brand. I don't think there are many hotels that can carry our brand-name. Mandarin Oriental is more than just a five-star brand; we would be devaluing ourselves if we were using the name on a typical business hotel in Cleveland or Houston or Mobile, Alabama. You cannot compromise on the promise. In the fashion business, certain exclusive brand-names have widened their appeal and you now see them everywhere. This certainly devalues the positioning. Some fashion brands have tried to become mass market, and it may be that they limit their life-cycles by doing so.

If you want to remain competitive and broaden your appeal, you need to adapt. There is a danger in assuming that in protecting the brand you cannot broaden the promises it makes. We cannot be the same Mandarin Oriental that we were in 1963. Then, eighty per cent of our business was from the UK, compared to the twenty-five per cent British business today. So, even if we're prepared to stay a niche player, we keep reminding ourselves that our customer changes every day and that we have to continue to broaden our base because there's more competition. Therefore your customer base, by its every nature, is always getting diluted. You're forced to broaden your base, but hopefully there are more people moving up: the achievers and the people who want to achieve – those who are on the cusp of achievement but aren't quite there yet. They are all part of our customer base.

Therefore, we must be selective with each new hotel. Or, if an acquisition could not carry the Mandarin Oriental brand, consider an alternative, such as our Excelsior brand for our first-class hotel in Hong Kong. Of utmost importance is not diluting the value of the brand by using it for properties which don't meet the standards. We must always be able to fulfil the promise and our customers' expectations. At the same time, we must understand the changes that are taking place with expectations so we can fine-tune our services to met the new expectations of tomorrow's customers.

A further danger is misjudging the attitudes of your market. Another Mandarin Oriental campaign was not totally effective with our Asian guests. It featured guests chatting and joking around informally with staff. It was strong in the sense that it was all about personal interaction. We started using photography featuring staff interacting with guests, which seemed perfectly natural for someone with an American bias. But we were so focused on shifting away from being stuffy to having personal interaction that we overstated the case. The research feedback six months on revealed it was not going down well with Asian consumers. Asians have a strong sense of politeness and it wasn't credible to them to sit in a restaurant and be over-familiar with a staff member. It wasn't something that warmed them. We were trying to tear down the stuffy image but went so far to the other extreme that they shrugged their shoulders and said 'who would want to do that anyway?'

As managing director, I take ultimate responsibility – for the brand – as any CEO must. Sometimes that requires hard decisions that may not be popular. A few years ago, for cost considerations, someone in our organization came up with a less expensive customer magazine. It was less expensive – and it looked it. So I cancelled it. The employee who suggested it had good motivation – we could have saved $100,000 a year by printing it on cheaper paper with lower quality editorial – but from a branding standpoint it's better not to have a magazine than to have one that doesn't match your standards. Recently, there was a hotel for sale in Los Angeles that many of our colleagues thought would be an appropriate acquisition for us. But I made the decision that it couldn't carry the Mandarin Oriental brand. It was a good financial deal, but it was only a four-star hotel: it just couldn't carry it off. In every organization, ultimately the CEO must decide on the final balance between short-term financial objectives and the requirement to build the brand with a long-term perspective.

14 | Mazda: The Journey Towards Harmony

SHIGEHARU HIRAIWA, *director
and president, Mazda Motor (Europe) and*
DAVID HESLOP, *chairman and managing
director, Mazda Cars (UK) Ltd*

Today marks a critical point in Mazda Motor Corporation's seventy-six-year history. In 1996, long-time partner Ford, the US car giant, took a controlling 33 per cent stake in Mazda, resulting in a management shake-up, with Ford's Henry Wallace appointed Mazda president – the first Westerner to head a leading Japanese car company. The past eighteen months had been a period of fundamental yet welcome change for Mazda. Despite a long-standing reputation for innovation – Mazda has developed some highly acclaimed technologies, such as the rotary engine, and its cars are widely recognized for their superior engineering – the company suffered falling profits in the early 1990s.

In 1994, vehicle production in Japan fell 22 per cent to 773,000 units, or nearly half the peak level of 1.4 million units just five years before. The reason was a lack of clear focus on branding, Mazda's management now concedes, that had a significant effect on the bottom line. Mazda is now working with Ford to harmonize product development strategies and marketing communications. Just how Mazda's traditionally individualistic approach will fit within a coordinated group strategy that aims to set Mazda alongside the Ford and Jaguar portfolios will become apparent in coming months.

A unique heritage

Mazda Motor Corporation, based in Hiroshima, Japan, makes a diverse range of passenger cars and commercial vehicles and is one of the largest employers in western Japan. In developed markets it has become synonymous with the revitalization of the sports car market following the launch of its successful two-seater convertible, the MX5. Mazda trucks and cars are exported to 153 countries and in each the same guiding principle prevails: the customer comes first. Customer service standards are set high and maintained by a 5,200-strong network of Mazda dealerships around the world and 2,700 sales and service outlets in Japan.

The company's Japanese heritage has been central in shaping the Mazda brand, at the heart of which lies customer friendliness. Research shows Mazda is a highly desirable and user-friendly vehicle brand. A recent German 'Customer Barometer' study (conducted by the Emnid Institute of Bielefeld in 1996, polled 32,000 members of the public on attitudes to 700 companies), for example, shows Mazda and Honda ranked ahead of Mercedes and Toyota. Another study carried out in Germany, by ADAC (General German Auto Club) shows Japanese cars are consistently at the top of the list in terms of reliability. The ADAC study, carried out in 1995, shows the Mazda 121 to be the most reliable small car in the German market, ahead of the best German car, the VW Polo, and the Seat Ibiza, Fiat Uno and Citroën AX. In the lower-middle-class category, the Mazda 323 came first, ahead of the Toyota Corolla, Suzuki Vitara and Nissan Sunny. In the middle-class section, the Mazda 626 beat the Mercedes 190 Diesel; the Citroën BX came in last. In 1995, Mazda's series 121, 323 and 626 won in three out of four categories for reliable engineering.

In one sense, the Mazda philosophy is a product of Japan – a country renowned for high-quality, high-standard products and modern technology. In another sense, it's a product of Hiroshima. Hiroshima is a mid-size, local city with a population of approximately 700,000. The people working there maintain a strong work ethic. Every single worker is dedicated to his or her job and committed to building the best quality vehicles. By contrast, Tokyo is a cosmopolitan city. In local cities in Japan, however, people move less frequently and stay there longer – they maintain values more easily than those living in cosmopolitan cities. Mazda cars are the most reliable and user-friendly. Customer satisfaction has become a core value and it must now be a key message because, historically, we have established and focused on product quality. This has been inherently at the core of Mazda. Sometimes we may emphasize sport, sometimes easy-to-drive features, sometimes fun – but always value.

This is a different approach to other Japanese car brands. And it has created a particular corporate culture. Mazda people have certain ways of working, of talking, of communicating. Certain values – a distinct sense of integrity – are the essence of how we live. We have open-plan offices. Our people communicate. They are cross-functionally linked in terms of seating arrangements and work groups. They take pride in developing themselves in order to develop Mazda.

The company has another guiding philosophy. It is committed to cooperating, wherever possible, with the needs of the international community. Mazda takes seriously the need to contribute to the further growth of the global automotive industry and the world economy. It is increasing its commitment to environmental research and development programmes to promote new levels of harmony among cars, society and the environment. To this end, it has developed hydrogen-fuelled vehicles, and pioneered a number of technological breakthroughs including a new plastic composite that can be recycled at least eleven times for structural material, and a decomposing catalyst for recovering gasoline and kerosene from all types of plastics.

However, a further aspect of Japanese culture – a belief that you do not need to shout – has had a less positive effect. For too long we have been product- rather than market- and marketing-led. This is now changing. And this change is being fuelled by the closer relationship with Ford.

East meets West

Mazda and Ford have had a long relationship. In 1969, Mazda, Ford and Nissan formed Japan Automatic Transmission Company – a joint venture to manufacture automatic transmissions (Ford subsequently withdrew in 1981). In 1979, Ford acquired a 25 per cent stake in Mazda, and in 1996, increased this stake to 33.4 per cent. Nineteen ninety-six was a year of restructuring for Mazda which involved a refocusing on customer satisfaction and a reassessment of the quality of our dealer network. In the light of fundamental changes associated with the Ford deal, one might have hoped, at best, for the business to plateau. In fact, year on year, European performance was up. In the USA, a major new advertising and marketing strategy got underway to boost image and stabilize segment performance. In Japan, volume share finally stabilized, after a seventeen-year decline.

The coming together of Ford and Mazda presents significant potential for culture clash. The power and dominant nature of American Ford is being linked to the incredibly cultured and structured society of Japan. In one sense, they are two opposites: the ying and the yang; East and West; formal and informal. However, branding is about people and, for a brand to work, the people within the organization have to have some purpose to drive consistency. That purpose is the vision and aspirations of the corporate body, where endeavour drives harmony. There are differences between the two organizations, but the corporation is a living, changing thing: the summation of every individual in the system.

Of course, when American culture is linked to Japanese culture, the result could be a confused mess, but there is another possible outcome. Through an organization's focus and willingness to talk and learn, such a union can become a building process – a way of developing a new and refined language. Brands are not static things, they have to evolve. This is our aim. Ford has its language, Mazda has another. All the time, we are talking and listening and out of this is coming a new understanding for the future. The process is forcing us to express ourselves better and, in turn, to develop a stronger understanding of our brand.

Global corporations transcend religion and culture. They drive their own consistency and actually create the corporate brand. Mazda UK isn't just 'Mazda Cars UK'. It is a group of people driving the success of the Mazda product and brand. The real structure is much more inclusive; it includes suppliers, agencies, customers, shareholders, bankers. And all the stakeholders must understand the Mazda culture.

Corporate harmony

The Double Concerto for Saxophone and Cello commissioned, in 1997, by Mazda for John Harle and Julian Lloyd Webber and composed by Michael Nyman has a harmonic plot. The subtext relates to the location of Mazda's headquarters, Hiroshima. The source of inspiration was a photograph displayed at the Hiroshima Peace Memorial Museum which simply and horrifyingly represents presence and absence simultaneously. The photograph depicts the entrance to a bank only 260 metres from the hypocentre of the atomic bomb dropped in August 1945. A person was sitting on some steps waiting for the bank to open. It is believed that they were facing the direction of the blast at the moment of the explosion and, without any chance to escape, died on the spot after being completely burned. The space where the person had been sitting remained dark, while the surrounding surface of the stone steps turned white due to the heat rays.

In the Concerto, the saxophone and cello soloists shadow each other and the jagged sound of the first section evolves into a more harmonic language at the conclusion. Kansei means harmony, the resolution by human intervention of the many conflicts of life into ultimate concord. It's a philosophy which has led to the design of some beautiful and practical cars. This philosophy is reflected in the Concerto's composition.

The attraction of opposites

Ford is a volume player and Mazda, while it wants to become more mainstream, is a distinctive player. Ford's brand positioning doesn't complement Mazda's, but it doesn't interfere with it either, which is what is needed in a portfolio of manufacturing brands. Jaguar, Ford and Mazda will be maintained in distinct and differentiated brand positions. There is collaboration in terms of technology and new product development, to avoid duplication. But there is also differentiation, distinctiveness and differences in branding and positioning. Through collaboration, we can also make sure we each remain distinctive.

There are obvious marketing and branding benefits from the Ford–Mazda union. Until now, our operations have been product-led. Our own people engineer and distribute our products. All our people love the cars and understand the differences between them and other products, ourselves and other companies. They in turn try to communicate this to the consumer. That is why there is such a close relationship between other countries' operations and Hiroshima. Everyone must understand the core philosophy, the core values, so importers and dealers are carefully selected and monitored. We encourage everyone to take pride in understanding the core values of the brand and, where applicable, to develop their own ways of communicating it.

Due to the structure of Mazda worldwide – with Mazda HQ at the centre, and regional Mazda executives, national Mazda offices and local dealerships representing business in each country – there is what we call a 'communications cascade'. It's like a waterfall. So, when we have a whisper in Hiroshima, it multiplies through the cascade until one whisper becomes a million shouts: a million customer experiences. This multiplier effect is the same for many global organizations. And it presents the same problem: how to make the whisper from Hiroshima live as an experience which is consistent with every customer, every dealer, every national office, every regional office.

There has been a breakdown in communication in recent years.

We have had misinterpretation and other weaknesses in the communications cascade. Historically, the difficulties have been with translating our understanding of the Mazda culture at regional and national levels. It meant there was an unclear understanding of the culture between Hiroshima and different continents. We had consistency of product, but not consistency in positioning.

To overcome this, the company must have a single, central vision. What a lot of marketers don't understand is the difference between the role of global strategies and the local experiences of customers. Global strategies are about economies of scale. Local issues are about flexibility and pace and consistency of experience. What we try to do in our organizations around the world is channel global visions, global manufacturing and all the economies of scale into local experiences. We drive this through global to local (you might say 'glocal') marketing, which gains the economies of scale of central manufacturing, while allowing for the local experiences of the brand. Certain cost and marketing mechanisms create efficiencies at different levels within the cascade: from Japan, Europe, UK, England, London, Swiss Cottage, the dealer to the customer. So, for example, customer databases exist most efficiently and effectively at a national level. Motor show stands are better developed and designed at a regional level – pan-European, for example – for the Paris, Frankfurt and Birmingham shows. One of the skills of 'glocal' understanding is knowing what is best done in a factory in Hiroshima and what is best left to the dealership in Harrogate.

The communications cascade is not a one-way process. Service is as important an element within it as product and marketing communication, and efficiency of service. We have a system where we go from the customer direct to the managing director to Japan, cutting out all the bits in between. The actual act of communication is critical to the brand, not just in the sense of marketing the consistency, but because we are listening. Our listening organization is a healthy one and we have to have a mechanism to get the critical point back fast. So, if the brakes aren't working properly on a car in the UK, our colleagues in Japan would know within minutes.

Think laterally

Traditionally, Mazda is strong in product and weak in marketing, whereas Ford is very definitely a marketing-led company. There is much more accumulation of know-how today, which is one great benefit of our closer cooperation with Ford.

Last year we created a marketing division at our headquarters in Hiroshima. Although there were some marketing activities in place, there was no dedicated strategic division. The aim is to coordinate brand messages around the world and control communication of our values. Real brand marketing is not about fabricated slogans, it's a total approach; which is why conventional above-the-line advertising has its limitations. We are now looking more seriously at communicating through the line and at other ways in which the brand interfaces with the driver. These other 'real' contexts will become more influential in the future. That's why we now believe we are no longer selling cars – we're selling customer experiences.

Our approach goes beyond traditional definitions of marketing. With the Double Concerto, for example, we wanted to highlight a debate in a way that no one else has ever done it before: it's a lateral step. What we try to do is write advertising to communicate our brand, product and message. We translate the language we've learned. That's what our agencies must do: to get the essence of the position, of the product, so they can translate this creatively into communication. We want people to talk about what we do. We want staff to talk about the brand and understand.

Branding is critical for Mazda. Immediate market concerns inevitably pose the challenge of tactical necessity against longer-term, strategic needs. It's chicken and egg. But we must communicate our brand values which, in turn, become part of the commodity price to the user so that when we are in the pricing game we can be a better player. It is dislocating if the brand image is not clear and may dilute reasons for a consumer to buy. We must ensure we do not jeopardize our brand values by tactical activities, such as price-cuts and discounting, while remaining highly competitive in value-for-money terms.

If we expect people to spend £20,000 on our product, we must get them to trust us. A relationship with the brand (and consumer) is essential. All the more so if you are Sainsbury and you want to be accepted as a bank. To be a bank in the old days, you had to have pillars and a bank manager who was difficult to get to see. Technology changed all that, and First Direct proved it could work. Emotional values give a brand stretch, because of trust. The battle-ground is choice rather than selling: that you *choose* to buy Mazda, rather than do so out of habit. Brand extension is the future of brands – it's about emotional commitment, the summation of the experience of a consumer with all the products and services and elements operating within our brand. It is an area we are now starting to explore.

The brand is also the language of a corporation. It offers the ability to communicate consistency. Mazda brand values are every-where around us, on a daily basis. We built out UK headquarters in 1983, with a garden, a pond with koi carp, and a car park sunk into the side of the hill – it's all part of the culture of how we relate to the material world. This affects every aspect of our communi-cation. At motor shows, we give our staff the opportunity to design their own clothes – it allows them to express their understanding of Mazda-ness through their own creativity. Our motor show stands are built from recycled bumpers. Environmental issues and recyc-ling are becoming an increasingly important part of how the car industry will survive, if it survives at all.

We spend a lot of time trying to communicate all this. People who create our insurance products, our warranties, our sunroofs, have to understand what it is that ties them together as a brand. The brand needs to be a communication mechanism to ensure disparate parts of the organization are united. We always think of end-user customers as the recipients of communication. But actu-ally, staff, suppliers, shareholders, bankers, all of these people are stakeholders and get the same message. If the brand is a chain of inclusive stakeholders – from manufacturer through distributor and retailer to the ultimate link: the consumer – it lives through each stakeholder's participation in that product and service. The way the chain holds together is a brand statement. The best brands work where the inclusion of every stakeholder is strongest.

Our current method of using advertising is also very much influenced by Ford. The Japanese traditionally assume an agency is 'only' an agency; they have a strategy devised by themselves, and the agency is called upon only to develop the creative work. We are now working to change our relationship with agencies to encourage closer cooperation and implement collaborative efforts, treating advertising agencies as if they were part of the marketing department. Agency staff become more innovative, stimulated and better motivated that way and come up with better creative ideas. We had already got to this point with all our other suppliers, but not in terms of marketing and brand development.

Mazda is starting a number of aggressive marketing strategies in Europe. One crucial decision was to retain the advertising agency JWT to support marketing communication throughout the region. This is a very sensitive area for us. For although we now have a pan-European strategy, Europe comprises regions and local communities, and each local market has its own character. I don't think we will ever be able to rely on just one standard strategy. We need happy harmonization between local and regional cultures.

Listen, and learn

As well as being more marketing-focused, we are becoming more market-led. In the past, we were not listening to the demands of our consumers. We are now asking whether we have done enough and where we have gone wrong. This involves talking to each other within the organization and talking with our consumers at length. We are making use of a broad range of research, from JD Power Customer Satisfaction data to tailored studies. All of this now shapes marketing and product planning, which it did not before. This is of course a time-consuming process, and we are still only one-third of the way there. But we are moving in the right direction. We encourage our employees to be aware of competitor initiatives and learn from their successes.

Engineers will traditionally lean towards making the top quality, whereas customers care about good value, the best quality for a certain price. There are a number of examples of where we have gone wrong. Mazda created many sports cars and speciality vehicles in the early 1990s. We thought the market demand was shifting and actually we ended up producing too many cars. This is one reason why Mazda has recently found itself in such a difficult financial situation. Also, we have developed many innovations that have been copied by others, such as a design to maximize interior space by folding down the back rest of the rear seat. We invented this in 1980. We also pioneered the wind deflector on the convertible, now a standard feature on rival models.

However, we were very poor at communicating the exclusivity of our products and features to our consumer. Part of the Japanese culture is that silence is golden and that the product speaks for itself. In modern Western culture, however, this is not sufficient. We must communicate loudly and we shall. Once the user experiences one of our cars, he or she will come to love it. But growth will be limited if only a small number of consumers know about our cars. That's the problem we must now overcome.

Our conclusion is that we didn't listen deeply enough. We must be more careful, more attentive. We have streamlined many product lines, focusing on core areas and growing segments in the market. For example, in the sports segment, we have the MX3, MX5 and MX6. No other company has such a wide range, and we could probably live with just one or two. Growing sectors include speciality vehicles, such as station wagons. We have a focus now on these growing segments and are shifting our emphasis accordingly. However, while Mazda must increase volume, it must not move away from its market positioning. Ford is a volume player, while Mazda has a distinct customer appeal: a feeling of distinction and exclusivity. Take the Ford Fiesta and the Mazda 121 – both are now made at the same Ford plant in Dagenham and basically share the same engineering platform. However, each is clearly and distinctively positioned.

If we refer niche back to product, from developing a broader range of model types, we could have around 90 per cent of the potential market. If we develop only a limited range, we're cracking only 10 per cent in product terms and, as we've discovered, we can't run a top ten manufacturer with that strategy. So what we have now is a shift in strategy. With a 2 per cent share of sales we're still a distinctive player, but we will attack mainstream opportunities in Mazda's unique and branded ways. Rather than building cars to attack only 10 per cent of the car market, we will build cars to attack 90 per cent, and yet appeal to this broader footprint with our unique interpretation of customer needs, expectations and experiences.

In order to grow Mazda's share we must coordinate activities with Ford, matching production cycle plans to avoid clashing with new product development. There will also be a clearer international strategy for the Mazda brand. This will be a major advantage, enabling manufacturer, distributors and dealers to be more sensitive to local needs. That is our longer-term goal: to produce a variety of products, satisfying a range of needs. At the core of this business will be the 323 and 626. We will also develop new models to diversify the range – recreational vehicles, wagons and diesels. Continued production and a widening range will ensure that Mazda is never relegated to being just another car at the back of a Ford showroom.

In late 1996 we launched a new speciality vehicle – the Demio – available only in Japan. We are ensuring it adheres to our core values of quality, style, user friendliness and excitement, and that the presentation of it to, and interaction with, the consumer communicate these core values. It's not so much a question of what we hope our brand will be in five years time. Our plans are clear: we must communicate our brand proposition to the consumer more effectively.

The road towards perfection

Another element to the Mazda brand is the Japanese concept of Kaizen. Kaizen is the concept of continuous improvement, without ever accepting that you will actually reach or achieve perfection. Instead, life is about the journey towards perfection. People may talk about the Mazda brand but, in fact, the Mazda brand today is slightly different from what it was yesterday. Because in just twenty-four hours, millions of people – employees and customers – have interacted with it. Let's say the sunroof fails on a car at twelve o'clock today, then that customer's experience of Mazda will dramatically change. And the experiences of consistency and value, structure and directive will change. We will then have to try and re-create a sense of harmony from that unfortunate event.

If we are good managers this happens in an evolutionary way, as it has over the many years it has taken for Mazda's business to evolve. During the twenty-five years Mazda has operated in Europe, we have been partially restricted by quotas, partially restricted by the model range, partially restricted by our ability as managers, funding, the commercial pressures and the currencies. All these factors have affected how well we have communicated, as have changes of government and fragmentation of media. In the old days, if you advertised on TV, the communication was very focused. Big brands such as Heinz, Unilever and P & G were built through being able to communicate with their end-users more effectively through the impact and focus of terrestrial television. Now, marketers are struggling. Suddenly you can hear radio messages locally, get cable TV and communicate using the Internet. Media fragmentation and new media make for a more difficult, complex world.

Such triggers can rock a brand. What we must do is learn and continually react to external factors better than our competitors by being more flexible, competitive, consistent. A healthy brand is one which can adapt quickly in the modern world. That is why this is a continuous process. The worst brand in the world is one which has arrived, because it if has arrived, it's dead.

15 | Federal Express: The Supremely Packaged Warehouse in the Sky

FREDERICK W. SMITH, *founder,*
chairman, president and CEO

In April 1973, the first night of Federal Express Corporation's operation, we had fourteen jets at our disposal and managed to deliver 186 parcels overnight to twenty-five North American cities. Today, our fleet of more than 560 aircraft – the largest all-cargo fleet in the world – travels nearly half a million miles every twenty-four hours, carrying nearly 3 million packages and documents to 211 countries every night. FedEx couriers log 2.5 million miles a day, the equivalent of 100 trips around the world.

We invented the concept of overnight delivery, creating a whole new market where previously there was none. But now, after nearly twenty-five years of rapid growth – we were the first US company to reach $1 billion revenues without mergers or acquisitions – our prospects are, if anything, even brighter. We started out in documents and small packages in the USA. Today, as the largest express transportation company in the world, we can ship virtually any package of virtually any size to virtually anywhere in the world.

For a growing number of major corporations, our air fleet has become their 500-mile-an-hour warehouse: we take over their logistics functions, allowing them to minimize their investment in stock and warehouses, and maximize the speed and flexibility of their service to their customers. And now, FedEx is ready to provide the distribution infrastructure Internet commerce needs. What the clipper ship and railroads did for nineteenth- and twentieth-century trade, we are ready to do for the twenty-first century.

The FedEx brand lies at the heart of the organization's success

– and its future potential. Many companies just wouldn't feel comfortable entrusting the management of their inventory, logistics and order fulfilment to an outsider. The FexEx name offers them peace of mind and quality service. So what makes the FedEx brand tick and how is it changing?

Anticipate customers' needs, innovate to meet them . . . and do it again

The biggest business opportunities rarely come from serving a need that has already been identified. The greatest opportunities arise when you spot the things that your customers didn't have a clue they needed until you offered it to them. That is what FedEx did with overnight delivery. When we launched, the idea of overnight parcel delivery as a viable, profitable business didn't exist. Yet we could see that moving small high-tech, high-value items such as computer and electronic components was becoming very important to the economy. And that skill – the ability to meet the needs customers don't know they have – is what continues to drive our business forward, as we open up new markets in logistics and electronic commerce.

The ability to identify an unidentified need, however, is nothing unless you can also come up with a way of meeting it. To be able to deliver a new service you have to innovate. The hub-and-spoke distribution system that lies at the heart of the FedEx network is one example of that sort of innovation. Another was the way we integrated ground and air systems from the very start. Up until that time people had operated surface vehicles or they operated aeroplanes, and the two were seen to be separate. We never felt that way.

Perhaps even more important was our recognition that, along with time-sensitivity, the ability to track the status of every item at every stage on its journey, from sender to recipient, would be crucial to customer satisfaction. We understood this even before we had the technological means to do it. As we have developed the means to do it, so information and information technology have become central to the FedEx offer, next to our fleet of planes and trucks.

Right from the very beginning we understood that FedEx stood apart from traditional postal carriers in two key ways. First we offer fast, time-definite delivery, whereas most postal services are non-time-sensitive. Second, our service is information intensive whereas theirs is non-information intensive – and we have worked non-stop to extend, deepen and innovate in the information side of our business. For example, our introduction of SuperTracker bar code readers in 1985 has helped to revolutionize the transport industry: a FedEx courier collecting a shipment scans it with a hand-held scanner identifying critical shipment information. Each item is typically scanned at least six times during its journey.

Also, we have continually developed each of our core competencies. For example, we have migrated our tracking system, from something which is internal to FedEx, into our customer shipping docks and into our customers' offices. To begin with customers had our own proprietary terminals, but increasingly the information is coming through their own computer terminals – so we have created an integral, on-line, real-time management system which is at our customers' fingertips.

At the centre of the FedEx information network is FedEx COSMOS®, which stands for Customer Operations Service Master On-line System. This is the central component of FedEx's strategic computer systems, allowing us to keep track of the status of every item as its bar code is scanned, from the moment it enters our hands until delivery. COSMOS currently tracks in the region of 45 million transactions a day.

Another essential part of the system is DADS (Digitally Assisted Dispatch System) which we launched in its original form back in 1980. When a package is picked up, the information gleaned by the scanner goes into a DADS transmitter which uploads the data into COSMOS via radio waves and telecommunications devices. We have a radio network linking our 35,000 couriers worldwide, to enable us to respond rapidly to customers' requests for tracking information.

This information is not only for internal consumption and use. Indeed, parallel to the development of our information infrastructure, we have always looked for ways to help customers access that information in the most convenient way possible. Back in 1978, we were one of the first transportation companies to introduce automated call centres to handle customer queries. In 1984 we introduced Powership, a dedicated desktop computer system that connects directly with the COSMOS network and allows customer to generate shipment documentation, streamline billing and track the status of their shipments virtually in real time. The next extension of this was FedEx Ship® software, which allows ordinary PCs to do the same. Both are offered free of charge to most customers, and now 60 per cent of all FedEx US transactions start electronically rather than starting on paper and having to be digitized later. We hope the Internet will help us automate the remaining 40 per cent.

In 1994 we became the first express transportation company to offer Internet connectivity for tracking and service availability transactions on the World Wide Web. Initially customers could use our Internet site to track the progress of their parcels simply by tapping straight into FedEx systems: no need to call customer service. The next step was to enable them to use it to initiate a transaction with FedEx InterNetShip℠ on-line shipping application – in a sense, making the Internet a seamless extension of COSMOS..

At the same time, we have always tried to innovate at the tactical level too. United Parcel Service (UPS) was at one point eight times bigger than us and began operations in the traditional post and parcel business – routine packages that were not necessarily fast, not time definite and with no information content. When UPS grafted an express system on top of their parcel post network, in response to FedEx's early success, we moved the goal posts. We went from next-day delivery to offering a money-back guarantee that we would deliver on time.

To defend your position, when competitors are coming in and narrowing the market, you have constantly to innovate and improve in order to maintain a leadership position. The focus of that quest to stay at the top currently fall into three areas: global capability, logistics and electronic commerce.

Offering 500-mile-an-hour warehousing across the globe

FedEx started out as a domestic US operator, but we soon realized that many of the items we were shipping, such as computer and aircraft parts, were essential to the operation of global businesses. So we started seeing ourselves as the clipper ships of the information age. Once, world trade depended on majestic sailing boats. Today, if you look at a news programme talking about world trade, you are likely to see some pictures of container ships in Long Beach, Liverpool or Le Havre. But in fact, the movement of goods by air, especially express carriers such as ourselves, is taking an increasing proportion of the value of the world's trade. We might be moving only 1 per cent of the items traded, but because they are high-tech and value-added items, they account for 40 per cent of the value of worldwide commerce. By 2020, it will be closer to two-thirds.

The expansion of our global network hasn't always been plain sailing. When we entered the European market we began by offering many intra-country and intra-Europe services, where the barriers to entry were low and where there were already many local competitors providing good services. We stuck to it for about seven years, and finally in 1992 we decided to restructure our operations there.

Our transportation infrastructure continues to expand rapidly. We now have eight hubs in America, three in Europe and two in Asia. In the last few years we have opened a new Asian hub in Subic Bay, in the Philippines. We have launched a new intra-Asia overnight delivery service and become the only US express transportation company to offer direct flights to China. We have created a new Latin American and Caribbean division reflecting our focus on the second fastest-growing economies of the world. Now we are the only transportation company that can connect 90 per cent of the world's GDP using our own aircraft and equipment.

This global transportation and the information infrastructure are the vital ingredients of major new developments for FedEx. The first of these is full logistics on a global scale. As part of our 'V3' (Vision, Value, Virtual) strategy, we are helping customers who manage complex logistics and transportation operations to reduce inventory, speed up their processes and improve customer satisfaction. In other words, to substitute information for mass. What we are saying is that we can speed up our customers' processes to such an extent that they can invest far less in warehousing and inventory; at the same time we are improving customer satisfaction, increasing their flexibility and their ability to respond to changing markets, thereby reducing the risks of obsolescence.

For example, in the past, if a company made aircraft parts in Arizona and wanted to sell those parts to people in Germany, it would have had a warehouse in Germany. Nowadays we can deliver to Germany within short time frames, so that a warehouse is no longer needed. That's why we sometimes say that FedEx planes are our customers' 500-miles-an-hour warehouse – or that our trucks are their 50 miles-an-hour warehouse. One of our customers used to have warehouses in twenty different locations, now it has three, and its inventory order-to-fulfilment cycle has been reduced from three weeks to three days.

We are using the same transportation and IT capabilities to position ourselves as a key part of the infrastructure in the emergence of Internet shopping, and in doing so we are providing a very powerful engine of commerce. The Internet should probably be compared to developments like the jet engine and submarine telephone cables: it will change the way the world does business. In particular, it will make time, place and infrastructure irrelevant in terms of selling and sourcing around the world – especially in business-to-business contexts. Another way of seeing it is to look at the link between the telegraph and the development of the rail system. The telegraph created the connections and the railroad allowed fulfilment. In the same way, where the Internet creates the connections we hope to provide the fulfilment.

In business-to-business transactions particularly, we believe there will be an enormous explosion of demand for products bought from catalogues over the Internet, and we have already developed the software to facilitate it. Called FedEx VirtualOrder[SM], this highly sophisticated system integrates order placement, billing, invoicing and inventory management to allow any company to sell on the Web. It lets our customers publish their business catalogues on the Internet and enables their customers to say which products and which of several FedEx delivery options they want. It helps the person shipping the item to know that there is a tariff of x per cent for products of that description, say, for Italy or Indonesia. It also notifies them electronically of the delivery. That means that a payment must take place, and we help facilitate that as well. Thus, you can sit in Leeds, Memphis or Wo Han in China and make it easy for someone on the other side of the world to order your goods and have them delivered and paid for, without the expense or hassle of finding a representative or a sales person or a partner there.

Build a service culture

Our goal is perfection, but we live in an imperfect world. It is probably beyond our grasp, given that we have to deal with hurricanes and snow, flying machines and trucks and traffic accidents. Nevertheless, we do our best. Every night an empty jet freighter leaves Portland, Oregon, for Memphis, tracking close to other FedEx airports on the way - just in case another FedEx jet can't fly that evening. If we do have a service problem we act promptly to try to make amends and make it right for people. Every day we make a huge effort to take what are already very high service levels towards perfection. In 1990, we were the first company in the service category to win the Malcolm Baldrige National Quality Award.

What makes FedEx stand out from most companies is our philosophy of People, Service, Profit (PSP). These three words are the very foundation of FedEx. They represent our belief that if you take care of people, they, in turn, will deliver the impeccable service demanded by our customers, who will reward us with the profitability necessary to secure our future.

This has been a core part of FedEx since its inception and it's been a very powerful business combination. We make it absolutely clear to everyone who draws a FedEx pay cheque that job number one is to create a 100 per cent satisfied customer, by 100 per cent on time deliveries and 100 per cent information accuracy. We want to make sure that customers understand that, in a sense, service is the only thing we sell. But the key is this: you cannot deliver the kind of impeccable service that is expected of FedEx unless you have satisfied and committed people working for the company. They've got to think that it's a good deal for them, they've got to be committed to the organization, and the organization has to be committed to them.

So how does this actually translate into action? First, every manager has to undertake a week-long training programme to learn the basics of PSP – at FedEx managers work for employees; it is a manager's job to help employees get their work done. Part of that training says that managers must seek to elevate human dignity and to reinforce a relationship of trust and respect with our employees.

Second, there are a number of programmes to make sure that employees feel they are fairly treated. We have a Guaranteed Fair Treatment Procedure that allows employees to raise grievances and have those grievances judged by their peers. We also have something called Survey Feedback, where we not only conduct annual employee surveys, but employee groups explore ways to improve on areas of concern.

Third, we have avoided layoffs when at all possible. This is good business sense for an operation like ours, where we are continually driving for, and need employee ideas on, extra efficiency through the use of new technologies.

Fourth, if the business is facing a tough time, the top people bleed first. Between 1990 and 1992, when many airline businesses in the USA were making substantial losses, executive salaries were cut before employees' merit increases.

Whether or not every sort of business needs to have a set of values like ours is a moot point. But, from the very beginning, I felt strongly that PSP was the way you need to treat people if we were going to have a high-performance organization. It reflects what I think is necessary to run this kind of business – and this is the kind of business I would like to run.

Building the FedEx brand

When I first started out with this business I didn't particularly consider branding issues. My mind was focused on filling a business need for moving the computer and electronic parts that were becoming so important to the economy. However, branding soon became a major issue. Initially, as we developed more front-office services, and now, as we move into Internet commerce, the FedEx reputation becomes invaluable. The fact that it is the FedEx world-wide express delivery system offering the opportunity of Internet commerce gives customers greater confidence than software coming from some other company.

Still, the core of the brand goes back to the idea of express networks that first emerged 150 to 200 years ago; they were networks through which you moved something very important under someone's custodial control and delivered it within a specific time frame. That is the heart of our business. Anything which falls under that umbrella fits the FedEx brand – transportation, logistics, the movement of goods – and everything we have done was a logical step for FedEx.

At the same time, because we are dealing with a service where expectations are extremely high, management of the brand becomes tantamount to providing customers with a degree of security. It's comparable to what American Express did in the early years of travellers' cheques. Our brand is utterly focused on what it identi-fies: express networks. At the same time it is selling something very general: peace of mind.

We are also broadening our offer into a wider range of services:

carrying different types of document, packages, freight for a range of customers from the very small to the very large. In a sense we are a bit like IBM. In its early days, IBM was many different things to many different people, making mainframes, mid-level computers, PCs, copiers, electric typewriters and so on. But it wasn't really important for the secretary who was very fond of his or her electric typewriter to know that IBM did all those things.

In many ways, competitors are able to come on the scene and close the gap on some of the transportation services we offer. So we have to look at where the battleground of the future lies, which is in information services. That is where all the added value is, and we're not going to let it be taken away.

We want to use our information expertise to strengthen and deepen the brand. Thus, as we broaden these services, we are deliberately using FedEx as a master branding device. We have, for instance, FedEx VirtualOrder, FedEx Powership® and FedEx InterNetShip. One of the main reasons we revised our corporate identity in 1994 to emphasize the FedEx brand was to develop the capacity to connote this panoply of services. We needed a better umbrella to deal with all these discrete segments.

Another very important reason was that 80 per cent of people had started calling us FedEx rather than Federal Express. There was a big parade out there and we needed to jump in front of it.

Working out the actual business value of making a change like that is difficult, but we do know that the new logo is much more efficient in terms of use of space. We have calculated that the impression that we will deliver would be worth about $60 million a year to us, simply because the letters are bigger and clearer. In other words, if we had to go out and buy the incremental impressions from the more efficient use of the same space on the side of the truck, the sign was worth about $60 million a year to us. It was also cheaper to maintain because of the amount of paint used; the extra time that the paint lasts on the aircraft and the trucks was also worth several million dollars a year to us. So it was a good business decision as well as a good marketing decision.

Communicating the brand

The nature of business determines the way we approach our sales and marketing. We use all the advertising and promotion techniques available to us, but when you are talking to Fortune 500 companies about redesigning their logistics, creating virtual companies with seamless technological access where your warehouse becomes a FedEx plane, a thirty-second advertising spot on TV is not going to convince them to change the way they do business.

Today, we have shifted our brand management and advertising focus away from time-sensitive delivery problems, to emphasizing our worldwide business capabilities. The brand management challenge is helping people understand that FedEx is much more than a document company. Many people don't know about the vast network we have in place and what its potential is. Also, while we have a twenty-year heritage in the United States, building the brand equity in Europe and Asia, where we are younger, is more of a challenge.

Today's advertising revolves around the slogan 'The Way the World Works'® in an attempt to address these challenges. We hope it provides a level of customer trust. It stresses our global capabilities, while providing an umbrella for more targeted marketing activities directed at different types of customer. And it's a big enough umbrella to cover the wide range of customers we now have: the way the world works *is* very different if you are shipping semi-conductor components from Malaysia to fifty different locations around the world, to moving manuscripts within the same city.

The next level of marketing reflects our intensive study of different customer segments' shipping needs: what type of shipments do they make, and how often? This also drives our automation strategy. For example, if our customer is a multinational company shipping 300 to 400 times a day from many locations, it may require EDI links, mainframe to mainframe. If it is a single location company making ten shipments a week, mainly paper-based, all it needs might be a bit of software on its PC. If a customer is shipping packages weighing 15 to 20 lb, he won't want to walk down the street looking for a FedEx retail outlet or drop box. But if it's just a document, he might be very receptive. For that reason, we actually have three sales forces: one for electronic commerce, one for freight, and one for the document and package business.

One of the best channels of communication we have is our own operations. By integrating our information systems and our transportation systems so closely with those of our customers, it becomes very difficult for them to think of an alternative. They have a symbiotic relationship with FedEx: when they turn on their PC, one of the first things they see on the screen is FedEx. To this degree, when we say we want to get close to our customers, we don't mean it in a metaphorical way. That phrase has become a cliché because there is no physical manifestation. We *do* mean it physically. We mean getting our systems integrated with our customers' systems. There is an interesting aspect to this. What started out as part of an offer of excellent service has become the ultimate sales channel. We have now got over half a million people using it to interface with us every day.

All these communications – advertising, direct mail, corporate identity sales force, couriers, information systems – play a part in developing the FedEx reputation. Maintaining this reputation and its brand image is a top priority for me, since it is one of the most valuable things the company has. Clearly therefore, acting as the brand guardian is part of my job as CEO. But that could be said of almost everything. You could say I am the safety officer too, because I have to make sure that everybody understands that safety comes above all else. So the operational responsibility for the brand lies with our senior vice-president for marketing worldwide, Mike Glenn.

At the end of the day, FedEx is not its logo or its advertising or its sales force. To the customer, FedEx is the person who comes to your door and doesn't let you down.

16 | Virgin: The Virtues of a Diversified Brand

RICHARD BRANSON, *chairman*

Trusted and totally accepted by consumers, young and old, Virgin is one of the most misunderstood brands in its home market amongst commentators and 'specialists'. In the main, brands are owned by large corporate entities, their creators lost in the mists of time, and are closely linked to a product or category. Virgin is different. Unconstrained and flexible, it is a virtual brand – it is not the only virtual, or attribute brand, but the others tend not to receive the same level of commentary. Yamaha, for example, successfully sells medical equipment, motorbikes and pianos world-wide. Virgin has got a long way to go yet.

Attribute branding is about building the reputation of a company over time and by association. The name Virgin was originally chosen to symbolize my ignorance of the business world, but it has come, to a certain extent, to represent the people's champion – a company challenging complacent markets and the status quo. This was not the intention.

In the mid to late 1980s Virgin stood for a different approach to music. Unlike the EMIs of the industry, who were vertically integrated, Virgin concentrated on signing and then marketing the musicians. Whatever business we are in, we concentrate our energies on the parts of it that really make the difference. In the music industry, pressing the vinyl and owning the vans that delivered it were not what mattered. We never lost an artist, and only picked those who transcended their time: Mike Oldfield, the Sex Pistols, Culture Club, The Rolling Stones and Janet Jackson are classic examples.

Virgin was a fun and friendly entertainment brand with huge

cachet. However, it was only when we moved into airlines that it also began to represent 'quality', 'value for money', 'innovation' and 'challenge'. Following our success with Virgin Atlantic, we began to target markets where the competition was not alert. We were not afraid to take on big, entrenched interests in such industries.

Taking on the big guys

From conversations with Freddie Laker we knew what we had to offer to succeed with our airline. His downfall was concentrating on price alone, which makes it too easy for powerful competitors to oust you. At the time, offering value for money and quality was unusual. It was one or the other, not both. The fact that we offered first class at a business-class price; individual seat back TV monitors throughout (we are still the only transatlantic airline to do so); an on-board massage service, etc., at far cheaper rates than the competition, built us a loyal customer base and travel industry acclaim. We were partly able to offer better for cheaper because of the way we have developed the Virgin brand. As in the music business, third parties have always been responsible for much of the operation. Only the customer-facing activities are Virgin branded or trained. Our cost base is therefore far lower than our main competitors' on most routes.

The 'consumer champion' position grew in leaps and bounds with the launch of Virgin Direct in 1994. Wherever we find complacency there is a clear opportunity for Virgin to do a much better job than the competition. We introduce trust, innovation and customer friendliness where they didn't exist previously. It is a successful formula which ensures that the brand gets stronger with each new launch.

As with the airline, we were able to offer the consumer more in the financial sector. In Virgin Direct's case, this was by cutting out the middle men – the independent financial advisers (IFAs). The cartel that had existed depended on practices that were not to the consumer's benefit. The 600 or so companies in the industry all had an identical price structure and were all trapped in the late-nineteenth-century practice of knocking on doors to sell. Direct Line had proved that there were far more effective and relevant ways of selling obligatory financial products. We decided to do the same with the non-obligatory ones.

Seen as our biggest challenge, Virgin Direct is the most successful new business we have set up yet: in 1997 we were the largest new personal equity plan provider in the UK, with nearly £2 billion funds under management. The PEP is designed to give customers, rather than the service provider, what they really want. It is made as easy as possible to invest in: telephone service; jargon-free literature; and a no pester promise. It is perceived as appealing, clever and irreverent. The business has been built by advertising, PR and word of mouth which consistently stresses that 'baggage-free' Virgin can offer better products cheaper. As a result, the industry is at last having the shake-up it needed.

Banking was a natural progression for Virgin Direct. The market was ideal for a brand organization like ours. The financial services sector is undergoing great change as a result of a combination of de-regulation, globalization and advanced technology. Almost anyone can offer a virtual 'bankassurance' company if they have access to capital and know how to manage risk. Traditional banks are only content providers; service providers are much closer to the consumer. As an information-rich industry, financial services can operate entirely within the global electronic network, unlike manufacturing where 'real' goods must be assembled and dispatched. This means that traditional operators and banks are put at a severe disadvantage by their expensive locations and cumbersome infrastructure. In October 1997 Virgin therefore teamed up with the Royal Bank of Scotland to launch our revolutionary One account, a combined flexible mortgage account with a single competitive lending rate for all purposes – mortgage, overdraft, car loan, credit card, etc. Critics perceive it as risky, complicated and of limited appeal. While I am the first to say that our first banking product will not instantly become a mass-market account, most of its critics avoid acknowledging the simple truth that it will save customers thousands.

Seizing the moment

Along with seeing where we can bring a little Virgin pixie dust to bear, seizing the moment plays a part in everything we do. It is true, as the critics claim, that Virgin sometimes seems to do odd things. Its idiosyncrasy is part of the brand's make up and charisma. Some of our activities are thought by outsiders to have over-stretched the brand or not built on its core strengths, but unlike a traditional FMCG marketer, we've never been constrained by the 'what business are we in?' question.

I am sometimes asked why Virgin Vodka happened. Well, why not? It was in the dull, dark days of 1991/2 that William Grant & Sons approached us with the plan for vodka. With minimal outlay from Virgin it has proved to be a useful learning vehicle and has brought in some profits from duty free shops and Virgin Atlantic.

Virgin Cola came out of the vodka learning and, again, Virgin has been criticized for this venture. If the product only tastes as good as a competitor's, is its existence of benefit for the Virgin brand? Financially, it certainly could be: if Virgin Cola were to capture only 1 per cent of the US cola market the returns on the resulting $1 billion business would be very attractive. And, in terms of the brand's development, we are certainly taking on powerful competitors. The Coke/Pepsi global duopoly is not an easy one to penetrate, but we love a challenge.

We are long term about the things we do. It was essential to iron out any glitches in our home market before attempting the US launch, and the two years we spent doing so have been invaluable. The vodka and cola developments have also been useful for the move into cosmetics and clothes. We are criticized for moving into areas where a Virgin shake-up is less relevant. However, we are building on our roots – the appeal to youth culture.

Things do not always happen exactly as you want them to in life and the same is true in the development of Virgin. When we took over the MGM cinema chain it was not ideal that they had to be Virgin from day one, but the MGM name had to come off and an interim one did not make sense. Similarly, on the rail franchise, we were obliged to brand the operation Virgin from the start. It might have been stranger to brand them Smith or Jones when everyone knew we were involved. The name Virgin naturally creates customer expectations, and both on the cinemas and the rail franchise it is a shame if, even in the short term, we disappoint. Ultimately we will of course deliver with both businesses, and it is good that we are under pressure to improve things.

With the cinema, we have been able to implement improvements very fast. Cinema had ossified in the 50s and become an operations-driven business where all that was delivered was a flickering picture, and often not even a comfortable seat. It was rarely a place of entertainment. There were so many factors that were crying out to be changed: the off-putting glass boxes you had to shout through for your ticket; the pointless curtain in front of the screen; no leg room; the lack of proper food or somewhere to eat it, to name but a few.

Improving the West Coast rail franchise is not a quick-fix option. It's the only time we've run into big trouble with the brand, and the only time I've wanted to get older quicker and turn the clock forward eighteen months. Rail travel is one of the most run-down businesses in the UK, and it is clearly a huge opportunity for us. The West Coast route links the key conurbations and comparatively few people use it at present. They are far more likely to do so when the new rolling stock comes on stream – this is the central plank of our turn-around strategy. Although most of the new rolling stock will only become available between 2001 and 2002, it will transform the line. As we increase the frequency and reduce the journey times, business travellers will not choose to drive or fly: whenever they turn up there will always be a train within half an hour. Attractive fare structures will also encourage the leisure traveller to leave the car at home. The switch to rail encouraged by the TGV in France provides a useful precedent: flying or driving Lyon–Paris has become a thing of the past. There are bullet train parallels with Japan as well.

In terms of its impact on the brand, I believe it will turn out to be the best thing we have ever done. By 2010, Virgin Rail will be looking after 54 million passengers a year, compared with 3.3 million on Virgin Atlantic in 1988. We, and our partners, are making a huge but essential investment: the cheaper, half-way house option of refurbishing but not renewing the rolling stock, which we reviewed but rejected, would not have provided the frequency of trains and reduced journey time that are clearly required.

Structured for constant regeneration

Until recently we did not think of Virgin as a brand. We were just having fun running companies – a record company, an airline or whatever. It's only in the last couple of years that we have realized we have something quite valuable. We found that when we wanted to launch an attack on the banking systems somebody else was willing to put up half a billion pounds to our half million, for only 50 per cent of the company. We're now taking the brand more seriously than we have in the past and being far more careful that it doesn't get hurt.

What becomes clear, reviewing the Virgin brand development, is that it is constantly evolving. There tend to be consistent elements in its make up but there is also a fluidity which allows us to take it into new areas. This in part results from how we perceive its potential internally. The majority of US and UK brands are fixed: their managers and owners have concentrated on core strengths, cementing them at every turn in the minds of consumers. In fact, consumers are far more open to the evolution of a brand than managers of other brands might imagine. It is easy to get too close to a brand and, as a result, to limit its potential.

This restricted outlook may explain why Virgin is the only recognized, new, global brand to come out of the UK over the past couple of decades. The general philosophy of the 50s, 60s, 70s and

early 80s was one of managing decline. Perceiving ourselves beaten
in the battle of technology, too many people fell into thinking like
civil servants. Many seem staggered that Virgin's collection of quite
small businesses can command such strong international recognition. The Virgin approach, however, can work for others.

How Virgin has evolved is due to a combination of factors –
intuition, hard graft and conviction amongst them. The brand is
regenerated, rather than extended in the conventional sense, by
each business we become involved in. We are in essence an unusual
venture capital organization: a branded one. Whereas most venture
capitalists are a financial resource, backing management teams and
their ideas, we offer a powerful branding and management resource.
We are also well placed to get any additional financial backing that
may be required. As part of the deal we control how the brand –
which we now know to be our greatest asset – is used. We therefore
retain at minimum 51 per cent control of most Virgin branded
businesses and are highly selective about what we invest in. Nine
out of ten projects we look at are potentially very profitable but if
they don't fit with our values we reject them. We put our principles
before short-term profits every time. Our customers benefit in the
longer term and so do we.

Our vertiginous growth from a modest music and entertainment
company with revenues of £50 million to a diversified global family
of companies with revenues of more than £2 billion has been
achieved through a core competence: the ability to manage high
organic growth through alliances, joint ventures and outsourcing.
The diversified group is bound together by five core values – quality,
value for money, competitiveness, innovation and fun. We have a
highly developed approach to negotiating and operating joint ventures in order to reap benefits for both parties which has resulted
in a lean and profitable organization, consisting of an ever more
varied array of wholly owned businesses, alliances, joint ventures
and outsourcing arrangements.

Virgin's structure is significant in the brand's development.
From our music business roots, where rights to 'properties' are
often shared through complex arrangements, we have the kind of

management mind-set that regards partnership with other companies as a perfectly natural way of doing business. By chance, we effectively combine Western and Japanese business practices. I was told by a Japanese journalist in 1984 that Virgin was like a *kereitsu*. There are indeed similarities: the Japanese *kereitsu* is a community of companies formed around a bank or an old family firm, just as Virgin companies are all off-shoots of, and supported by, Virgin Management. Each business is discrete: there is no annual aggregation of results. Companies in a *kereitsu* function autonomously, but regard themselves as allies with shared ideals, interest and goals. The benefit of such a grouping is that it predisposes the managers of each company to co-operate with the others, and adopt the kind of flexible management style that facilitates external co-operation. It also implies a system of beliefs and behaviours about how a loosely confederated group of different businesses might work together for mutual advantage. It is because these beliefs and behaviours are embedded deep in the Virgin culture that this approach works so well. It is a factor in our ability to start new ventures with what seems to other companies like astonishing speed. *Kereitsu* has created some incredibly strong, global brands.

We are a federation of businesses. In contrast to many traditional businesses Virgin is a group of companies with a global presence that has no head office, virtually no management hierarchy and minimal bureaucracy. The flat management structure keeps costs low and it keeps us nimble. This structure also allows us to be bold. Our ideas are not made bland by committee. Each business stands or falls on what the individuals within that business do – we try to retain the small company feel so everyone feels they are managing their own businesses and using their own judgement. It's a decision-making rather than a blame culture. As a result there is a tendency for everyone to be fiercely independent and fiercely protective. Such empowerment is essential in such a widespread, diverse and decentralized group, for it decentralizes decision making and creates nodes of real responsibility right through the enterprise. There's a collegiate feeling, a creativity and a buzz about the place.

One of the things people like about Virgin is that it is unstuffy.

We're in business for fun: we offer consumers something better; we need to make money; are we going to enjoy doing so? Many companies just make money – they develop the most efficient model for doing so and run it to death. We aim for our approach to be special and different.

We are committed to the regeneration of the brand. When Virgin decides to start a new business we make no assumptions, take nothing for granted and rely only on our own research. We draw on talented people from all parts of the group to confront and solve problems in new, practical ways. This often involves locking the chosen team in a room until they can blow our socks off. We have to continue to innovate internally as well. We are constantly on the look out for ways to re-energize our businesses. It's a process of continuous improvement.

Sometimes it's simply a matter of repackaging. With Virgin Atlantic, for example, we were treating our business customers to a delightful Range Rover experience followed by the usual brief but grim Heathrow check-in on arrival. An enterprising Virgin manager suggested we use the Range Rover computers to check passengers in so they'd have a 45-second drive-through (à la McDonald's). He also grabbed the requisite tiny piece of ground we needed at Heathrow.

Sometimes it's a new product like Virgin limo-bikes which all but eliminate the traffic factor for the time constrained. It's a mix of practical solutions and a sense of fun. Our small, entrepreneurial teams make sure we remain customer-focused. They make things happen.

Our culture is one of corporate artists: challenging conventions is proving to be one of the best ways to bring about success. Our approach to managing each business is based on our roots. Instead of musicians, the artists Virgin now manages are the individual companies and, of course, the Virgin brand. Virgin Management is fully involved with launching new companies, reviewing the opportunity, setting up the business, and providing a creative team of managers who are seconded to new Virgin companies for as long as they are needed. Fledgling Virgin ventures thus acquire the trademark Virgin management style plus unique skills and experience from all parts of the group. After the business has been set up, however, it is the responsibility of the individual company's management. As time goes on we anticipate that there will be seven or eight separate Virgin companies: Virgin Atlantic; Virgin Direct; Virgin Retail; Virgin Rail; Virgin Trading; etc. All lease or will lease the brand from Virgin Enterprises.

Exploiting the intangible assets

The brand identity is a powerful one. For the consumer, the word itself encapsulates our core values, and the signature acts as a flourish of individuality. Red, white and yellow are the dominant colours in our youth, music-related and travel industries. Somewhat subtler shades are being developed for sub-brands such as Virgin Bride and our cosmetics offer, Virgin Vie. Our name is well suited too to the way the organizational structure has evolved via alliances and joint ventures: excelling in 'virgin territory' is integral to the brand.

The brand manifestation is one factor in Virgin's distinctiveness. How we promote it is another. For us, each new company is like a new CD – we've got to get out there and tell people about it. When we launched Virgin Direct we found word of mouth, fuelled by a small public relations campaign, was more than thirty times as effective as the small amount we spent on advertising. As a result we are perceived as warmer than companies with a distant chairman. My promotion of Virgin Direct may indeed have been the impetus for Peter Davies to start telling people he's the 'man from the Pru'.

The *Economist* commented that Virgin is 'more of a phenomenon than a brand, feeding almost entirely off the publicity-seeking antics of one man'. It is true that Virgin has high awareness. In the UK 96 per cent of the population are aware of Virgin, and 95 per cent can name me as its founder. It is also true that my activities seem to capture the public's imagination and get press coverage. It is an unusual way to develop a brand, but one that can be relevant to other brand managers. With an attribute brand, reputation is all, and a key aspect of Virgin's reputation is trust. Recent TSB research showed that the young and old seem to look to me as a role model. In fact, the only area where the Branson factor missed it completely was amongst the under sixteens, where I'm dismissed as 'part of the establishment'. People know about Virgin and expect extraordinary things from us, which puts us in a unique position of trust and strength, but also gives us a responsibility not to let them down. A recent newspaper poll reported that more Britons would trust their savings to Virgin than to the Bank of England.

The Branson factor is only one of many that the team at Virgin have within their armoury of marketing tools. So far it has proved a useful one, particularly at the launch of a new business. We have often had to make a noise because we simply did not have the advertising budgets of our competitors. (Barclay's £25 million to Virgin Direct's £2.5 million is a typical example.) We do not shy away from exploiting our intangible assets – rather, we embrace them.

Ultimately, the Virgin brand will go where we can have fun and where there's an angle. We will constantly need to find new areas where industry cartels are looking out more for themselves than for their customers or where it's 'just always been done that way' when it shouldn't be. Once we launch the alternatives, the constant regeneration process within the resulting businesses remains the constant challenge.

Our exuberance seems to capture more than just the UK public's imagination. Although it is still early days for the brand from an international perspective, Virgin is among the fifty best-known global brands. In some countries the Megastores provide the launchpad for other Virgin companies. In others, Virgin Atlantic is the lead brand. The Internet is also providing a powerful way of developing the brand globally, as is Virgin Radio. All the individual companies will play their role in our aim to be the leading British global brand of the twenty-first century.

17 | Vodafone Group: Refreshing the Brand to Maintain Market Leadership

CHRIS GENT, *chief executive*

By the mid 1990s it had become clear that the mobile phone market was in the midst of fundamental changes, moving from a market that was technology and supply led, to one where the winners would be those with a strong and recognizable brand backed up with superior customer care and value for money. The time was fast approaching when Vodafone would no longer be able to rest on its laurels as market leader: the competition was getting much tougher, and we could see that the strength of the brand was going to be one of the few sources of sustainable competitive advantage. We knew this was going to present some daunting challenges: we had to review our brand values and identity in the context of a radical rethink of the overall company structure in order to make the Vodafone brand powerful enough to create real customer loyalty – and do it quickly.

The birth of the brand

The mobile phone market has grown up in a very short space of time. Now worth £35 billion, it only began in 1985 when the UK government awarded licences to two mobile phone operators. One was Cellnet, a joint venture between what was then British Telecom and Securicor. The other licence, which was put out to competitive tender, was won by a consortium led by Racal Electronics, a company with expertise in communications, mainly in the defence industry and professional electronics, which developed the Vodafone brand as a mobile phone operator.

Not only did we have to launch a new brand into what was essentially a new market, but we also had to tell people who Racal itself was. And we had an additional complication: under the terms of the licences, both Vodafone and Cellnet were prohibited from selling products and services directly to customers, and had to go through independent third parties which became known as service providers. The concept of service provision was introduced by the government to ensure that the market was competitive and that customers were given a choice.

Being a trail blazer is never easy, particularly when you are faced with a complex distribution system which stands between you and your customers, but by 1986 Vodafone was the market leader, in part because we had such good relationships with our service providers. This was, of course, something of a double-edged sword, since the service providers owned all the customer data, and controlled the selling environments, and were thus in essence the controllers of the brand, able to repackage and rebrand Vodafone's products and services. All we as the operators had were the records of telephone numbers and airtime used. Nevertheless, the brand swiftly gained a widespread penetration of the market.

New competitors emerge

And that market proved to be far more successful than anyone could have predicted. So successful, in fact, that by 1989 the government decided to license two more operators: One2One from Cable & Wireless; and Orange from Hutchison Telecom. Even though their prices were 30–40 per cent lower than either ours or Cellnet's, neither of us dropped our charges because we both realized that it was in our interests to let the newcomers get a fair start so that we could not be accused of predatory pricing. Nor did we want to be compared to companies which could not offer the same high level of service as us.

However, the nature of the game began to change dramatically because under the terms of the new licences the new operators were allowed to go directly to customers and bypass third-party providers. That meant they could start building up their brands from scratch in a very focused and energetic way. Orange, for example, did something which was quite new for the mobile phone market: it branded itself through a colour, emphasizing emotional values more than functional features. Its message was less about the phones or the networks than its brand values.

These values came through very clearly, even though the breadth and quality of their coverage was nothing like that of Vodafone or Cellnet. That was very clever: Orange created the perception that it had more coverage than it actually did. It was also risky, because a mobile phone network can be compared to a stretched piece of gum: occasionally it breaks apart and leaves holes. But Orange was perceived to be an innovator.

The other new entrant, One2One, followed a lower risk strategy by first concentrating on operating within the M25 and then spreading slowly as it built up its coverage. Despite this it still suffered teething problems: for example, it had to back away from one of its most publicized promotions – free evening and weekend calls – because this created great problems in terms of overload for its network.

Meanwhile, Vodafone had been developing in a number of other ways which consolidated our market position but also made strong, consistent branding more difficult. For instance, we had acquired a number of service providers including Vodacom, Vodacall, Vodac, Talkland, Astec and People's Phone. So by the mid 1990s distribution was increasingly complex because not only were we selling through six different companies which we owned and which were competing against each other in the marketplace, but we also continued to sell through independent dealers, high street retailers and some other shops. Nevertheless, owning those service providers meant that at least we now had access to the data of almost half our customers.

The market shifts to consumers

One of the main incentives for us to undertake an in-depth review of who we were as a brand and how we were perceived, was that we could see a shift in our market. Until the beginning of the 1990s our main target markets were corporate and large business organizations, where we were market leader and which was reflected in our tariffs, but gradually the market began to turn from one that was mainly business oriented, and centred on price and technology, to one where consumers were becoming key targets. Cellnet and Vodafone started to recognize this as early as 1992 when we both introduced a low monthly rental but higher call cost, aimed at consumers. The advent of Orange and One2One accelerated this shift.

The problem was that not only did the market begin to seem very cluttered, but the sheer volume of different products and deals was confusing, and both irritated and alienated many customers. This meant that to succeed in this next phase of the industry we had to pay far more attention to marketing, and, in particular, use a strong brand identity to cut through all the uncertainty that characterized the market. We had to forge relationships with our customers, and make sure our promise of customer care was backed by our customers' experience of it. Strong brands were becoming crucial to consumer recognition and loyalty. At this point, in early 1997, a market of 7.4 million customers was at stake, which was forecast to grow to 20 million over the next ten years.

Rethinking the brand

We decided that it was essential to review the whole operation and see how we could streamline all the key elements, including tariffs, the brand/corporate identity and distribution. There was a lot of work to do: we were operating with twelve different brands, eighty-seven different tariffs, six customer-care systems and five different billing platforms, as well as over 240 retail outlets. Although we were still maintaining a reasonable market share, research showed that our brand had no obvious position: customers could not come up with clear brand attributes. This, however, was not the case with our competitors: Cellnet was perceived as 'big', Orange as 'innovative' and One2One as 'value'.

The attributes associated with the Vodafone brand were not encouraging: it was business focused, not consumer oriented; it lacked modernity and currency, being seen almost as old-fashioned; it was big, but not loved or respected; it was a follower rather than a leader; it was responsive rather than pro-active; it was expensive and non-specific.

This rather sedate image was underlined by other research carried out by our corporate identity consultants, which found that if you compared the four rival networks to cars, Vodafone was a Ford Mondeo, characterized by a businessman in his mid-fifties who sells life insurance. Cellnet, on the other hand, was an Audi, perceived as a businessman in his mid-forties, forward looking and responsive to change. The buzz that Orange had created was shown by the fact that its brand was compared to a Toyota MR2, seen as a young businessman in his mid-twenties, in advertising or PR, and described by words such as 'dynamic' and 'leading edge'. One2One was young, the most female, informal, friendly, relaxed, and compared to a Vespa.

The first stage in the renaissance of the Vodafone brand was to establish just who our target market was. It soon became obvious that this could be defined as anyone who is or may be interested in mobile phones, including existing customers and the competitors' customers. It also meant that the market would stretch from individual consumers right through to large multi-national corporations. Armed with this information, we set ourselves the following objectives: to re-establish brand leader status; to emphasize that Vodafone is the 'best' network; to move the brand image from one seen as corporate, expensive and old-fashioned to one that is characterized by adjectives such as modern, reliable, personal, good value and biggest; to show Vodafone as a caring company; and to develop real brand equity which would mean something for existing and new customers, appealing to audiences as diverse as the teenage mobile phone user and the telecommunications analyst.

We had to agree the values that we wanted to be associated with the Vodafone brand, and describe them through key words that went to the heart of the brand. Defining these values would be the basis for our new identity and also give us a benchmark against which we could develop future products and services. The key words were: innovation (pioneering, creative, visionary, leading edge); thoughtful (helpful and intuitive, customer service excellence); dependable (reliable and trustworthy, quality-focused); and integrity (honest and sincere, trustworthy).

In essence, the extent of the changes could not have been more far-reaching. They would affect every department, every piece of literature, every communication and every employee within the Vodafone group of companies. More importantly, for this to succeed, it had to be accompanied by a cultural change that would take in the new brand values and significant organizational change, the like of which we as a company had never seen before.

Taking the plunge

So we embarked on an ambitious programme of change in January 1997. We realized that a key element in reaching our goals was to make sure we had the right agencies and consultants, and that they worked with us as part of our team – we put a lot of effort into hiring them. We were lucky in that we were already working with a good advertising agency, BMP, with whom we began to work on our brand values.

It was equally critical that we chose the right corporate identity consultancy to develop a new image which would enable us to appeal more strongly to the consumer. The consultancy would have to meet our very demanding time scale: we wanted to be ready to unveil the new identity in six months. That month we appointed Springpoint. Their brief was challenging. It was to define the best branding relationship between Vodafone and other companies in the group, define new positionings for Vodafone and the group companies, and create a new corporate identity which would encapsulate the new positioning – all in the space of six months, instead of the twelve to eighteen months normally taken to create a new identity. The process began with in-depth interviews with Vodafone management plus existing and potential customers, to help develop a picture of the group's needs. That included research on the existing logo which we had used since the beginning.

Giving the brand clarity and clout

The consultancy recommended that we should reduce our twelve brands to one, to ensure clarity for customers and give marketing effort maximum focus and weight. And while we didn't want to discard the sense of the brand as one with a history of expertise to draw on, we were adamant that the new positioning should be a bold leap onto the emotional high ground of the market. It had to be radical: we felt that an evolutionary design change would not get the brand where we wanted it to be quickly enough. While competitors were dramatizing the process of mobile communications and the technology of networks, Vodafone wanted to be associated with the idea of dialogue, the richness and variety and liveliness of human discourse – indeed, communication in all its forms.

We were advised to use this single, dominant brand identity across all shops and services, as well as the network itself, to get the message across loudly and clearly. The new identity uses speech marks in the two letter 'o's of the word Vodafone, inextricably linking the ideas of expression, communication and exchange with the Vodafone name. In addition to the word Vodafone the icon uses an opening speech mark symbol as a mnemonic, which was shown by research to add to the brand's impact. We do not regard the identity simply as a badge to identify the company and its services, but see it as a powerful tool to engage both business and personal users and to build true and genuine brand loyalty. We believe the new identity is modern, flexible and multi-layered, reflecting the vitality and depth of the group. Over time we would like that symbol to become as well known and universally understood as the brand marks from companies such as Shell and Nike.

Making Vodafone the single dominant and consistent brand to represent all group activities meant we had to make some major changes to our distribution structure. Part of our radical overhaul included reorganizing the six service providers (which were at that time targeting overlapping markets and trading under their own brand identities) into three new businesses, all branded Vodafone but concentrating on separate market sectors: Vodafone Corporate for corporate customers; Vodafone Retail for individual consumers and small businesses, with over 240 stores refurbished and rebranded in less than six weeks; and Vodafone Connect, also focusing on individual consumers and small businesses, but in addition managing sales through third-party retail channels, from specialist dealers to High Street multiples and affinity partners. The total cost of changing premises to the new identity, including all the shops, literature and vehicles, was set at £15 million.

Getting the message across

One of the most critical factors was to get all the employees on board in a relatively short space of time, and make sure that when they were told 'we are going to rationalize our distribution' they were aware that the job cuts would be minimal – which is the way it actually turned out.

As chief executive, I spoke to every employee in the UK throughout June and July of 1997 to get the message across, while we also produced an employee communication package, including a video, to tell them what was going on. You do not want any of your employees to read about such profound changes in the newspaper.

We had to work so fast because we needed to be ready for the launch of our new advertising communications at the end of

September 1997 – the period between then and Christmas is the peak selling period for mobile phones. We committed £35 million to promoting the single brand concept through advertising and sponsorship. Owning a theme or link to the brand became fundamental to our strategy. Our brand tracking study had shown us that whenever Cellnet advertised above the line, Vodafone's sales increased, and when developing our brand and advertising strategy, we needed to understand why, when Cellnet advertised, it created a need for a mobile phone, but not necessarily a Cellnet mobile phone. We believe that, as with all products, the advertising should create not just a need for the product but, more importantly, a need for that particular brand of product.

We had to ensure that the creative idea would always link the advertising to Vodafone, no matter what the media. This was a problem both Orange and One2One had overcome by the use of their names, and, in the case of Orange, a colour. Obviously this was not a viable route for Vodafone. Instead, we use the speech marks to help forge a solid link between what we are trying to say and the brand.

To put the creative idea into context, we liken it to the way in which DHL or UPS approach their markets, as a transportation system for parcels, or, with British Airways, as a transportation system for people. The new identity brings the company name to life, since 'voda' is based on 'voice' and 'data'. Vodafone is in essence about the way in which people talk, their conversations, their expressions and all their forms of dialogue and communication. Words are not just spoken, but can also include data words and fax words and e-mail words, all of which the Vodafone network carries for our customers. The creative idea goes deeper than just words, because words themselves carry with them the emotions and feelings of one person to another.

The word is Vodafone

The creative strategy is therefore based on the proposition that at Vodafone we understand the value of your words and all that goes with them, centred around the theme of 'the word is Vodafone'. It emphasizes that Vodafone has developed the best network, one that takes greater care in transporting your words more clearly, uses innovative methods of transporting them, and does it for a price that represents good value for money.

We decided to do three television commercials, using the first to establish the new brand identity, as well as to begin to develop some of our brand values. We wanted this commercial to deliver a warmer, softer, more caring image, and to establish Vodafone as a company that, despite not offering a tangible product, satisfies an emotional need.

The second ad communicated that we had our superior overseas coverage in place well before Orange and One2One did, while linking back to the first ad through the use of the creative theme. The last ad was devised to launch our 'Pay As You Talk' service which was our key Christmas gift promotion, targeted at the 17–28-year-old market, which research had shown to be new and incremental. The campaign also included our biggest ever poster campaign, worth £2.5 million, and a six-week £1.25 million press campaign to support the new brand look and to communicate Vodafone's advantages with a clear, brand-reinforcing message.

Our new-look shops gave enormous impact to the Vodafone brand in the High Street, and put us in a strong position relative to the other three networks. The shops offered the kind of service that it was impossible to deliver in retailers such as Dixons and Carphone Warehouse. Radio was chosen as the most appropriate way to get this message across during the crucial Christmas period. Although we used a different agency, both because of the volume of work and the need to put greater emphasis on the offer and the shops, the advertising linked into the brand advertising both through music and the strapline 'the word is Vodafone'.

Sponsorship also had an important role to play. For sponsorship to be effective you not only need a strong identity, but you have to sponsor some activity that stretches from the top to the bottom of the market: from the broadsheets to the tabloids, if you like. We already had a close association with horse racing through sponsoring The Derby. Then, in early January 1997, we had the opportunity to take over the sponsorship of English cricket at all levels, including sponsoring the England team. We have committed £13 million to this over five years.

Travelling across borders

One of our biggest strengths as a company is that we have been steadily expanding internationally, into countries such as Australia, Greece, Holland, France and Malta. That strategy was set in place early on by our first chief executive and founder, Sir Gerald Whent, who came from the defence side of Racal. He saw the advantages of moving into overseas markets step by step, with the result that we now have substantial and profitable investments abroad. Whereas the game three to four years ago was to get involved in overseas licences through taking small stakes, now the plan is to increase those stakes over time to a level where we can consolidate the profits into our accounts.

In Greece we have moved from an original 45 per cent in the Greek mobile phone operator Panafon to total control with 55 per cent, while in the Netherlands our stake in the network operator Libertel has risen to 61.5 per cent from 35 per cent. In France we have a 20 per cent stake in the French digital network operator. We have found that the earlier we can get into these networks, the less it costs, but we cannot move into new markets as easily as other types of company. If you decided that you were going to invest in Portugal tomorrow, you could not just decide to be a mobile phone operator, open a chain of shops and call that Vodafone. You need government permission with a licence and a band of frequencies.

We are taking a market-by-market approach to branding these overseas investments. While we will move to using Vodafone in

Malta, for example, we have no plans to change the name of our Greek company, Panafon, or Vodacom in South Africa. In fact, over time we want to give both Panafon and Vodafone in Australia a more national image through public offerings on their local stock markets. We have no intention of pushing the Vodafone brand where there is no real commercial benefit.

One of the big advantages we have had from being in other countries is that we can pick up ideas from other cultures. We also keep a close eye on all overseas network operators because we can learn from them – for example, we might see an innovative way of handling tariffs. If we benchmark Vodafone against anyone, it is probably the US operator AirTouch. Like us, they have a home network but also a number of overseas investments.

Keeping the customers

Retaining customers is now the major priority. We firmly believe that the network that wins will do so by encouraging loyalty through offering superior customer care and value for money. This industry has taken a while to learn that, in part because the sheer rate of growth hurt our collective ability to handle customers properly – our concentration was on gaining new customers and the billing network. But reality has now dawned that unless you have an excellent customer care system, your rate of churn – or customers leaving – will rise.

That puts the focus on making sure our employees in the shops are well trained in customer care, because they act as our foot soldiers on the High Street. We want to make sure that whenever customers come into a shop, for whatever reason, they are handled to their satisfaction. That is why we place a premium on staff motivation. Because many of our people have only joined the company in the last few years through acquisitions, we want to make sure we earn the same loyalty from them as we have from our longer serving staff. It helps that a large proportion of our employees are shareholders.

A happy conclusion

Our radical rebranding has paid off quite quickly. Our September through December quarter in 1997 was the most successful in our history. We achieved both more gross and net connections – net connections take into account those customers who leave in the time period being measured – than any of our competitors. In particular, the new 'Pay As You Talk' service, which was our key Christmas product, had sales well above expectation. It was very gratifying to see that because of the advertising, even retailers such as Woolworths, which had never sold phones before, experienced heavy demand.

Our brand tracking analysis also highlights the improved health of our brand. Each month on our behalf Millward Brown interviews 480 customers with the authority to purchase, across the UK. The results up to 7th December 1997 showed the impact the integrated approach had made: spontaneous awareness of the brand had risen by 10 percentage points during the quarter, while spontaneous recognition of the speech mark icon was already in excess of 20 per cent. It was also very gratifying to receive the 1998 Marketing Society Brand of the Year award.

Critically to our business health, our share price reached an all-time high in December, following steady increases since our restructuring and rebranding announcements. Worldwide, in our half year to September 1997, our customer base hit a record level of over four and a half million subscribers, while our UK operating profit was up 18 per cent, with our total UK customer base exceeding three million for the first time. On turnover, up 51 per cent to £1.16 billion during that period, our operating profit overall rose 33 per cent to £317.5 million, including the £19 million cost of restructuring.

And that performance is a sure sign to us that all our efforts have been worth it.

Index

HarperCollins Business

The Fish Rots from the Head

The Crisis in Our Boardrooms:
Developing the Crucial Skills of the Competent Director

BOB GARRATT

An organization's success or failure depends on the performance of its board – an ancient Chinese saying is that 'the fish rots from the head'. Yet the vast majority of directors admit that they have had no training for their role and are not sure what it entails.

As boards' activities are made more and more transparent under national and international law, there is an urgent need for a transformation in the way directors' competencies are developed.

Bob Garratt argues that directors need to learn new thinking skills to apply to the intellectual activities of direction-giving and implementing strategy. They need to develop a broader mindset to deal with the uncertainty of higher-level issues such as policy formulation, strategic thinking, supervision of management and accountability.

The Fish Rots from the Head is the first book to clarify and integrate the roles and tasks of the director and provide a programme of learning. As the tide of regulation swells, no board director can afford to ignore it.

'An important contribution to the corporate governance debate and clear and intelligent advice on how to improve the performance of a board'
    TIM MELVILLE-ROSS, INSITUTE OF DIRECTORS, London

'This clear, very readable book should ensure that many more fish swim rather than rot'   SIR MICHAEL BETT, CHAIRMAN, Cellnet plc

0 00 638670 9

In Search of Excellence

Lessons from America's Best-Run Companies

TOM PETERS AND ROBERT H. WATERMAN JR

The international bestseller

American know-how is alive and well and growing stronger daily. *In Search of Excellence* distills the art and science of management used by leading companies with records of long-term profitability and continuing innovation. No-one concerned with international business today can afford not to read what makes leading US corporations successful.

'One of those rare books on management'   *New York Wall Street Journal*

'Required reading'   *International Management Magazine*

'Receiving serious attention in business schools and corporate boardrooms'
     Washington Post

0 00 638402 1

HarperCollins Business

The Tao of Coaching

Boost Your Effectiveness at Work by Inspiring
and Developing Those Around You

MAX LANDSBERG

Coaching is *the* key to unlocking the potential of your people, your organization and, ultimately, yourself.

The good news is that becoming a great coach requires nurturing just a few simple skills and habits.

Max Landsberg, responsible for professional development programmes at McKinsey & Co in the UK, takes you through the stages needed to master and implement coaching to maximum effect. He shows how to:

- nurture an environment where coaching can flourish

- develop a team of people who relish working with you

- enhance the effectiveness of others through learning

- create more time for yourself through efficient delegation

By investing small amounts of time to provide constructive feedback, mentoring and encouragement, managers can substantially boost both their colleagues and their own performance.

With the current emphasis on helping individual employees to realize and deliver their full potential, the techniques of coaching are fast becoming essential tools for managers and other professionals. This is the first book which, in a highly entertaining and practical way, shows how to go about it.

'I'm making this useful guide required reading for my executive team'
GEORGE FARR, VICE-CHAIRMAN, American Express Company

'Practical, readable and relevant'
ARCHIE NORMAN, CHAIRMAN, Asda Group plc

0 00 638811 6

HarperCollins Business

The 22 Immutable Laws of Marketing

ALI RIES AND JACK TROUT

Al Ries and Jack Trout, two of the world's most successful marketing strategists, call upon over forty years of marketing expertise to identify the definitive rules that govern the world of marketing.

Combining a wide-ranging historical overview with a keen eye for the future, the authors bring to light 22 superlative tools and innovative techniques for the international marketplace. The authors examine marketing campaigns that have succeeded and others that have failed and why good ideas didn't live up to expectations, and offer their own ideas on what would have worked better. With irreverent but honest insights, and often flying in the face of conventional, but not always successful, wisdom, they give us:

The Law of Candour
be honest with your audience, point out the negatives, and improve your credibility

The Law of Line Extension
don't try to be all things to all people; companies that overextend themselves consistently lose market share

The Law of the Ladder
the battle isn't lost if you fail to be No. 1

The real-life examples, common-sense suggestions and killer instincts contained in *The 22 Immutable Laws of Marketing* are nothing less than rules by which companies will flourish or fail.

0 00 638345 9